CONNOISSEUR VOLUME 1

ENGINEERED BY DAVID SCOTT HAY

HEADLESS

A WHISK(E)Y TIT PROJECT

Published in the United States and Canada by Whisk(e)y Tit: www.whiskeytit.com. If you wish to use or reproduce all or part of this book for any means, please let the author and publisher know. You're pretty much required to, legally.

ISBN 978-1-952600-64-7

Cover design by Liam Callahan
Engineered by David Scott Hay

INTRODUCTION

SADIE HARTMANN

What a delight to be invited to write the introduction to this anthology by my friend, and the editor–excuse me, "engineer", David Scott Hay. I quite like that subtle title change from editor to engineer. Feast: Curated Horror for the Discriminating Palate, is the first official project of the new literary horror imprint from Whiskey Tit, called Headless. The origin story is quite fascinating and something I think many horror readers will relate to.

David was a Bram Stoker Award Juror in the short fiction category and as I understand it, he was quite blown away by all the stories he consumed. Of course, at the end of the day, there could only be one winner and one winner was ultimately selected but David wondered about the visibility and availability of all these amazing tales he read from the Bram Stoker Awards recommended reading list.

Somewhere along the way, he imagined compiling his favorites in the same way one might make a Greatest Hits Album. The packaging is square, resembling a double album. **Side A: Tomorrows** features 6 stories. **Side B: Pink Houses** with seven more.

The second record, **Side C: Rage, Rage** and **Side D: Fables** both contain 6 stories.

When David excitedly texted me with this whole concept and his desire to get these stories out to the general public, I found my heart resonating with his infectious excitement.

As the co-owner of the horror subscription service Night Worms and the Bram Stoker Awards winning author of two non-fiction books about horror books, I know a thing or two about the fierce drive to stoke the flames of horror fiction fire and put the right scary stories in the hands of the right audience. I feel incredibly lucky that David chose me to preview the curation and catch his vision for the formatting—even the way the stories are ordered and chosen for each section. It feels intentional and knowing David

personally, this is no surprise; a man of exceptional taste.

Side A: Tomorrows features dark stories exploring themes of the unknown and uncertain futures. Everything from gun violence and school shootings to spontaneous combustion in the context of an intimate relationship. I remember reading Tananarieve Due's story, **The Biographer**, in her short story collection, The Wishing Pool. A post-pandemic-apocalyptic story about chronicling the lives of every single person. A biographer comes to stay with a subject until the biography is complete. But what if you don't approve of the way your life is represented by this stranger selected to record your personal history?

I love the way all the stories in this section harmonize so uniquely to demonstrate the fear of the unknown and the lack of security we have about the promises of all our tomorrows.

Side B: Pink Houses starts off with a story I will never forget, *YOUR DASHER HAS ACCIDENTALLY AWAKENED THE CRAWLING CHAOS BY GAZING*

Lastly, **Side D: Fables** I don't think I'm allowed to pick favorites but I can tell you I grew up reading a lot of fantasy, fables, and fairytales. I didn't know then what I know now, which is that fables and folklore are meant to be dark and even horrifying. They're often cautionary tales; little nuggets of wisdom like,

"Watch out for gentle wolves, friends. No wolf was ever gentle."

"If love is honesty, honesty is sometimes unpleasant."

"Consequences are part of learning."

Go with the Starman.

Get your vaccines or else you'll learn why they're called "goosebumps"

"When the ocean is angry, it coughs up the best trinkets." Oh, but also, "The more skilled the ghost, the more valuable you are." That's an important one.

Finishing this anthology, I feel full. It's so satisfying to know that I have twentyish more horror stories locked inside my reader's brain. They're mine now. The images haunt me, the wisdom has been imparted to me, and I have wrestled with my fears. Now you get to jump in and fill yourself up too, friend. What a delight. A big thank you to David for collecting all these horrors in one place and to all the authors for breaking open the dark parts of their brains and spilling it out on the paper. We love you for it.

Sadie Hartmann 'Mother Horror"
October 31st, 2025

SIDE A

TOMORROWS

THE EPIDEMIC OF SHRINK-RAY-GUN VIOLENCE PLAGUING OUR SCHOOLS MUST END

PEDRO INIGUEZ

Their atoms dust the floors
of every school in the country;
those frightened children
we can no longer console.

Their cries have faded
into inaudible wavelengths
inside a quantum world where
hugs and spacetime both cease to exist.

They have dissolved into mere fractions
of their corporeal selves,
their particles swept into dustpans
and mopped into oblivion.

Blame those new blasters inundating the market,
stowed inside scores of scruffy backpacks;
the preferred choice of disgruntled
circuit-heads throughout the nation.

As parents, we stand before you
requesting prompt legislation to end
the rampant wave of shrink-ray-gun violence
endemic to our culture.

We beg you.
Think of the children,
screaming
beneath the soles of your shoes.

WE COME APART AND THEN WE ARRIVE

ERIC LAROCCA

We were told that my beloved husband, Arnold, was to perish—*detonate, blast apart, explode, whatever you want to call it*—at precisely two-thirty-three in the afternoon on Wednesday, March the 7th.

Of course, it was merely an estimation; however, they told us with such certainty that we believed them and believed them in such a way that we asked very few questions.

There would be no acolytes of the government in attendance when he passed even though it was usually customary for a representative to be present at all home-based detonations. Instead, I was tasked with the responsibility—not necessarily the *honor*—to care for him and to report his explosion to those in charge when the time came—when his body was to be ripped apart by the small explosive device embedded in the black collar belting his neck.

Naturally, it was a surprise to the both of us as we had always expected Arnold would detonate long after I was gone seeing as I was four years his senior. After all, it had always been common for older folk to move to the front of the line with regard to their scheduled demises. Since most detonations are ordered to occur before a civilian reaches the age of fifty-six, I had always presumed that my turn would come sooner than his considering I was rapidly approaching the age of the final limit. After all, I had just celebrated my fifty-third birthday.

After we had been informed of the date and time he would unquestionably meet his end, Arnold and I took all necessary precautions to see to it that his affairs were accounted for and orderly when he finally expired. Of course, to think of his death as such a calculated and meaningless matter to be overshadowed by paperwork and our government's bureaucracy was nearly unbearable for me.

Regardless, we made our plans accordingly and did everything we could to see to it that Arnold had all his business affairs settled by Tuesday the 6th.

I had nearly expected him to become glum about the mouth—to pout or, even worse, uncontrollably mourn the control he had lost over his circumstances, his very livelihood. But, to my astonishment, he never did. Even though he was fully aware that was a small clock ticking away inside him that would eventually detonate and send the life we had built together to smithereens, he never questioned his fortune or petitioned for a second opinion.

I often wondered if it truly hurt me to think of how Arnold seemed to lazily accept his sentence. I wondered if I might prefer him to shriek, to condemn the government, to resist the ruling and to do everything he could to overturn such a mockery of our pathetic lives. After all, to the government, we were nothing more than infinitesimal beings existing in the delicate and tenuous space between two major life events—birth and death. Our lives were forever trapped on a conveyor belt gliding down a dimly lit corridor toward oblivion.

After several dread-filled days and sleepless nights, Wednesday the 7th finally arrived and brought with it a sunny morning that almost seemed like an insult to the grim tone that echoed throughout our apartment.

Our morning routine went un-interrupted and, eerily enough, was fairly typical despite the fact that I knew full well I would be eventually playing witness to my husband's violent detonation in the afternoon. As we sat at the kitchen table, I observed Arnold while he scooped some melon from the bowl and ladled the pieces onto his plate with a fork. He ate without comment and would occasionally glance at me with a look that seemed to say: *"Why aren't you eating more of this delicious melon?"*

Of course, I thought of asking him how he could act so absentmindedly. I thought of asking him how he could be so calm and reserved when he knew full well his life was about to come to an end in a matter of a few hours. But I didn't want to spoil his breakfast. Moreover, I felt that asking him such things—giving a firm voice to such loathsome truths—would make the situation even more insufferable for the both of us.

We spent most of the morning in silence, as I had expected. After all, what was there to say? Everything I thought of to mention seemed so small, so trivial, so inconsequential. Of course, I could tell him how much I loved him—how much I cared for him and the beautiful life we had built together—but every word I invented in my mind seemed so trite and utterly contrived. For some reason, every bit of love and affection I could offer Arnold seemed so hollow and terribly hopeless for me. In fact, there was a part of me that wondered if I secretly enjoyed the prospect of Arnold being detonated.

I wondered if I, for some reason, reveled in the opportunity to send him on his way. After all, why did I feel so numb? Why couldn't I offer something more meaningful to him during his remaining hours? All I had given him was a warm cup of tea and a few slices of fresh melon for breakfast. Did I really love him? Did I truly and completely care for him the same way he had always nurtured and loved me? I couldn't be certain. Moreover, it nearly decimated me that I couldn't be certain if I loved my husband the same way he had loved me over the years.

We had become good friends with several of our neighbors when we first moved into the apartment building, and we had come to learn that one of our neighbors had been married to a young lady that was ordered to detonate at the young age of twenty-seven. Only three years into their marriage and the poor thing was expected to care for his beloved wife in the final days leading up to her government-ordered demise.

As Arnold and I sat at the kitchen table, mindlessly eating the sliced melon, I recalled how I had once asked our neighbor, Mr. Kedrick, about his experience with his wife's demise. I remembered how his lips pulled downward, his brittle voice thinning to a mere whisper as he spoke, and how he spoke so slowly and carefully—as if any incorrect word or syllable might insult the memory of his once beautiful wife.

He told me how after the ordeal was over—after his wife had been detonated and her remains had been splattered all over the walls of their living room—he sat there for what felt like hours and thought of the moment when he and his wife had first met at the local park. Of course, he knew when he married her that there was every possibility that the two of them would meet their demises in such short time spans, but he told me how he never regretted his affection toward her. Mr. Kedrick loved her unabashedly and still loved her no matter what.

After several hours of silence passed, I glanced at the clock and noticed how two-thirty-three was rapidly approaching. It felt so strange to think of a mere clock as a director of our agony, a shepherd of my beloved's inevitable destruction. For half an hour or so, Arnold and I seemed to exist in the seconds, the milliseconds of each passing tick—our hearts seeming to echo the beating of the clock as time moved forward like an unstoppable tide, an agonizing current that was unmistakably headed toward a never-ending void.

Finally, when I was certain it was time to say 'goodbye,' I told Arnold how we should move into the spare bedroom we had covered with plastic tarps. He shifted, seeming to agree, as he ambled from the kitchen and into the room without furniture. Once we both arrived there, I closed the door and moved into the center of the space with him.

"I don't want you to get hurt," he told me, pushing me away whenever I would try to draw too close to him. "Who knows if it will set off the detonator in your collar if you're too close to me?"

I rolled my eyes at him, silently wishing he wouldn't be so careful all the time. "I'm sure they've taken precautions to see to it that the devices aren't so sensitive."

"You don't have to stay with me, you know?" he said to me.

I knew what he would suggest next. He would urge me to leave the room, to lock the door, and to wait for the ordeal to be over. I knew he didn't want me present for his detonation. Whether it embarrassed him or made him feel hopeless, I couldn't be certain. Regardless, I would sooner cut out my tongue than leave him to endure the agony all on his own.

Finally, the time came we had both been dreading. Arnold seemed surprised when I pulled him close as the time drew nearer. Of course, he attempted to push me away, but I did everything in my power to hold onto him even as he resisted me. I glanced at my wristwatch and noticed the time had reached the moment we had been fearing—two-thirty-three. I pulled Arnold tight against me, closed my eyes, and waited for the explosion to rip through us, to send me sailing away from him, to launch us both into the air like confetti and blast through us like an errant locomotive that was always fated to destroy us.

But much to my surprise, nothing happened.

Instead, silence filled the small room.

I could hear both of our heartbeats hammering away like organic clocks made of sinew and tissue.

I pressed my fingers into the firmness of Arnold's arms, making certain he was still there, was still breathing.

To my astonishment, he was.

For whatever reason, he hadn't exploded.

I winced slightly, regarding his face and wondering if the explosion was to happen when we would least expect it. Of course, I figured the government employees who calibrated the equipment in our mandatory collars were evil enough to play horrible games with us. But I wondered if they really hated us to the extent where they would give us a false sense of hope—a pitiful sense of faith when there was clearly none to be had.

We waited another minute.

Nothing.

Another minute.

Nothing.

Another minute.

No explosion.

I pulled Arnold tight against me.

"You're still here," I whispered to him. "You're still here."

Arnold shuddered in disbelief, clearing the nervous catch in his throat. "This—must be some mistake. It was—supposed to happen."

I pecked him on the cheek, too ecstatic to even think correctly. Too stupid to be scared. "But it didn't. You're alive."

I buried my face into his chest, inhaling the familiar scent of his cologne. The bristly hairs on his chest tickled my nose. When I pulled myself away, I regarded him and noticed how he observed me with such horror, such unrestrained terror.

"For how long?" he asked me, hiding the tremor in his voice.

I thought for a moment. I immediately knew what he meant. I knew the fear he felt. It was the same fear I sensed coiling its way around my heart and squeezing tight until I could hardly breathe—that familiar, all-consuming sense of dread that always seems to serve as a terrible overture for what's to come. I knew, in my heart, that something horrible was on its way. Even worse, I knew that until then, Arnold and I would merely exist in a tenuous space—the same space where others dwell who know that violence is on its way toward them.

✝✝

As soon as we reported that Arnold's detonator failed to cooperate at the day and time proposed by the council, my beloved Arnold was whisked away to a private room at the consulate where he was interrogated by several members of staff. He told me how there were several officials who ran various tests on the equipment he had been outfitted with and how they adjusted his paraphernalia only to no avail.

Perhaps the most insufferable aspect of our ordeal took place when both Arnold and I were brought to a private room at the consulate. We sat in a pair of identical chairs across from a man with a pockmarked face who loitered behind an impossibly large desk. When we asked the representative what would happen to Arnold, he seemed incensed by our curiosity. He seemed as though he thought we should be grateful to even be graced by his presence with the way he sneered at us and tapped the end of his cigarette in an expensive-looking ash tray situated at the corner of his desk.

He told us how there was, unfortunately, no way for those tasked with calibrating the equipment to properly ascertain when the device would finally detonate. Of course, Arnold and I were shocked by such a revelation.

"How could they not know when it will go off?" he asked the official, leaning forward in his chair and straining his voice. "That doesn't make sense."

The official merely told us how very often some of the gear they've assigned to certain civilians fails to detonate in time. According to him, the device continues to count down toward a specific day and time that, for some reason, is not visible to those calibrating the equipment. He told us how there have been a few reports from others based in the nearby districts of detonators finally imploding after several hours, days, weeks. The unfortunate part of the ordeal —the explosion occurs at random and the subject in question is forced to live in a transitory state of limbo while the device recalibrates.

I expected Arnold to say something, to question the official as he told us the hopelessness of the situation—how Arnold would be forced to exist in a purgatory-like state until the gear would finally explode at random. Instead, he said nothing. I watched him carefully as his eyes opened and closed mechanically, his tongue sliding across his lip. He straightened from his chair, thanked the man on the other side of the desk, and then motioned for me to follow him out of the room. I walked a few paces behind him, eyeing him as he ambled down the corridor and toward the emerald-glowing exit sign above a nearby doorway.

I noticed how my pace began to slow as I let Arnold move further and further ahead of me. I didn't think anything of it until we made our way into the facility's covered parking garage. Arnold turned around, as if wondering what was keeping me and why I was moving so slowly after him. I straightened, hastening after him and eventually catching up. But, all the while, I wondered why I had been so cautious to move close to him. After all, I had once held him, embraced him in what was supposed to be his final moments. I obviously didn't care about my safety then. Why did I suddenly pay mind to it now?

There was a quiet murmur snarling deep inside me that seemed to confess my sudden hesitation to be around Arnold.

The truth was—I had already suffered through the agony of preparing to lose him once. Why should I do it again?

It was a question I certainly couldn't ask Arnold to answer. Instead, I figured it would be answered in the solitude—the precious space between moments—when we were both unguarded and fully prepared to melt through one another the same way sand travels through an hourglass or the same way running water trickles through fingers.

++

The first few hours of Arnold's homecoming weren't as unbearable as I had predicted while we were driving in the car. Although Arnold had offered to drive, I reminded him of his predicament, and he agreed to sit in the passenger seat while I drove instead. It had felt so unusual to remind him of something so grim, so decidedly awful—*There's a chance you might explode, love. Wouldn't want to be driving on the highway when that happens.*

Eventually, we arrived home and Arnold passed through the front door of our apartment like a bereft specter that knew full well it did not belong here but simply had nowhere else to haunt. That was exactly what Arnold had become in the few hours since his equipment malfunctioned—a wraith of his former self. I watched him wander aimlessly from room to room, eyeing our belongings—as if trying to recognize a modicum of familiarity in a world that most likely seemed so immeasurably different to him.

"Perhaps you should stay in the spare bedroom?" I said to him as I watched him mill near the kitchen window, gazing outside at the makeshift garden we had made on the balcony.

Of course, I felt so foolish for suggesting something so heinous, so unkind and cruel. But what else was I to say? After all, we had made provisions for his demise. We had removed all the furniture from the spare bedroom and stacked different pieces in the master suite. We had spread out plastic tarps all over the floor and pinned them to the walls as well so that there wouldn't be too much of a mess to clean when it was over. Why shouldn't I suggest Arnold spend most of his time—what little of it he had left—inside that particular room?

"I can bring you something to eat in an hour or so," I told him. "Something to drink, too."

His eyes lowered, lips moving with muted words that were probably far too agonizing for him to utter.

I watched him as he drifted into the empty spare bedroom, the plastic tarps covering the floor crinkling gently as he moved into the center of the space and stood there like a disciplined toddler. He glanced around the room—the nothingness that had been waiting for him there—and he regarded me with a pitiful look of such longing, such quiet desperation.

"Is this my life now—?" he asked me, his voice trembling slightly as if fearful of my answer.

I didn't know what to say to him. *After all, what was there to say?*

I couldn't help but notice how in the few minutes we had returned home from the consulate, Arnold had begun to twitch involuntarily at every horrible chirp his collar made. I had always teased him how oblivious he had always been to such an irritable sound. But, for a reason I knew all too well, his attention seemed far more hyper vigilant than it had before since we returned home. I felt my heart quiver

slightly as I observed him wince a little like a child that was being approached by a heartless school official brandishing a wooden paddle.

Even worse, I noticed how I began to shrink a little at every chirp his collar made—as if expecting each and every sound would be the very last thing we would hear before the damned thing finally went off.

For a moment, I watched Arnold pace back and forth inside the bedroom like a captured beast. I wondered when it would happen. I felt guilty for needing to excuse myself to go to the bathroom and I wondered if I would suddenly hear a horrible blast in the next room while I was seated on the toilet.

It was then I made the horrible realization that I yearned for such a thing. I didn't want to be present for his death any longer. I wanted to shut him in that empty room, lock the door, and simply wait for the walls of our apartment to shake when the detonator finally went off. I thought of going to the door and securing the latch so that I knew he couldn't escape. But I couldn't follow through with it. I knew I was capable of doing horrible things, but I never considered myself to be so monstrous that I would lock Arnold away from the world. Still, the thought teased me again and again throughout the remainder of the night. *What if I left him in there? What if I pretended to forget about him? Would it even matter?*

The thoughts frightened me, and I hurled them away as soon as they made their presence known, fangs and all. Despite the fact that I banished these awful ideas, I kept them close enough to listen to their whispers—their incessant growling—late at night when my inhibitions were unprotected and when I felt completely and utterly unmoored.

It was nearly three in the morning when I secured the latch on the spare bedroom door. I could hear Arnold snoring on the other side of the door, probably dozing on the makeshift cot I had prepared for him. I wondered if he heard me. But I didn't care. To me, he was finally dead to the world—a whisper sealed off inside an ancient sarcophagus, a terrified shriek forever echoing throughout a deserted tomb.

✝✝

Morning arrived and I awoke to the sounds of Arnold beating his fists tirelessly against the locked door. I hadn't slept much during the night, so I was surprised I was even able to doze off for what was probably twenty or thirty minutes. Realizing that I was now tasked with the unfortunate business of informing my husband how I would not be releasing him from his bedroom, I popped one of my anxiety tablets and chased it down with a gulp of tap water.

"Darling," he called to me from the other side of the locked door. "I can't open it. I think it's been locked."

I inched close toward the door leading to the spare bedroom. I sensed myself quiver slightly, afraid of what Arnold might say when I finally told him what I had planned for him.

"Yes. The door's locked, dear," I said to him, my voice shuddering a little while I spoke. "I locked it."

"Why have you locked it?" he asked me, almost pitifully sounding.

"I think it's best if you stay in there, darling," I said to him. "It will be less strain on the both of us."

"Less strain?"

He sounded annoyed.

I rubbed my hands together, searching my mind for a semblance of an excuse I could use to explain why I had deserted him, why I had forever locked him inside that small tomb.

"I've already gone through the agony of preparing to lose you once before," I told him. "I—don't want to go through it again."

I could hear Arnold stammering on the other side of the door, unable to speak as if I had seized him by the tongue.

"You're going to stay in there until it's over," I said. "It's better this way."

There was a long, pain-filled pause from the other side of the locked door.

"We're not going to be able to say 'goodbye' to each other," he whimpered.

I felt tears webbing in the corners of my eyes, my throat suddenly closing as if a secret valve inside me had been tightened.

Finally, I forced the words out: "We've already said 'goodbye' to one another."

Before Arnold could respond, I moved away from the doorway and drifted down the hall until I was out of earshot. If he cursed me, shouted at me, or condemned me, I wouldn't have heard it. I didn't want to hear it. In my mind, what I had done was entirely justified.

Of course, there was a part of me that recognized the cruelty of what I had done to my husband—how I had condemned him to a slow, agonizing and painful death—but how could I possibly live with him and know that at any moment he could be ripped apart before my very eyes? How could I comfortably live in the space between now and the random time of his violent demise without fear, without trepidation? I knew it wasn't possible. I couldn't exist with him, meanwhile knowing that his doom was imminent and fast approaching.

That was more than I wanted to bear.

Days passed and eventually Arnold stopped pummeling his fists against the locked door.

Of course, I yearned for the moment when he finally accepted what was to be. However, there was a quiet, mournful part of me that grieved his vitality, his desperation to survive. To me, it appeared as though he had given up. A small wound was opened in some secret cavern deep inside me when I realized I had truly and successfully undone most of his longing to live. I had removed that all-too human desire to survive from him. For the first time in my life, I felt like a monster. I felt unclean and rotted.

In one of my more maudlin moments, I searched the living room for the photo album I had patched together over the years. I found the old thing in the trunk my mother had gifted us for our fifteenth wedding anniversary. As I began to flip through the pages, I recognized how there was a light reflecting in both of Arnold's eyes that seemed to dim softer and softer throughout the years since we had been first married. I wondered: *Had I done that to him? Had I robbed him of happiness and joy prior to his sentencing by the government?*

It was excruciating to observe just how noticeable Arnold had transformed over the years, accepted his visible unhappiness with a visible calmness in drooped shoulders and glum, half-hearted expressions that were supposed to be crude imitations of joy and delight.

I could hardly believe just how much integrity and joy I had sapped from him over the years since we were first married. Feeling foolish for not realizing it sooner, I thought of poor Arnold wasting away in that small spare bedroom—dozing on the tiny cot I had prepared for him, pacing the room while the plastic tarps crinkle and chirp beneath his weight.

How could I have abandoned him like this?

I had prepared myself to love him unconditionally and to the very end, just like our neighbor Mr. Kedrick cared for his wife.

Wondering if I was too late to undo all the evil I had done, I swiped the keys from the kitchen counter and hastened toward the spare bedroom door.

"Darling," I said, calling through the door. "I've made a mistake. Will you forgive me?"

There was no response.

I pushed the key into the lock and twisted it.

"I want to hold you," I said to him. "I'll never forgive myself if I leave you here like this."

But just as I was able to turn the door handle and step inside the small room, there was a disgusting thud that sounded like a large bag of potatoes being dropped on the floor. I waited a few moments. Finally, something else, something truly horrible answered me—the sound of an explosion. I lurched back, the walls of our little apartment quivering slightly and then finally settling after a second or two.

I heard nothing beyond the locked door. That silence told me unmistakably that it was over.

As I stood in the narrow hallway, my hand glued to the door latch, I thought of how my beloved Arnold and I seemed to always exist at a threshold—the two of us seemingly forever cursed to be skittering across the barrier of a great divide between two life-defining moments.

We lived in a permanent state of nervousness—on the precipice of some other critical moment—for so long and now, much to my sorrow, we had finally arrived.

TEMPEST

EMMA LOUISE GILL

In space, no one can hear you scream. Thank fuck.

I turn off my comms and scream in my EVA suit until my voice turns hoarse, then pant, sweat dripping down my brow, silence blessed silence filling the void between gasps. Of all the sound in the universe, my own voice is the least aversive. It's not egotistical. It's mental. It must be. The product of a faulty brain that nothing back on Earth could cure.

The ringing in my ears subsides gradually. Soon enough the only sound is my breath, my heartbeat, the measured vibration of air molecules oscillating through my ear canal and setting off electrical impulses to my brain. My HUD is off, the helmet close but comforting, and the darkness of forever stretches like an empty canvas dotted with light.

I can't hear the stars from here, though I know they have voices. Their EM frequencies—translated to 'music'—drove me mad at grad school. Diagnosed with misophonia, I escaped via remote classes. But every living thing, every atomic vibration, every chemical process makes sound, if you know how to hear it.

It's a fact I wish I could forget.

++

I make my way through frozen passengers in their cradle clusters, guided by the soft blue light of cryo-displays. I envy their sleep. My funds were insufficient to join their ranks, though the Company described it differently. Instead, I have to work for this journey. I brush a hand over the cool surface separating me from an inanimate face. Do they dream in there?

If I'd had this year to dream, it would be of drifting through a silent void, and I wouldn't want to wake up.

A curse from behind makes me whirl. "Why the hell you working in the dark?" It's Smith, his irate, over-loud voice grating. "I can't see for crap in here."

He must have walked into a cryo-cradle, unused to the low light I like to work in. I frown. Smith's getting better at creeping up on me. Usually I flinch at every noise.

Rising from the examination, I lock the cradle and face him, not bothering to hide my irritation. "What do you want?"

He shrugs, black shirt just another shadow in the large room, eyes reflecting screen lights like the glowing orbs of a predator. "You weren't answering your comms. Again."

I'd turned them off to avoid Smith's obnoxious music, since he insists on sharing it with his colleagues. "I needed to concentrate. You know, actually do some work."

"What, this? Riiiight." He laughs and this time I wince as the hair on my arms rises in response, as my body shies from the sound. I'm more on edge than usual today, disturbed by noises last night that couldn't possibly be real. Scraped steel and howling ghosts. Staccatoed knocks like stone on glass.

"Sleeping beauty ain't going anywhere." He shakes his head. "Leave it alone, Ray. Hewett made some kinda scran that smells half-decent for once. You know, she might be getting better."

I don't want to eat with them, be forced to endure the sound of other people swallowing, smacking lips, tearing food with wet, sharp teeth. Don't want to listen to their inane chatter, or be subjected to Hewett's reality show reruns on the mess screen. The *Pilgrim* is reality enough for me.

"No thanks." I crouch down beside the next cradle.

Smith continues to stand there, clicking with his tongue. It echoes in the room, and I hunch my shoulders in disgust. Gross. "Fine," he says. "But keep your comms on."

He switches the light on as he leaves, blinding me for no reason other than he can.

++

I've struggled with noise all my life. It isn't easy to tune out a society insistent on making its presence heard. Generators; communicators; advertisers; animals; the discordance of people inhabiting a space designed for billions fewer. Humanity turned its back on silence.

This ship offered escape. A new world at the end, a place to make a quieter home. Yawena. All I had to do was monitor passengers. Yet this year trapped in a vessel with two colleagues and a thousand sleepers is worse than all my time on Earth.

There is no escape from my torment. No place to hide.

Smith broke my noise-cancelling headpiece. An accident, he called it. Malicious intent, I believe. It's not like I take them out often. But after my last spacewalk—the one with the scream and the sweet, sweet relief from its absence—I came back to find them gone from my locker. Three days later, I was forced to confront him on the bridge.

Smith acted innocent, but I could read the smirk in his eyes. "Did you check the trash 'bots? They're always picking up stuff they shouldn't." His affected drawl was pitying. "Maybe you should find a more permanent solution, Rayan. Ever thought about a career change?"

I glared. "I'm just as qualified as you and Hewett to run this ship. All I need is my gear back."

He glanced at Hewett but the Captain, focused on her terminal's readouts, barely acknowledged me. "If you can't find them, you'll have to deal with it."

Smith turned back to me. "Seriously, Ray. Shit makes noise. I don't understand your problem."

No one ever does.

When I find my mangled gear in a trash 'bot, I know it was Smith. But there's nothing I can do. The *Pilgrim*'s printer doesn't carry specs for personal medical devices, and though Hewett eventually dredges up an old design, the replacements muffle barely half the decibels I need.

Amongst the *Pilgrim*'s constant hums, whirs, clicks and beeps of operations, its interior vibration sounds off-key lately. Almost painful. I stray into MedBay, driven to run checks. But my jaw and teeth are fine. No decay, no reason for the deep ache other than sound. Unceasing, unbalanced sound.

The loss of my gear hits me in a new wave of grief. It's a good thing I don't have a screwdriver nearby. Jamming one in my ears and *twisting* is so very appealing.

The airlock is open, the door too wide for me to block Smith's view. He crept up on me again. The joke's old now, though. Old and idiotic. I step in front of him, arm out to slow his advance. "Go away."

He raises an eyebrow and attempts to push past. "What are you doing?"

Finding vibrations. "Recalibrating," I say. The inner door controls hang exposed, wire guts spilling from their wall cavity. "The airlock won't seal properly. I'm fixing it."

Smith's eyebrows unify. "Like you 'fixed' the printer in engineering?"

"It wasn't working. Now it does." Mostly.

"It looks like you took a wrench to it." He eyes the door controls like they'll bite him any second. "You shouldn't be touching this."

"The extruder was half-melted before I ever touched it." The wrench was an unfortunate side-effect of two hours fixing a machine that didn't want to be. "Besides, the *Pilgrim*'s door controls have been buzzing for two days. If I don't fix this airlock, we're all going to die."

"Or we'll die because of your meddling. Let me through."

"No." I need him to leave. I can't concentrate, can't fix this if he won't leave my space. My chest tightens, like the buzzing in my bones is calcifying them, weighing me down. "I don't interfere in your 'work', Smith. Stop *interfering* in mine."

He is supposed to be our other Systems Tech, but the most I've seen him do is program 'bots to do his work for him. That, and play music whenever and wherever he feels like. I tried adding a disruptive frequency in my new headset, but it couldn't match the tones fast enough. I record it all anyway. Even if our Captain doesn't recognise my complaint, someone might.

Hewett is glued to her consoles recently, only appearing for dinner—but I take mine and leave when she does. The other two are too much. I no longer sleep in my own cabin, since they've also been making a lot of noise in theirs. Together.

Crew quarters aren't designed for getting cosy.

"Go bother Hewett," I tell him. "At least *she* wants your attention."

Smith clicks his tongue. "You're just jealous I get more Captain time than you." His grin makes me feel sick. I want to punch it off his face. Then he frowns, putting on a concerned uncle face even though I'm older and definitely wiser than him. "You have to stop breaking shit for

attention, Ray. The airlock this time?" He shoulders past me.

"Hey. I don't need—or want—anyone's attention!"

Only three months left until we reach Yawena, unfreeze everyone, and I can set up my Habitat. The Company promised me a spot three klicks from the main colony. I've earmarked the supplies I'll need so that I won't have to see or talk to anyone for at least six months. If I'm lucky, I'll never have to talk to Smith again. But then, I've never been lucky. "I just want to get to this planet in one piece."

"Yeah, well you'd better let me deal with this, then." Smith scans the wiring and turns to me. "Why don't you just go to MedBay, Rayan, seeing as you clearly need your head checked. Again."

He's been in the personnel files, no other way to know about my tests, my diagnoses. "Fuck you."

I knock his hand away from the wires, but he doesn't let go, he pulls, insisting he knows better. We struggle, arms locked together, me stomping one foot onto his, Smith elbowing my ribs, grunting and swearing at each other. I'm pushed backwards. Door controls dig into my upper body. I twist away but Smith yanks me, and something catches, and the controls rip off the wall as I fall, alarm blaring, lights flashing. *Shit.*

The door.

Smith pushes me off him as the secondary iris slams inward. Metallic doors slice together into a perfect seal, cutting off the corridor, and the air pressure takes a massive dive inside the chamber. Smith's eyes bulge as he registers what's happening, and my head splits apart with excruciating pain as my eardrums burst, as the pressure drops further, as the air is sucked out through the escape valve that's meant to equalise atmosphere with that of the outside—but there is no outside, there's only space, vacuum, nothing, and we're so so fucked—

I jump as a crash reverberates from behind, followed by Smith propelled backward by his attempt at smashing the door. He's got pliers in one hand but his mouth is open in a cry, blood streaming from his ears, his nose, fists—and I can't hear him anymore, only see the horror on his face, hear the ringing, loud so loud I think I must explode. Metallic bubbles form and burst on my tongue like my mouth has been filled with sherbet made of fire. I'm burning, my eyes are burning,

vision blurred by steam as water boils from every orifice, and though it's only been seconds I know we're about to die and I think, *at least I know I was right.*

Then I pass out.

Sometimes I imagine I am suffocating in a sea of sound. Confined to a tainted vessel, an echo chamber of my own making. I crave silence. But there is nothing to prescribe for my affliction, no action more extreme than leaving atmosphere.

Or so I thought.

I stare at Smith's burns, following the lines on his face where depressurisation ruptured and broke his skin, exposing subdermal vessels, scarring even as the MedSuite works. I once saw a lightning strike victim with Lichtenberg figures, feathery lines tracing their body where current passed, reminiscent of lightning itself. This is nothing like that. This is the cold death of vacuum. It isn't pretty.

He blinks. I swear, shying back, becoming aware of my own MedSuite confines at the same time. My voice is raw, a sharpness choking my throat. Everywhere is pain.

Cargo pants and a green coverall steps into view. Hewett. She presses the Suite's screen and a robotic arm darts sedative into my thigh.

"Don't worry. It will all be fine." Her voice should lull me into the silent darkness of sleep, but the edge in her tone is darker still. I do not remember my dreams.

Day three hundred and forty. Tomorrow our destination will be visible on the short-range scanners. Weeks of forced rest in MedBay, enduring Smith's raspy breaths and Hewett's infrequent, cursory 'checkups', have driven me close to the edge. I'm ready to fall, ready to let go and slide, slide, like a skier before an unstoppable avalanche. This is my last chance to reset my baseline before the final weeks, before landing. To luxuriate in blessed silence, so that whatever else may come is manageable.

The first time I ventured outside the *Pilgrim* was for a solar sail check. Usually Smith's 'bots did it, but that day they were all too busy. Lucky me. I was suited up and ready before Hewett could say 'watch your step'. Adrenaline in my veins, respiration rate a little excessive, but the empty horizons were pure mana to my stressed-out mind. I completed my task then luxuriated in the still quiet until Hewett had to call me back in.

Soon the silence entered my dreams. I volunteered to go out any chance I could. Smith told me to slow down, give some poor 'bot a chance, whatever. I ignored him; practised suiting up alone countless times. Early on, I figured out how to turn off the Heads-Up-Display and remain connected. It's not something you get taught for EVAs, probably because it's not a great idea to let newbies know they can clear the screen and be distracted by stargazing when they're out in space. But it's also one of the best things about being out here. That, and the chance to *breathe*.

I'm feeling so good when I come back in today that Smith's music blindsides me. He's not supposed to be up and working yet. Jaunty synths mock me, break my calm and set my pulse rushing. My HUD beeps in alarm. I turn off the comms, turn off everything except O2, lock the doors to the chamber, and curl into a corner, raging. Muttering. Shaking.

Hewett finds me two hours later. She removes my helmet, waking me from a dream of drifting in blessed silence, and her disapproving expression is enough to make me want to go straight back out the airlock.

"I've got enough to deal with without your crazy shit, Ray. Get up."

So nice to know the Company Captain cares.

She doesn't listen to my explanation, just declares me unfit for work and marches me back to MedBay. Keeps me there for another week with a carefully programmed 'relaxation' scene projected on the Suite, carefully monitored drugs calming me down, and a careful reevaluation of sharp or heavy objects within my reach after I take apart the first 'bot to enter the room. Violently.

After that, I do feel calmer.

And that scares me.

✝✝

Smith doesn't lose his superior attitude after the airlock incident; he continues to make my life worse just by his presence. Since he returned to duty before being fully-healed—also apparently my fault—Smith has a new raspy way of breathing that makes my own chest tighten. Hewett also has a new habit, tapping her fingers on the nearest available surface. I'm sure she does it on purpose. The 'bots and chirps and thrums of the *Pilgrim* continue to harass me, coming and going in waves. Once or twice I've felt the weirdest sensation like I'm in an earthquake, as rumbling passes through the entire ship, shaking my body and leaving me reeling. Other days I've spent hours searching for cascading knocks that I swear I've never heard before. Hewett insists it's all in my head.

We're five days out. Yawena is a dot around its star. Nearly there.

I lose my cool one afternoon and take off to engineering for some time alone. Smith's music still manages to drift in, and that's when I snap. The virus takes an hour to build; it'll take five more before it can worm its way into the system. I don't need to be subtle. I've had enough. It's either this or tossing his hard drive into the nearest star. Tempting.

✝✝

I'm deep into the complicated process of unfreezing expedition specialists when Smith and Hewett enter the bay. The cradles are thawing, dry steam hissing, condensing, dripping for hours. I've been battling the urge to walk away, stop the process, or just pull the plug and empty them all into space. My skin itches with remembered pain from the broken airlock. My jaw and joints hold an interminable ache. My eyes water. I'm multiple stims and waking nightmares into a twenty-hour shift and all I want is to step into my EVA suit, float in the void, and scream until I pass out.

Smith coughs, Hewett taps a cradle.

"What do you want?" I'm not in the mood for confrontation.

"I need you to stop what you're doing and fix this." Hewett walks toward me, her customary half-distracted derision replaced by something like fury. I've never seen her this off-balanced.

I sigh. "What?" I'm trying to concentrate on the next step, checking vitals, lining up thaw time and medical data and assigned job priorities—

"Stop." Hewett yanks my hand from the terminal. I'm forced to look at her. The carefully constructed lists in my head fall into a heap; it'll take ages to get back into rhythm after this interruption. "Stop and listen for once."

Seriously? All I ever do is listen. My imprisoned fingers clench. The beeps and background hums of the ship become louder, clearer. If she'd just let me finish, there'd be other people in this cacophony of noise. Someone else to take on this burden. Someone else to drive to madness.

"You need to restore the files you erased," Hewett says.

"What are you talking about?" I frown and pull away. "I'm on a tight deadline here—"

"The fucking music, Ray! You destroyed my music!" Smith's face is ruddy, his ugly skin peeling.

I can't help the grin, though I mask it in a second. Finally something gone right. "Nothing to do with me," I say. "Maybe some 'bots did it."

Hewett gets up in my face, breathing heavily. "The music's not important." Smith protests, which she ignores. "The rest of it is. All sound data is gone from the ship." She shoves a handheld terminal at my chest. "You're pathetic, Ray. A superfluous, whining *child* who doesn't know when she's not wanted. I'd shove you out an airlock—Smith too, for his part in provoking you—except that I *need those files back*."

I recoil, clutching the handheld in defence. She eyes the datapad, voice low and doom-filled.

"Yawena is more volatile than predicted. Probe data on approach identified an asteroid impact sometime in the past decade has set off a cycle of atmospheric disturbance and seasonal variation. Combine that with mineral composition of the proposed site, it's a significant threat to the new colony. Not something that would usually matter to me, but I can't leave Yawena until there's saleable material."

Of course she's only worried about the short term—she's contracted to captain the *Pilgrim* back to Earth. What happens to Yawena will be someone else's problem by then.

I stare at the readouts in my hand. "How long have you known the planet isn't viable?"

"That's not important. And it's *not* unliveable."

Smith snorts. He's not surprised. *He knows*. My pulse rises, cheeks warming from the rush of blood to my head. "What does the Company say?"

Hewett shakes her head. "Data takes too long to return to Earth, more to process. The *Pilgrim* was sent on the basis of initial surveys. This volatility developed after key decisions were already made. It couldn't have been predicted."

She reaches for the data pad, but I step back. "Aren't there contingency plans? Other sites?"

My promised Habitat is fading from near-reality to distant dream. I shove the nightmare aside and check her data. Even if we shield our equipment from being torn apart by storms, the wind resonance will be amplified by the canyons protecting each site, like a giant speaker system. But life support systems, energy fields—in fact, most machines necessary for the new colony to function—are vulnerable to stress and tension from that level of vibration. I've seen it happen in TeachVids. Every engineer knows about it. Our ships and our materials are designed to combat resonance, among other things.

Except Yawena has a noise problem we weren't prepared for, and our roster of colonists lacks an industrial materials scientist. I should know. "Why didn't you just turn around when you found out? Why keep going?"

We're days from the planet. Hewett has doomed us all.

She scoffs. "Once that bottom line is signed, all risks belong to the colonists. The Company lent you the *Pilgrim*, the data for a Goldilocks planet ripe for the taking, initial fabrication and colonisation materials. Yawena Colony owes a planetary-sized debt."

One that can only be paid once they begin producing and shipping raw materials. And Hewett values her paycheck. A perfect Company captain.

Smith jabs the nearest cradle like I'm the one inside it, not some defrosting colonist. "Basically, we're all gonna die or go mad like you, Rayan. Probably both."

I round on him. Sleeping with Hewett, yet he didn't stop her. "I can't believe you *knew* and still let her bring us here!"

"Shut up," snaps Hewett. Smith screws up his face; I glare.

"I need those sound files to counter the resonance," she continues. "A sound wave barrier, broadcast at the appropriate frequency, pitch and volume, might afford protection for the colony until you all figure out something permanent. Basically, an interference shield. I've been testing the idea." She gestures at the handheld. "But you've just wiped out all sound-related data on the *Pilgrim*."

"It wasn't me." The response is automatic. I turn away, staring at the nearest console while I think. Vital signs dance across the screen. Lines of life that, if translated, make their own eerie music. Hewett taps her fingers, sending needles across my skin. The *Pilgrim*'s hum shifts, off-key again. I wince—

—and freeze, mind set to racing. Snatching up the readout, I scan them, bile rising. Yawena's winds won't just destroy the equipment. The planet's minerals are natural resonators that ring out when vibrated at certain frequencies. Some of them...hum. At pitch and amplitudes unpleasant to sensitive human ears.

"That data is vital to survival," Hewett is saying. "Months of work identifying frequency compatibility, modifying parameters—"

"Why *did* you keep this from me?"

Unease flickers over her face at my scrutiny. I almost choke as I realise: Hewett hasn't just come up with a plan.

"You've been testing these predicted sounds...for months." My chest gains a hollow void, rapidly expanding. "How?"

She sighs, her expression patronising. "Subject exposure and analysis. To gather data on sound variation, impact, and mitigation potential."

"Subject exposure." I struggle to repeat her words.

"Yes? I needed to know what to expect when we got here, and whether interference would effectively reduce mental deterioration rate over time." She sighs again. "The planet's noise is particularly…unpleasant sometimes, shall we say."

I'm as cold as the frozen colonists around us. "You've been broadcasting the sound of Yawena as an experiment. To see *what that does to people?*"

I turn to pace; find my path blocked by Smith. "Is that why you're always playing music?" I accuse him. "Because you know whatever Hewett's doing will fuck with your head?"

He sneers. "I play my music because it's damn good music. Or it was, until you *deleted* it all."

Hewett scoffs behind me. "I didn't need to test it on him. I already had a subject who was sensitive to noise." I spin back to her. "We figured, if *you* didn't go crazy from the sound then the rest of us would definitely be fine. For a short time, at least."

I stare, speechless at her callousness.

She shrugs. "It's not like you were useful for anything else."

"Though it does turn out that Yawena's sound makes crazy people crazier," Smith adds.

Hewett said it was all in my head. Hewett kept me in MedBay 'out of concern for my mental state'. She banned me from EVAs and any relief from the constant barrage. 'Offered' shoddy replacement noise cancellers when mine were deliberately broken…

"Just stop whining and repair the files," Smith says.

I clutch at the closest terminal, knuckles white.

Hewett points at her datapad, limp in my other hand. "Fix it so we can all live on that planet, and I'll even let you have that weird Habitat. At least then you'll be somewhere I can't hear your complaints while the rest of us actually deal with the noise."

Rage, humiliation, and pain consume my vision in a dizzying tumult. Floundering, I manage a single syllable.

"No."

I stumble from the bay.

It doesn't matter that I might be condemning us all. The void has swallowed me, taking with it any capacity for forgiveness, rational thought, anything. I leave them to their accusations and gaslighting and lies. Months of unnerving sounds have scoured my soul to bare bones; now Hewett's revelation has set even those aflame. Nothing on Earth or in space can make me help her now, Captain or not.

Smith comes for me in the corridor. "Just tell me what you did and I'll fix it," he says, blocking my way.

"Why, so you and Hewett can play 'Let's see how long it takes before Ray breaks' some more? I don't think so."

"Can't you see the big picture?" he says. "Someone had to be the guinea pig. Sucks to be you, but—"

I laugh at him, without humour. "Moron. I saw the data. Whether I or anyone else can stand Yawena's sound up here doesn't matter. That planet's a freaking *amplifier*." I swing my arms, turn in a circle. Whatever I've experienced on the *Pilgrim* is nothing compared to the hell waiting on-planet. "We're. All. Fucked."

It gives me a kind of satisfaction, that Hewett will soon know how it feels to be driven mad by sound.

"Calm down, Rayan." Smith steps closer. "Calm down and fix the damn

virus." He grabs me and when I protest, drags me down the hall to the nearest terminal.

I curse and pull to no avail. I need time to think, I need space. Smith pays me no heed.

A maintenance 'bot trundles towards us, an unknowing saviour. I stop resisting, and when Smith turns in surprise, I knee his groin, and grab at the 'bot. At its handy tool belt for engineers.

Smith manages a strangled, "What the fuck, Ray?"

I brandish the screwdriver, ready to run. "It's not as easy as that, asshole. I can't just 'bring back the data'. You'll never leave me alone, you can't help it. You and Hewett have treated me like an idiot, a freak, when I can run this ship as well or better than both of you! And you've been *running experiments* on—" Tears scald my cheeks. I can't run. I can't hide. The 'bot beeps and I shriek. "Why can't you all just *leave me in peace!*"

Smith lunges. But the screwdriver is heavy and sharp. The stab it makes in his arm is deep, his shout of pain a shock and yet so very, very satisfying. Blood flies, hot and dark. Fear and adrenaline and fury fill my mouth, acidic. Sweet. He knocks me away, punches the side of my head so that I stagger, light and pain blinding me. A moment later, I'm back up. I need to break free but I also need to give in to this violence, this revenge. My pulse pounds with the ship's heart, with the cascading arrhythmia of Yawena's soundtrack. I drive the rod into the soft muscle above Smith's knee, bringing him down, wrench it out and stab again, catching an ear, nicking his neck as he rolls. We're screaming, both screaming, as I cut at him again. Both his ears are bleeding, one hanging oddly, a lump of misshapen, unnecessary flesh. I yank at it, my hand coming away bloody and full. Then Hewett is at the end of the corridor yelling, coming fast, and I can't take on both of them. I run.

My tears are hot and angry, yet also ecstatic, and horrified, and everything in between. I ignore the shouts as I make it to the aft ladder, down to engineering, along the next corridor. The screwdriver and ear fall along the way.

There's only one place left that's safe. Only one place I can go for what I need.

†

It takes longer than usual to don my suit. The *Pilgrim* vibrates beneath my magnetic-soled boots, a deep, low thrum that never dies, only changes. It is familiar now, reminiscent of her sound when I first came aboard. The *Pilgrim* is happy. Hewett must have turned off her experiment, for how long I don't know. I stroke the walls with shaking, bloody hands.

My seals are intact, door locked by the time Hewett and Smith arrive at the evac point. I've already expelled the air from this side. Smith yells through the viewport, eyes crazed. I can't hear him. Bright yellow and black door paint distracts from the purple apoplexy of their faces. I scroll through the data on my HUD, ignoring blood pressure alarms, the cold weight sitting on my chest. I don't see my once-colleagues leaving, only their absent ghosts when I glance back once more. It doesn't matter. They can't get me here. Not yet.

I package what I can recover of Hewett's data, sending it to the soon-to-be-waking colonists, the external relay. A short video goes with it: my testament. I doubt I'll be around to tell my side of events when they're reviewed.

Hewett's 'experiments'. I laugh sourly. She'd gotten her results all right.

Mechanical, technological and mental erosion, the spiralling anguish of my waking and sleeping hours. My stomach roils. I rub at a dark red stain on my suit. A lifetime of overwhelm, of short fuses and triggered rage, seeps from my pores. I need to scream. I need to end it. All I can aim for is silence, the vast expanse of blessed nothingness whose cocoon calls to me.

I turn off my displays and comms, palm open the airlock door. Vibration shakes my limbs as the hull slides apart, then disappears as I disengage my boots, lifting into weightlessness. Silence wraps me in its welcoming embrace. I hold my breath, taking it in.

A suited crew member swings around the door from space-side and barrels toward me. In my surprise, I don't react quickly enough. They crash into me, gripping tight, momentum carrying us both backwards into the airlock, onto a floor that a moment ago was a wall. Déja vu hits as I crash hard, rebounding, grappling, gloved hands slipping on bulky suit. Smith's name is stamped on the chest before me, face hidden by the copper mirror of his visor. He must have pulled himself over from the other airlock, the broken one we sealed off after the accident. I bash at his

helmet and kick with my heavy, too-slow legs. I cannot get away.

We whirl. With each rebound Smith pulls me towards the exit though I try to twist away, disoriented but knowing I don't want to go out there, not with *him*. He thrusts our helmets together, visor to visor, and then I hear it: "Stop this, Rayan. Stop, Ray. Stop!"

It's Hewett in the other suit. It has to be; it's Hewett's voice and she's yelling in her helmet, sound that travels to my ears because unlike the vacuum outside, air and helmets are made of molecules, they vibrate.

"Stop, Ray. Don't do this." I'm caught; nowhere to go. No way to block her out. Why's she in Smith's suit?

Hewett pushes off a surface, sending us back toward the inner door. Her voice fades in and out. "It'll be okay. Smith can analyse…it's you we need. Don't you see?…from the start. It's only sound, Ray…it'll work…it will. Just have to repeat…" She pulls back, reaches for the controls to shut the exterior door once more, to repressurise and reorient and—

"No."

We can't hear each any longer, but it doesn't matter. I won't do what she wants. I won't let her repeat those experiments, or chance Yawena's surface. She'll destroy this ship, these colonists, before they can figure out alternatives.

She'll destroy me.

I grab Hewett's back, her oxygen supply tube. Wrap my thighs around her tank and brace my feet on the wall and *pull*. She resists, and I shout my exertion, and I won't let her do this, I won't, and I'm not holding a screwdriver—I dropped it, I dropped it—but my rage remains. Hewett is the problem, the problem not the solution, and as she falls backward I kick out too, reverse my direction and shove her forward. Helmet into door, the force of my upper body behind her head.

Smack.

I yank her head back, forward again.

Crack.

Again.

She *has* destroyed me.

A section of tubing snaps free; I pull and twist and shove her back against the door, again and again, and I scream, and her helmet splinters, her suit rips on the upper arm, air spews, all in silence except loud, so loud. I don't need to hear to *feel*, to see the broken fabric floating past my face, to witness the red coating her visor. I grasp her helmet in both hands and headbutt it, yelling nothing at all. Blood spills through fractured glass, viscous, globular. Hewett's face is behind the crack, her eyes bulging and red, mouth wide in a snarl, a scream, a panicked terrified unsatisfied gasp. There are no 'bots to open the door this time. No MedSuites and weeks of recovery, of preparation for further *testing*. I take hold of the front of her suit, turn and push with all the strength I have remaining, and send her through the airlock into the void.

There is no time in space, only the moments between one breath and the next. One heartbeat; the next; the next.

Time and breath and heartbeats.

Tears, wetting my cheeks.

I find my centre.

Rows of cradles stretch out before me, shells of frozen potential, of life: disruptive, disregulated, and oh so *loud*, but life, nonetheless. I punch the stasis button on every one, defrosting reversed.

"Sleep well." I won't wake them for Yawena. The planet is a lost cause. But we have supplies and fuel to spare, and Hewett earmarked two planets as possibly habitable before her ill-fated scheme took over. Sixteen months' travel to the closest, twenty more for the other. Risky, but doable. Better that than return to Earth, unwanted and unwelcome. Or condemn these thousand sleeping souls to a brief, excruciating existence in the wind-stricken hell of the planet below us.

I lock up and head to MedBay. Smith may recover, though his hearing will never be the same. I've fixed his loss of music with a new simulation of Yawena's soundscape. He can listen in the cryo-cradle I've assigned him.

The *Pilgrim*'s robots are well-programmed to replace my former colleagues. The ship only needs one technician awake, after all. I pat the walls fondly as I do my rounds, buoyed by the familiar, regular vibration. It's soothing, this hum. Helps me think.

THE SEVENTH INSTAR

KAY VAINDAL

We are three larval worms inside a tall man's ear. We watch him sit in his office and stare at a screen too bright for us to see, click click tap tap, but we're too cold to leave. We've grown up here, in this wet cave. Our mother lovingly oviposited us here, and then spread her fluttery wings and flew home to Venus.

Today, we're munching on a fresh supply of earwax. The tall man has been instructed by his doctor to stop using Q-tips, and we're delighted. We lost a good, smart brother to Q-tips at the end of our second instar.

The doctor can't see us. The tall man can't see us. His ears are so very itchy. When we see his stubby finger, squared-off fingernails ready to pierce our squishy abdomens, we huddle back near his eardrum. Three or four times before this

his doctor shined a flashlight into his ear canals. We hid, at first. But then our stupidest brother crawled eagerly toward the light, presented his body and his bristles to the doctor's warm otoscope, and still the doctor said, "All clear in there, Mr. Dimiglio."

Our greatest danger now is the prescription anti-itch ethyl-alcohol lubricating drops that Mr. Dimiglio puts in his ears every evening. Our brothers are suffering. We, the three smartest worms, the first of the eggs to hatch, the first to grow bristles and eyes, came up with our solution just yesterday. It's timely. We know soon we'll outgrow our warm wet cave.

Last night we tunneled into Mr. Dimiglio's brain. It's soft and pink and smells fresh. It's through here we can watch today's doctor's appointment. The doctor is saying *psychosomatic*. The tasty serotonin in Mr. Dimiglio's tissues shrivels up. Springs of cortisol bubble up in the wrinkles of his brain and make us feel like happy, bouncy worms. We bounce and play in pools of hormones while Mr. Dimiglio's doctor refers him to a psychiatrist.

The most delightful thing about being worms living in Mr. Dimiglio's head is that Mr. Dimiglio is rich enough to show us all sorts of lovely tastes and sights. He flies in a plane twice a week. He loves steak. We love steak, too. We think our mother picked him out on purpose for us. We think she flew low and slow, suffering the frigid Earth, until she found just the right man for us to grow inside.

Soon, we can make Mr. Dimiglio do things. We can make him turn his thermostat up and stop using his lubricating drops, and we rub our bristles against his pituitary gland so we can shiver and play and bounce. We hear our brothers' cheers from the ear canal the first night the cave stays sober. Our plan is working.

But still, we need more. The cave is too small to host our many cocoons, and the air is too cold. We make Mr. Dimiglio fly to the equator. We book him a week-long stay at a resort in the rainforest, where he meets with dozens of other wealthy tall humans and they play tennis and his ear sweat nourishes our brothers with salt and spice. We think about ordering a stupider brother into this warm atmosphere, but we know it isn't hot enough here.

Back in Houston, Mr. Dimiglio eats a large pile of wet beef and Googles what is the warmest place on this planet. The four of us book a flight to Las Vegas, and we rent a big, warm car to take us to Death Valley. In Death Valley, we feel almost comfortable. Here, we select a brave, stupid brother to exit the ear canal. We watch him with Mr. Dimiglio's eyes. He rolls his bristles on the sand in front of him. Raises his head to smell the fresh air. Our brother plays and bounces in the sand for only a minute. Then he dries up like a raisin.

In the cave, our brothers cry and cry. We make Mr. Dimiglio do jumping jacks until his ears sweat, and we leave our brave dehydrated brother in the sand.

It's in the awful winter months that we have our breakthrough. We've been inside Mr. Dimiglio's head for two years now. We're so bouncy and playful and we're running out of space. The thermostat is set to 84. Mr. Dimiglio has a lovely dinner of cow ribs soaked in the gooiest of oils that night, eating with his hands in front of a big television screen. We love Mr. Dimiglio's television almost as much as we love his computer. On the television, we see three sad tall people in lab coats chaining themselves to an oil rig. We see vibrant, colorful plumes of smoke from a tower. A shiver runs across every one of our bristles, in the brain and in the cave. Even our

stupidest brothers understand. "Mr. Dimiglio," we say to our friend, "this is just what we need!"

Mr. Dimiglio buys us the oil rig. It only costs him three billion dollars. We bring him to the top of our smokestack and we stick his face in the rainbow plume of gases and it's the most delicious air we've ever tasted, warm and fresh, and our bristles tingle like they never have. We hear rumors from the cave that a bold brother enters his sixth instar then and there, bristles settling against his soft flesh hardening into keratin.

We spend the night at the computer. By morning, Mr. Dimiglio's eyes are dry and twitching, and his brain misfires, and he owns an oil company called Fundy Fuels and a majority stake in a news company called Media Corp. We let Mr. Dimiglio sleep only after he's befriended a tall man geo-economist and published sixteen of his rejected papers on why CO_2, our favorite glittering rainbow gas, is good for the human economy and human health and human bones.

Mr. Dimiglio sleeps and we think about amassing more money like piles of fresh wet beef. We love piles. Thinking about piles makes us bouncy and playful and we stretch and roll. Mr. Dimiglio's pile of wealth is growing and growing and so are we. People like the sad lab coat people are very angry about that on the computer. We don't blame them. If we had no piles, we'd be so so sad.

We are friendly worms now, ready to navigate the world of mammals. Mr. Dimiglio never wakes up. As he sleeps we untie the nerves in his brain and we replace them with our brothers, who snap electricity back and forth along their spines. The first day is difficult for us. We wear our smile too wide and too often, and some of the employees look nervously at each other when we bounce and play and roll in the halls.

We go to lunch with Vice President Andrew and five other tall people, and we approve a plan to extract oil from a new place. Oil turns into our favorite gas. Our favorite gas turns into warms. We know for sure now that our mother oviposited us in Mr. Dimiglio's ear for this purpose.

It's so so lonely to be a brain made out of worms. We play and bounce in private, behind the closed door of Mr. Dimiglio's office, but it's different to play and bounce in a human body. We miss the warm wet cave. The stupid brothers take shifts as nerves. The worms who aren't nerves slither to the cave to play and bounce and nap in big heaping piles, cuddled with their brothers' many legs. But we three smart worms sit on top of the brain day and night, directing traffic and planning our escape from the skull.

Mr. Dimiglio has a big business meeting soon. We'll meet with a group of more established humans eager to meet us, and we'll see if they can help us get more warms. Andrew stressed to us the importance of this meeting. Back in Mr. Dimiglio's penthouse, we practice a charming smile in the bathroom mirror. Then we put the body to sleep and we play and play all night, even the smartest of us, rolling and bouncing in Mr. Dimiglio's ear nose and throat.

In the morning, we take an airplane to the meeting. Elated by the color of the sky, two more brothers enter the sixth instar, hardening into keratin and freshly exempt from duty. Nerve shifts grow longer each day.

Off the plane in a new city, we check into a comfy cozy hotel room with a big glass window that lets in so much warm sun. It's freezing. It's the iciest hotel room on the planet and the thermostat won't budge the temperature. We press ourselves against the window and shiver shiver. We pull blankets up onto our shoulders and over our head and we tug them in tight and we march down to the front desk and we demand a warmer room.

The desk woman is meek and pliable. She agrees to come with us to look at the thermostat. We are friendly worms but we're no pushovers, and we demand she send a big, buff, massive maintenance man instead. The maintenance man she chooses is large and orange. He's a pile of skin and fat and he rides the elevator back up with us. We smile at him like how we practiced.

The maintenance man cannot fix the thermostat. It's summer now, and the thermostat can only be on the chilly-cold setting. This is terrible! We beckon him into the bathroom to check the tub. We smile at him like we practiced. Then we hit him over his head with his wrench, and we shove his warm pile of body into our mouth piece by piece. This takes hours. Mr. Dimiglio's body hums with warmth after, beads of sweat nourishing our off-shift brothers. After, we clean ourselves in a hot hot tub until Mr. Dimiglio's skin turns pink. The meeting is in one hour, in the conference room downstairs. We arrive just

on time, in a fresh suit with no blood on our lips.

Twelve other tall men with pink skin! We sit at a round table and give them the smile we practiced. All the pink men grab hot coffees from the dispenser and we close the double doors. One man has bloodshot eyes, and where he goes, we watch and follow. All twelve of us fall into step behind this bloodshot individual.

"Gentlemen," says the bloodshot pink tall man, "Welcome!"

"This is a cold hotel," says another tall pink man.

"A very cold hotel!" says a third.

We smile so so much as the rest of the tall pink men take their seats around this round table. The bloodshot one walks in a circle around our perimeter. We all watch him. He goes from tall pink man to tall pink man, brushing his gentle hands through our fine gray hairs.

A bold pink tall man reaches to rub our leader's fine gray hairs back. "Would you like," says the bloodshot tall man in the bold pink tall man's ear, loud enough for us all to hear, "to bounce and play?"

We bounce and play all afternoon! It's like we're in our second instar again, rolling and squirming and jumping and shouting.

When we're finally tired enough to sit back down, all of us grinning the way the humans call too wide and too long, our smartest bloodshot leader tells us to crack open the earth. "Our favorite gas is inside," he tells us.

Another pink man, beside us, presses his fingers to his lips. We've seen humans press their fingers to their lips. All these worms perform humanity at a higher level than us. Are we the youngest worms present? Our head bristles are less gray than theirs. Our skin is a shade less pink. How many piles have these friendly worms amassed? How much of our favorite gas have they contributed to the frigid air our mothers left us to swim through?

"Do you worry about the humans?" we ask our smart cousins.

The bold pink tall man chuckles. He brushes his wet hand on our less-gray hairs and produces a smile more practiced than ours. "You ate one this morning, cousin."

The round table gasps. Our bristles point at the white dome above our heads hanging low.

"You can't just eat humans, cousin," says the bold pink tall man. "Humans don't buy products from humans who eat humans."

"We're sorry," we say.

Our cousin brushes our not-gray bristles with a soothing shush. "You didn't know."

A cousin across the table nods. "We ate a human once, years ago," and a chorus of others agree. "When you're cold, and they're warm, it seems like the right thing to do."

The tall pink man with the bloodshot eyes stands again, smoothly like he's all nerves and no worms. "The humans love the warms too," he says as he adjusts his tie. "They'll thank us once they see our beautiful wings."

We nod, and hesitate, and nod again, and add, "We mean the humans who chain themselves to our oil rigs."

Our bloodshot-eyed cousin smiles at us very well. We want to be just like him, so spiffy in his black-and-white. "We've been here a long time, cousin. The humans can't make piles like we can. You've seen these insides. Juicy and fresh and soft. No diapause for humans. Buy buy buy. Forget to buy food, die. Forget to buy water, die. Forget to buy happy ice cream for serotonin? Die. Work work work to buy buy buy. Even the ones with piles like ours are wet beef in waiting. This world is so ruled by piles. And we are pile-making worms. This is why our mothers oviposited us here. To build piles and warms until this world smells delicious and they can come and bounce and play with us in the sky with our great big beautiful wings, like home."

"Home," we say.

Our smartest, friendliest cousin proposes sliding a metal proboscis into a piece of land he owns in a US state called Idaho. Then we'll use Fundy Fuel's special horizontal drills to poke poke a massive mantle plume where we'll find bubbling reserves of our favorite gases, liquified by pressure and waiting thousands of years for us to set them free. Our cousin discovered this on the Discovery Channel. All at once the explosion will carry out what our cousins have been waiting on since the humans started burning. A toasty, cozy earth, warm and full of good air.

We put our piles together and we have a mountain. Our cousin says only thirteen humans in the whole world have a bigger mountain than us, and seven of them are in the energy sector, too. We meet in Idaho the following Thursday, all of us excited and bouncy and our bloodshot cousin's eyes bulging three centimeters outside of his face. Idaho is cold, cold, cold. Great bumps of earth sit stoic on the horizon. *Release us*, they say.

We've kept the drilling so secret. Human Vice President Andrew moved our special horizontal drills by night on the highways, drivers paid more than they deserved to keep their little lips sealed. The humans will be fine, we're sure. We remember our vacation in the rainforest and the humans who laid under the sun collecting warmth until their skins glowed shades of brown and orange and pink. They'll love this.

We put the drills in place and put our special hero humans on the drilling platforms with the big checks they'll never cash, and we get on our smartest cousin's jet and fly to a place called Italy. There, we sit at a villa at a beautiful lake and wait. Our cousin's eyes are looking yellow now. His skin is less red now, pale. We hear another cousin whisper that if even one more worm in that brain enters its sixth instar, the whole skull will explode.

We're disappointed when it happens. From Italy, we can't hear the blast or see the ash. Humans at the resort look at their phones and whisper in shock. We see one look at another with a sort of smug satisfaction. Laughter on the tennis courts. They go back to hitting balls.

In the morning the clouds arrive. Dark and delicious. The humans wear masks over their faces and clear plastic glasses on their eyes and leave the resort in speedy little vans. The air tastes so good and the staff at the resort tell us they'd like to evacuate, too. "To where?" asks our cousin with the bulging eyes. "This is a global event." He smiles. It looks less practiced than it used to. The staff stay and serve us little pork sticks.

Something is wrong. We monitor the temperature at the lake each morning. The air tastes so yummy but the sun won't pierce the ash clouds and the earth is cooling fast. We feel sluggish and tired. We rest Mr. Dimiglio's dead body in the sauna for a while.

The electricity goes out one week after we let the gas out of the earth. The staff disappear that night. Our thermostats drop back and our rooms get chilly chilly chilly. With our last scraps of energy we drag our bodies to a conference room. Some of our cousins have blood on their chins and the collars of their suits. "This is a cold hotel," says a cousin.

"What happened?" says another.

"How long until it gets warm?"

Our smartest cousin's skull explodes. Bits of gray brain splatter the walls and the table. Seven beautiful moths emerge between shards of bone, great glorious golden wings extend three feet across. They flutter and breathe and gasp and shiver.

Our free and beautiful cousins fly toward the ceiling, to the corners of the room. They flutter straight through a glass window and under the black sky. Then they freeze. Their wings stop fluttering and their shivering ceases and it's like they go to sleep, so peacefully drifting down out of the sky, falling like leaves into the layer of black dust on the resort sidewalk. Ash settles over their golden bodies.

We shiver and watch from the window. Then we turn and join our cousins beside our smartest cousins' remains. "It will get warm soon," says a cousin. "The models say so." We huddle in the dark and nibble on our cousins' host's skin, cooling fast.

THANK YOU FOR PARTICIPATING

TJ CIMFEL

» Hello. Thank you for participating in the Gardner Empirical Institute's Sleep Study (GEISS). This is the first in a series of brief daily online questionnaires. Please respond to every question in your own voice. Be as thorough and truthful as possible. Delayed, incomplete, or misleading responses may result in dismissal from the study and prorated remuneration. This is a real-time study. GEISS Researchers will review your responses each evening and may tailor questions in subsequent portions of the study. Please think of this as a conversation. And have fun!

In your own words, please provide a baseline description of a typical 24-hour period in your life. Be specific.

I usually get up around six to record, but I struggle to get going, so a lot of times I read my phone and drink coffee until I wake up, which sometimes means I'm not really laying down any tracks at all before I have to shower and get the day going. My wife is a stay-at-home mom, but she suffers from severe depression, so I'm usually the one to make the kids' lunches and get them ready and take them to school. I'm usually late to work because of that, but no one really cares about that stuff anymore especially because it's a given that I'll be working late. I spend most of the day coding, but we have occasional meetings. I usually get home in time to make dinner for the fam, do bath time, clean up, put the kids to bed, maybe watch TV if my wife is feeling up for it. If I'm lucky, I have the motivation to get back in the studio for a couple of hours, but lately I just lie in bed and stare at my screen until my eyes close. It might be the side effects of my other meds, so I'm curious to see what will happen with this whole thing.

How much sleep do you get on average?

I typically sleep five or six hours a night. I know it's not healthy and that the average is supposed to be something like eight or maybe even more, but there's just too much on my plate.

On a scale of 1-5 (with 1 being poor and 5 being excellent), how would you rate your ability to fall asleep?

Two. I normally can't fall asleep without trazodone.

On the same scale, how would you rate your ability to remain asleep?

Three. I'll sometimes toss and turn in the middle of the night and wonder why I can't fall back asleep, and then I realize after a while that it's just because I have to pee. I'd say about 50% of the time I fall back asleep without issue. The rest of the time, I just stare into the dark and twirl about whatever's going on in my life. It's a hopeless feeling.

On the same scale, how would you rate your ability to wake up in the morning?

One. I've started setting multiple alarms because I don't trust myself with the snooze button. And like I said before, even after I wake up, I'm basically a zombie for the first hour of the day. Which sucks because that's the only time I have for myself.

Do you ever get sleepy during the day?

Hahaha. That's an affirmative. Mornings are fine. Caffeine is a helluva drug. But after lunch, it's all downhill. I have trouble paying attention in meetings, and there are times at my desk when I prop my chin on my hand and zonk out for a few minutes. There's a corner of my cube where no one can see me. It's frustrating because I never feel that way at night when I am supposed to fall asleep.

Do you ever feel your daily functioning is compromised due to challenges with sleep?

I guess I'd say no. I'm still able to do everything I do. I guess I'm just not doing everything I want to. Does that make sense? Although I'm not sure if that's a sleep issue or a "my life" issue.

What do you hope to get out of this study?

Better sleep. Better energy. More time to focus on my true passion.

Have you discontinued and destroyed all other medications you are currently taking?

I have.

» Please take one capsule now and submit.

» Hello. Please complete the following questionnaire as thoroughly and truthfully as possible.

On a scale of 1-5, (with 1 being poor and 5 being excellent), how did you sleep last night?

One. I got in bed at the same time I usually do and read my phone. I thought I might be getting drowsy, but my oldest had a nightmare, so I had to talk him down because my wife was already asleep. I guess that's one of the good things about her depression, she doesn't have any issues with sleeping. Anyway, I probably drifted off around one, but I couldn't really regulate my temperature during the night. I kept taking my pajamas off and then putting them back on. I'd be sweating my ass off (Hope it's okay that I use colorful language. You did say I should answer in my own voice.), then I'd kick off the covers and immediately get the chills. I figured it was a fever, but when I took my temperature, it was normal. When I did eventually fall asleep asleep, it was probably after three. I woke up groggy, too, and it took me longer to clear my morning brain fog.

Did you experience any somnambulism (sleepwalking) or somniloquy (talking in your sleep)?

No.

Did you dream? If so, what about?

No.

What are the names of your wife and children?

I put this in the release form already, but my wife's name is Jennifer, and my sons are Abe and Phineas.

» Please take one capsule now and submit.

++

» Hello. Please complete the following questionnaire as thoroughly and truthfully as possible.

On a scale of 1-5, (with 1 being poor and 5 being excellent), how did you sleep last night?

Okay, so this was interesting. Like, the quality of my sleep was actually a four or five, but the duration of my sleep was a hard two. Early on, I had the same issues as the previous night. Temperature and all that. I probably wasn't out until three in the morning or so. My mind was racing about my wife. She's really not doing well. But this time, once I fell asleep, I was down for the count. When my alarm went off, that was the best part. My eyes popped open, and it was like there was no grog whatsoever. I went downstairs, brewed a pot of coffee, and worked on some overdubs. Stuff sounds great!

Did you experience any somnambulism (sleepwalking) or somniloquy (talking in your sleep)?

No.

Did you dream? If so, what about?

I think I did, but I can't remember what it was about. I just remember being outside.

What are the names of your wife and children?

Is this a copy/paste from yesterday? Jennifer, Abe, and Phineas.

» Please take one capsule now and submit.

++

» Hello. Please complete the following questionnaire as thoroughly and truthfully as possible.

On a scale of 1-5, (with 1 being poor and 5 being excellent), how did you sleep last night?

Ten! Holy shit. I closed my eyes at one and opened them at six. No temperature issues, no nothing. It was amazing—like I blinked and woke up. I know it was only five hours, but if I could sleep like this all the time, I wouldn't even care!

Did you experience any somnambulism (sleepwalking) or somniloquy (talking in your sleep)?

No sleepwalking. But my wife did complain that I was mumbling some stuff in the middle of the night. Like nonsense babble. I have no recollection of this. By the way, I am totally going to name one of my songs "Somniloquy."

Did you dream? If so, what about?

Yes! I was in my backyard. It was a beautiful day. All the colors were super saturated—our house, the grass, the trees. I don't know that I've ever noticed color in a dream before. Are you dosing me with LSD? If so, keep it up! I was playing my Strat. It wasn't hooked up to an amp, but it was loud and clear and I could change its tone just by thinking about it. The thing was, I could only play in tritones. No matter what I tried, how I placed my fingers on the frets, it was always tritones. It was super weird too, because even though tritones are one of the gnarliest chords in music, it was beautiful. Like, the most beautiful progression I'd ever played before. There were a bunch of little blackbirds with yellow eyes. They were next to me on the ground, and it was like they were watching me play. I don't think they were crows. They were smaller. Hold on, going to Google. Grackles. I think they were grackles. After a while, I noticed the ground in front of me would shift based on the

dynamics of my playing. If I played quietly, it would ripple a little. But when I let it rip, it was almost like the ocean. The birds bounced when I played. It was hilarious.

What are the names of your wife and children?

Jennifer, Abe, and Luke Skywalker.

» Please take one capsule now and submit.

» Hello. Participant is reminded to answer all questions as thoroughly and truthfully as possible. Failure to comply could lead to loss of remuneration and/or revised study parameters.

On a scale of 1-5, (with 1 being poor and 5 being excellent), how did you sleep last night?

Five for quality, one for duration. I think I'm getting less sleep each night, not more, which is weird. I maybe got two, two and a half hours. This drug is supposed to help me sleep, isn't it? Don't get me wrong, I feel rested, I feel sharp. I'm drinking less coffee, too. I'm not nodding off in the afternoon. But this can't actually be healthy, right?

Did you experience any somnambulism (sleepwalking) or somniloquy (talking in your sleep)?

My wife told me I was out of bed for a half hour. I asked her why she didn't come get me, and she said she just thought it was more insomnia. I have no recollection of being up, and like I said, I felt like I slept like a baby.

Did you dream? If so, what about?

I did. I was in my backyard again, and I was playing that same song on my guitar. The grackles weren't on the ground anymore. They were hovering in midair like hummingbirds, only their wings weren't moving. The ground rippled each time I played a chord (tritones only still), and after a while I realized the grass was actually folding in on itself little by little, like there was a sinkhole opening up and my guitar was making it happen. Eventually, there was a hole big enough to drive a car into. The grackles started moving in a circle above it—not flying, just kind of rotating through the air. Bizarre stuff.

Did you look in the hole?
WTF?

What are the names of your wife and children?

Jennifer, Abe, and Phineas.

» Please take one capsule now and submit.

» Hello. Participant is reminded to answer all questions as thoroughly and truthfully as possible. Failure to comply could lead to loss of remuneration and/or revised study parameters.

On a scale of 1-5, (with 1 being poor and 5 being excellent), how did you sleep last night?

I've been trying to get ahold of you. I tried calling the study hotline and the Gardner main line and only got automated responses. No one replied to my emails, and your chatbot was a joke. How did you know I dreamt about a hole? How did you know that I dreamt at all? Or even slept? I sat there staring at my computer screen yesterday worried I was losing my mind. And it's not helping that I can't reach a single human being at your facility. Could someone please get in contact with me immediately? I slept an hour. I don't understand why I'm not tired. Rank that however you want.

Did you experience any somnambulism (sleepwalking) or somniloquy (talking in your sleep)?

I babbled. I walked around. And that was during an hour of sleep.

Did you dream? If so, what about?
Yes, about the field and the song and the grackles and the hole. And no, I didn't look in the hole.

Did you look in the hole?
What is this bullshit?

Do you love your wife and children?
Jennifer, Abe, and Phineas.

» Please take one capsule now and submit.

» Hello. Participant is reminded to pay close attention to all questions to ensure the most thorough and truthful responses. Participant is reminded to not use the study questionnaire as a means to communicate information outside the purview of the study. Should assistance be needed, please contact the study administrator via the provided hotline.

On a scale of 1-5, (with 1 being poor and 5 being excellent), how did you sleep last night?
I didn't. And I called the damn hotline is what I'm trying to tell you! All freaking day. You get sent through this lunatic audio maze and wind up at the same place every damn time. I know you're supposed to be some cutting-edge scientific institution or whatever, but that won't mean shit if you can't understand the basic rules of customer service.

Did you experience any somnambulism (sleepwalking) or somniloquy (talking in your sleep)?
No. That would require actual sleep.

Did you dream? If so, what about?
Your drug doesn't work.

Did you look in the hole?
I'll give you a hole to look at, fuckface.

Do you love your wife and children?
What the FUCK is that supposed to mean? Why the FUCK do you keep asking me about them and how is it relevant to this study? I'm not taking another capsule until I talk to a live human being. FUCK YOU.

» Please take one capsule now and submit.

» Hello. Please complete the following questionnaire as thoroughly and truthfully as possible.

Are you aware of the risks of not participating?

Yes.

Would you like us to schedule a follow-up from yesterday's one-on-one with our outpatient administrator?

No.

Do you love your wife and children?

Please don't hurt them.

» Please take one capsule now and submit.

✝✝

» Hello. Please complete the following questionnaire as thoroughly and truthfully as possible.

When was the last time you slept?

I believe it has been about 72 hours now. I swear to God I will remain compliant with the study as long as required, but please understand that the stress and anxiety (and now physical pain) I am dealing with as a result of my participation may be skewing the results for you. I would like to discuss a safe way to withdraw from the study. I'll make a healthy donation to your foundation. I'll recruit others to take my place. Anything.

Did you experience any somnambulism (sleepwalking) or somniloquy (talking in your sleep)?

No, but I am experiencing constant anxiety and pain from the extraction site. My hands are trembling really bad. I've been getting light headaches the past few nights, but that may be because of caffeine withdrawal. I haven't had a cup of coffee in at least two days. I feel scatterbrained, like I can't hold any one thought for too long. Or maybe that's wrong. I can hold a thought, but others crowd in around it, like I'm having multiple thoughts simultaneously. How is it that my brain can operate without sleep? What are you guys giving me? Like, at work, I'm performing better than ever. I squashed a bug that had been stumping the team for weeks, and I'm processing code twice as fast as before. I've been recording at night while everyone else sleeps because it calms down my brain and it's something to do and I always used to complain about not having enough time or energy to do what I really love. The thing is, now that I'm doing it, it's like all my old songs don't sound good to me anymore. They feel juvenile, overly simplistic. I went back into one of them and started tinkering and realized what was wrong. I started re-recording some tracks with just tritones and it was like something clicked. It's so fucking good. So fucking beautiful. My oldest came in and interrupted me last night, and I shouted at him. I felt terrible, but also a little good. I'm so goddamn tired of bottling things up.

Did you dream? If so, what about?
I didn't sleep.

Did you look in the hole?
No dream, no hole.

Where are your wife and children?
I WILL KEEP TAKING THE MEDS.

» Please take one capsule now and submit.

» Hello. Please complete the following questionnaire as thoroughly and truthfully as possible.

When was the last time you slept?
Tuesday. I really wish someone would reach out to me.

Did you experience any somnambulism (sleepwalking) or somniloquy (talking in your sleep)?
My headaches are worse. I'm really irritable. I called into work, but that was a mistake because I can't really be alone at home.

Did you dream? If so, what about?
I don't know how, but I think so. I was in the studio, middle of the night, working on a new song. It's the only thing that helps with my head. I was playing this beautiful progression of tritones and layering them onto other tritones, and I started copying and pasting them over and over, just making this wall of sound in Logic Pro, and I felt this euphoria I've never felt before and suddenly I was in the backyard. Like, I was literally standing in the backyard. There was a grackle floating next to my right shoulder, and I swear it turned its head and looked at me with its yellow eyes and said, "What's your true passion?" Only it was my voice that came out of the bird. I could tell the birds were waiting, so I played my guitar and was playing all of the tritones at once, like in my recording. Like, I would strike two fucking strings, two fucking notes, that's all, but all of the notes played and when they did, the air kind of vibrated, or the birds vibrated in the air and they started moving in a circle above the ground like before, not flying though. And I kept playing and the ground fell in on itself and the birds moved in the circle faster until the hole appeared. And then the birds flew in. The next thing I remember I'm back in the studio playing music, only I notice there's dirt and grass on my guitar. What is happening to me?

Did you look in the hole?

If I do, can I be done with this?

Where are your wife and children?
Why are you doing this? Are you doing this to others or is it just me? My new therapist told me this was a specialized study, but I'm scared. Is this because of what I told her? I didn't mean it. It's just how I feel sometimes. I'm a good person. Can we be done now? Please?

» Please take one capsule now and submit.

» Hello. Please complete the following questionnaire as thoroughly and truthfully as possible.

When was the last time you slept?
120 hours ago.

Did you experience any somnambulism (sleepwalking) or somniloquy (talking in your sleep)?
I can't stop shaking.

Did you dream? If so, what about?
I went to clean off my guitar and found blood and hair on it.

» Thank you for participating in the Gardner Empirical Institute's Sleep Study (GEISS). As a participant in Cohort B, you have been receiving an inactive formulation that includes starch and sugar. You may now return to your previous medication regimen.

THE BIOGRAPHER

TANANARIVE DUE

The Biographer arrived much sooner than Olivia expected.

The young woman on her doorstep that morning was wearing a wool coat too threadbare for the snowy trek up the hill to Olivia's house—which was fashioned after a castle with its pale stone facade and a half-frozen moat filled with koi swimming beneath the ice. The stranger was breathless after climbing so many steps, but Olivia hesitated before opening her door.

She wouldn't have expected a Biographer so early, which seemed counter to the strict protocols Biographers were famous for. Through the viewfinder, the stranger had a studious look but was also much younger than any Biographer she'd heard about, maybe in her mid-twenties, so Olivia at first thought she might be only another of the faithful on a sojourn to say she had met her face to face. Usually these people were harmless, but one could never be too careful about opening one's door.

Then the young woman held out the golden envelope and crimson seal for a clear view on her security camera. Olivia had heard about the "Golden Appointments," as they were sometimes called tongue-in-cheek, but it looked the way it had been described in rumors. The envelope reminded her of a story her mother had told her about from her youth involving Golden Tickets, but Olivia could not remember the story or author because it was from Before, as if a wildfire had consumed her childhood. Everyone had the same experience if they had been born before the Plagues, but it still made her feel tainted and empty at times—like now, facing a Biographer at her door and having so little to say. And far too early to say it.

"Olivia Burns," the young woman announced. "Congratulations—you have been assigned a Biographer. Now your story will be told."

Olivia hadn't had her wake-up tea yet, so it was hard to feel celebratory. She had turned only sixty on her last birthday and had fully recovered from her bout with the virus, so this encounter had the markings of a bureaucratic error. But she wouldn't make the young woman wait outside in the cold, so she pushed the wall panel button to unlock her door, which slid open on a silent track, letting in a bracing smack of cold air across her face although she was several yards from the doorway.

Before entering, the young woman ceremoniously fitted herself with a snug medical mask covering her nose and mouth in skintight fiber designed to better display facial features. Second Skin, they called it. The skintight mask created a bizarre flattening effect across her features, especially her mouth, but Olivia could still make out the nub of the young woman's nose, rounded like hers. She'd heard that Biographers were assigned subjects who were similar to help create rapport. And it was true—the young woman's brown skin, windswept corkscrew hair, and old-fashioned round frame eyeglasses reminded her of herself at that age, which seemed both long ago and as if she could find that youthful face in her own mirror.

"A mask isn't necessary," Olivia said. "Wear it if you prefer, of course. But my house is sanitized. And I've long recovered. I can swab and show you my med file…"

"Not necessary," the woman said. "Oh–!" She tripped slightly on the small step into the house, and the large plastic file box she was carrying slipped from her arms, scattering files and photographs on the stone foyer floor. Olivia bent over to try to assist her, but that made her hiss and wave her away, so Olivia took a step back and watched her collect her research, all of it protected in plastic sleeves. She glimpsed a photograph of herself on the set of her most famous film, *Sick*, that she had not seen before. She only saw the image in a glance, but her face looked oddly contorted, and the image filled her with unease.Before she could ask for a better look, the Biographer had deftly refiled it in the box.

"I apologize for my clumsiness," the Biographer said. "Please rest assured that the story of your life will be treated with my utmost care and respect."

"Yes, about that…" Olivia said. "Aren't you early?"

"I'm sorry about the hour. I tried to time it—"

"No, not just that…" Olivia twirled, her arms raised like a Phoenix's wings in her bathrobe. "I'm perfectly healthy. I've recovered. Remember that old quote by Mark Twain…?" From the way the Biographer's eyebrows lowered, she had no idea who Mark Twain was, or his once-famous quote about reports of his death being exaggerated. "The point is, I'm not dying. So you're a bit early. I'm sure I have three or four good films left in me."

The Biographer smiled, a misshapen leer beneath her tight mask. "That's just a misconception, Master Burns. We—"

"Dear God," Olivia said. "'*Master?*' Please call me Olivia."

"Of course…Olivia…" – She said her name as if it were an unfamiliar language– "Especially for someone of your stature, the Academy of Biographers believes that it's best to get an early start to create the most thorough scholarship."

Dammit. So she wouldn't be able to send this young woman away and enjoy a quiet cup of tea before getting back to work on her script after all. She had never heard of anyone sending a Biographer away, especially not so soon.

"I'm sorry, so…how does this work? Obviously, this is my first time."

"I'll be staying with you for a short while," the Biographer said. "I'll go back down the hill now and get my bag. I had to be sure I would find you. This will surprise you…but sometimes people hide from us."

It didn't surprise Olivia at all, if only because of the disruption. She almost protested that she didn't have a guest room, but the size of her house would have called her a liar. Truthfully, she had never explored some of the rooms on the third floor. The Biographer would have to sleep up there with the dust and tarps that probably had been there since the original owners died of Plague forty years before. And how long was "a short while," anyway? Olivia had hoped to finish her shooting script within the week.

"What's your name?" Olivia said.

"I'm sorry, but too personal a relationship between Biographer and subject can taint the scholarship. You can make up a name for me, if that makes you feel more comfortable."

Olivia resisted the urge to roll her eyes. The stories of the ridiculous protocols were true. "Fine. Go get your things. I'll fix you a cup of tea."

"No, please," the Biographer said. "It's our honor, and a requirement, that we cook for you and serve you during our stay. If you just give me a minute…I'll fix the tea for *you*. I know just how you like it."

✝✝

Olivia Burns would have been an unlikely candidate for a Biographer if not for pure luck—if "luck" was the right word for her dystopian film about an oncoming global Plague (which she had only meant as a metaphor for climate change and bigotry) that unfolded almost exactly the way her film had predicted it.

Sick had been her first project out of film school, funded by an arts grant her film school mentor had told her about after she started sleeping with him. The grant had been minimal, with most of the shoot taking place on deserted shrublands of the Mojave desert. The ten-day shoot had been miserable, between the heat, failing camera equipment and a temperamental crew unaccustomed to hauling their own gear. The cast was so small that she'd had to play one of the parts herself—Cassie, who was so traumatized by the loss of her family in the fictitious plague that she rarely spoke a word (which was the best fit for her limited acting ability).

Sick's release hardly had the hallmarks of any kind of classic. Despite her grant, she'd spent her last money in post-production and struggled to find a distributor. Finally, she'd thrown it on the

Internet at the mercy of fate. At the time, she'd considered the film a failure: too "arty," too pedantic, too grim. But it survived the Plagues. She'd kept her physical copies pristine alongside her water and food supplies even during the worst times.It also didn't hurt that she was one of the few filmmakers who survived the first Plague years.

Sick hadn't made her a profit—but it made her a prophetess.

And that, it turned out, was a story worth telling.

Olivia's throat tickled with a cough while the Biographer was outside retrieving her bag, so she quickly flicked the inside of her cheek with a swab from her foyer drawer and was relieved when the pleasant tone signaled she was still free of the virus. But the cough was hard to kick—some patients had spasmodic coughing the rest of their lives even after the virus was gone, but Olivia was lucky. She'd coughed until her ribs hurt for the first week, but the new serums were deft at fighting back against infection. Researchers had not vanquished it completely—and probably never would,

the Cabinet of Science confessed—but the current virus's destruction bore little resemblance to the early days from decades before, when Plague had changed the face of the world. "It isn't just here to kill us," her main character, Sadie, had said in *Sick*. "It's also here to set us free." (Her friend Lakisha, who had played Sadie, complained on the set that the dialogue was too on-the-nose, but Olivia had insisted on keeping the line. Couldn't even death be considered a kind of freedom?)

Olivia couldn't have known then that those words would later be enshrined at the base of statues in her own image at the Survival Monuments in London, Dubai, New York, Tokyo and Mexico City. She would never have believed how close the Plagues would have brought humankind to extinction, and that so much would be different in the After, including an indie filmmaker's ascension to dizzying heights of esteem. When she'd learned through the Art Authority that she would receive a lifetime stipend and this castle on a hill, she'd laughed herself to tears.

For all her riches, she had only six wayward cats to keep her company. And now this strange Biographer who would not even reveal her name.

"Life is a mystery every day," Sadie had said in *Sick*.

Maybe her dialogue *was* bland and on-the-nose. But that didn't mean it wasn't also true.

††

"One lesson we learned from the Plague," the Biographer said when she returned and had served Olivia a mug of perfectly brewed Chai, "is that each human life is a miracle worth chronicling."

The sentiment was lovely, so Olivia decided not to bring up the obvious fact that less than a quarter of the population could expect to be assigned a Biographer, by her estimate. Clearly, most lives were deemed far less miraculous than others. Still, it was a clear improvement over the old times, when biographies had been written by chance by obsessed scholars acting independently and filled with bias, not organized through an Academy with training and a creed.

It also amused Olivia to hear her Biographer use the word *we*, since this youngster clearly had been born long after the worst Plague years. She had grown up in the new world and had seen few glimpses of the old one: the wars and senseless fires had swallowed so many libraries, museums and treasures.

"So how does this work?" Olivia said when the last of her tea had cooled and the Biographer had run out of platitudes. Their long silence had veered beyond "awkward" to troubling. They were sitting across from each other at Olivia's vast dining room table, which had seating for eight—ironic, considering that she entertained only rarely.

"Ah!" the Biographer said. "I observe you. That's the core of all biography."

"Observe me doing what?"

"Whatever you would ordinarily be doing."

"As in…finishing my script?"

The Biographer smiled, that horrid grin again. "That would be my honor, of course."

Olivia was relieved, quick to rise to her feet. She felt a cough try to rise in her throat, but she suppressed it for the sake of politeness. And she certainly didn't want to give her Biographer the impression that she was frail at sixty, when the observation would be enshrined into history.

The Biographer rose as well, mirroring her motions, a tablet computer ready in her hands. "I'll be right behind you."

In her office, Olivia suffered impulses to squirm in her straight-back chair with this young woman perched in her window seat five yards away, watching her like an owl. Occasionally, the Biographer whispered an observation into her recorder, scattering Olivia's thoughts although she couldn't make out what she was saying—or especially because she couldn't. The *clack-clack-clack* of her retro-styled typewriter usually chased away sounds unrelated to her stories, but she could not unremember the presence of someone chronicling her every move. She glanced up and found the woman taking a photograph of her. Olivia chastised herself for not dressing in day clothes instead of staying in her bathrobe.She had lived alone for too long. History would remember her as a lunatic hermit who didn't practice basic daily rituals.

This would not work. Not at all.

"I write better when I'm by myself," Olivia said after ninety minutes of struggle.

"Oh!" The Biographer sounded more surprised than disappointed. "Of course. I'll make my way around your kitchen and start working on your lunch. But may I ask one question?"

"Ask away." The sooner she started her interviews, the sooner this woman would go.

"That typewriter. I've read that you have an attachment to it because your father used an antique IBM Selectric when you were young, from 1987, I believe. But you had a manual one built, modeled on one from 1939."

They were statements, not questions, but Olivia guessed what she was asking. "When I was a young woman in my late twenties, I went for long periods without a home, without electricity or solar panels. An old typewriter I found in an abandoned warehouse helped save my life. Writing was always the way I felt most alive, even when I was surrounded by death. When I didn't have paper, I typed on the back pages of flyers and posters I found hanging on the walls."

"Do you still have any of the old manuscripts from that time?"

Olivia felt a physical flash of pain in her chest as she remembered the fire that had devoured the subway station where she'd lived for six months with her typewriter—deliberately set by police, as far as she knew. She still had a burn on her shoulder blade from her narrow escape. Even the memory of losing her typewriter and its fruit wearied her.

"No," she said. "All that's lost now. I was barely able to save a copy of my film."

"What were those scripts about?"

"The same thing most of my stories are about," Olivia said. "Surviving."

Only later did it occur to Olivia that the Biographer took frenzied notes during her observations, but didn't use her recorder or take any notes when Olivia was mining such difficult memories. Shouldn't her personal history be the life blood of her biography?

"Did you get all of that?" Olivia prompted.

The Biographer nodded, tapping her temple. "Yes. I'll remember." She noted Olivia's puzzled stare with a huff of impatience. "You're confused."

"A bit."

"So here it is in small bites, Master…" Despite the artificially respectful moniker, the Biographer's tone was so condescending that Olivia flinched against her chair. This arrogant little bitch. When she'd been this woman's age, she'd been trapping squirrels and wild hares for food in the woods, and a man with snowy dreadlocks who looked eighty had taught her how to tan rabbit hides to make them into warm vests. Surviving in ways she could not imagine.

"…You need to understand that we're not journalists. These won't be interviews. And you're a storyteller, so we can't have you telling your own story, can we? That's an *auto*biography—completely your right, but unregulated, as you know."

Tradition or not, Olivia came close to telling her to get the hell out of her house. The words tickled her tongue. Instead, she said, "*You* asked *me* about the typewriter."

"And thank you very much for your answer. That was lovely. I promise it was."

I promise it was. Olivia couldn't suppress the cough she hid behind her palm. What a bad actress this woman was! Or worse—she couldn't be bothered to try to hide the disdain nestled beneath the surface of her professed admiration.

"I'll make you some honey lemon tea for that cough," the Biographer said.

The unpleasant young woman gave a bland curtsey before she turned toward the door.

Time passed slowly with the Biographer in her house. Olivia usually was restless in her sleep before dawn, eager to begin her days at her typewriter, but now she wanted to linger on her silk sheets, avoiding the strange girl as long as she could.

First, the girl was dirty. Olivia barely had noticed the crud under the woman's fingernails when she first served her tea because of whatever long trek she had made. But by the second and third days, it was clear that the Biographer did not change her clothes or bathe. Her blouse grew so rumpled that she must be sleeping in her clothes too. She also had taken to walking barefoot, and the soles of her feet looked like they had been painted black. The unmistakable odor of unwashed skin was baking from her more strongly each hour, making Olivia's throat pinch shut when the woman leaned over her to serve her meals at the table.

And the food! The meals she fixed felt like food for the infirm: soups, mashes of indistinct vegetables, dry toast, apple sauce. When Olivia complained that she was feeding her like a patient, the Biographer only gave her the placid smile that was her substitute for interaction. Olivia got up late

the second night to cook herself the foods she craved from her freezer, only to find that her lamb cubes, chicken breasts and caramel chunk ice cream had been removed. When she asked the Biographer why she had moved her food without permission, the grubby young woman gave her a blank stare and insisted she had never seen them.

✛✛

"How long will you be staying?" Olivia finally asked on the third day.

"Not much longer." As vague as possible. As usual.

"Is there an average stay for a Biographer?"

Olivia shrugged. "The duties sometimes take more time, sometimes less."

Duty was a strong word, Olivia thought, since all the woman seemed to do was sit staring at her, or chronicle the books on her shelves, or cook her another mess of a meal. (On that note, at least Olivia was losing weight.) Her cats avoided the stranger, so she rarely even got feline comfort since the Biographer's arrival. The kitties even stayed hidden at night, when Olivia was sure she could hear the

Biographer walking aimlessly through the house, occasionally bumping into things. One night she broke a ceramic bowl, waking Olivia after midnight, and left the pieces at the foot of the stairs, almost as if she hoped Olivia would trip over the ruins of her life. No apology. No explanation. Olivia didn't have the energy for a confrontation, so she threw the bowl away herself. She noticed that the trash can outside of her kitchen door was overflowing with other items from the house—many of them old and rarely used, but still. The nerve!

But telling the Biographer not to touch her things was of no use. The woman smiled and nodded after every correction, then carried on exactly, if not worse, than before.

By the fourth day, Olivia was so frustrated that she researched on her computer to try to learn more about Biographer protocols—because she was sure this woman must be in violation of several. The Academy of Biographers had a website with an official seal picturing an old-fashioned fountain pen inside a wreath, but the site did not have a way for non-members to access any of its files, or even a welcome message, so she gave up on finding official accounts. She found plenty of complaints elsewhere online about the caste system declaring some people worthy of biographies and not others, and a few rogue biography organizations boasting more egalitarian goals and "Happy Endings for All," but the long threads (many of them heavily redacted) offered no information about sanctioned Biographers and how to be rid of one.

Olivia was a bit disappointed in herself that she had never taken notice of the quiet controversies about Biographers, since she had never believed such matters affected her—and wasn't that so much of what was wrong in the world? Weren't lack of empathy and apathy a big part of the reason the Plagues had taken hold with such unrelenting might? Hadn't that, in fact, been a big part of her inspiration for *Sick*?

On the fourth night, while the Biographer was warbling an unrecognizable song at the top of her lungs while she clanked pots and pans together in the kitchen, Olivia noticed her that the Biographer's file box was unlocked, a glimmer from one of the plastic sleeves peeking through. Olivia quickly opened the box and pulled up the sleeves one by one:

many held photographs, some held documents and letters.

The first photo was from the set of *Sick*, capturing a moment Olivia had nearly forgotten: that day the pressure of long hours and little money had caused her to scream at her best friend, Lakisha, her face contorted with rage that made her barely recognizable. Dear Lord! Lakisha was long-dead—nearly everyone of her generation was-—but Olivia hoped the Biographer had interviewed people who knew her truer nature as mild, even shy. Sleeve after sleeve painted a less flattering portrait of her, from overdue water bills to discarded manuscript pages she thought she had destroyed to the deluded letter from her mentor blaming her for his destroyed marriage because of their three-month affair. She had only been nineteen, and he was a grown man of forty! Again, Olivia was sure she had burned the letter as soon as she read it…but somehow the Biographer had it in her files. One photo was nearly unrecognizable, mounds of ash and charred walls. But in the center…

Oliva gasped. Her old typewriter! This was her subway station shelter after it had burned.

Olivia's fingers were trembling, so she slammed the file box of horrors shut. Why was the Biographer only cataloging her worst moments? Her biggest failures? Her sharpest pain? Her most deeply buried shame?

"Are you all right?" the Biographer said.

Olivia didn't know how long she had been standing behind her, but the woman was sure to guess that Olivia had seen her rifling through her files. But she didn't care about being caught.

"Have you started my biography?" she said. "I'd like to see a few pages. I don't like the direction it seems to be taking…"

The Biographer barked out a laugh so loud that she covered her mouth with both hands. Tears of glee peeked from her eyelids. "Subjects can't read their biographies!" she said, muffled. And laughed some more.

A new shame overtook Olivia: She had never read a biography, she realized. Not once. She had seen Biography sections in the National Library behind golden doors, but she had never been curious enough to apply to read one. How could that be? *Everyone* had a story.

"You look a bit pale to me, Lakisha," the Biographer said. "I'll bring you some tea."

"You know damn well my name isn't Lakisha," Olivia said.

The Biographer's eyes danced with glee at irritating her. "Oh, that's right. Lakisha was your best friend since childhood. She was the best part of your film, you know. It's a shame the way you treated her."

"I want you to leave," Olivia said, fighting her own tears. Her friendship with Lakisha had never had the time to recover from the trials of the movie shoot, a regret she had smothered over the years. "This match isn't working. I'll ask the Academy for another Biographer."

The woman ignored her, turning back toward the kitchen. Olivia noticed a thin veil of smoke through the kitchen doorway. She coughed, a reflex. Whatever was burning did not smell like food. More like…papers?

"That's a nasty cough!" the Biographer called. "Your hacking has been worrying me."

"That's ridiculous. I can count on one hand how many times I've coughed since you've been here," Olivia said, but the Biographer walked on. "And you're burning something in my kitchen. Anyone would cough."

By the time the Biographer returned with a cup of tea that smelled like mint—at least she could brew good tea—Olivia had calmed down by reminding herself that all things came to an end. The Biographer might not leave today, but one day she would. And then this horrible ordeal would be over.

The tea was sweeter than usual, but Olivia didn't complain. Unlike the meals the Biographer served her, at least her tea had something like flavor.

As usual, the Biographer sat across from her watching her.

"Let's keep things pleasant between us," Olivia said to break the silence. "I'm sure the Academy was exercising wisdom when it chose you."

"Not at all," Olivia said. "I was the only one willing."

Her staring eyes were more unnerving than usual now. Olivia had only taken three sips of tea, but she put the mug down on her table. Her coasters were gone. The Biographer had left at least half a dozen faded rings in her good oak from tea mugs and glasses since she arrived, so the tabletop was already ruined.

"I'm going upstairs to do some writing," Olivia said. "I'll need to be alone."

"Still trying to write on the typewriter your father gave you?"

Olivia tried to stand up, but an alarming wave of dizziness rocked her back. "I've told you…my father always used an electric typewriter. He didn't give it to me…"

"Are you sure?" the Biographer said. "That's not how I remember it."

In fact, Olivia suddenly *wasn't* sure. Sitting still didn't soothe her dizzy spell, and her mind was reeling, unmoored. Whose typewriter had it been? Was the smoke in her house from the subway fire? Had she ever lived at all? Her mind fumbled to answer the simplest questions.

"You did something to my tea," Olivia said, understanding. "You drugged me."

The Biographer stood up and walked to Olivia, squatting to meet her at eye level. When the Biographer removed her mask, Olivia was shocked at how wrinkled her face had grown underneath, unless it was only her imagination—or was she looking into a mirror?

"It's against the rules…" the Biographer whispered. "…but I like you,

Olivia, so I'll give you a preview of your biography. You have faithfully used your long-dead father's typewriter, which survived the Plagues…"

"That's…not true. I had it made—"

"…and you might have had three or four more films left in you, but you got sick."

"I'm not…sick," Olivia said, but she had to gasp to draw the air for speech. "I recovered. I had a… mild case. That was… weeks ago."

The Biographer was so close that her stench clogged Olivia's nostrils. "You were cut down by the very Plague you prophesied in your film."

"Why…are you doing this?" Olivia choked. The room was dimming.

The Biographer leaned close to her ear, her breath hot and putrid. "Why do you think?"

Olivia knew the answer. She heard herself laugh even as her lungs cinched, starving for oxygen. Olivia reveled in one last marvel of irony and tragedy, a fiction more true than reality, the escape from her suffering. She opened her mouth and coaxed out what her Biographer would accurately chronicle as her last words: "It's a good story."

The Biographer squeezed Olivia's damp, cooling hand between two dirt-crusted palms. "I shouldn't say this, but it's one of the best we've written."

Oh, yes, it was good. Someone might even venture past the golden doors to read it one day. Olivia almost smiled before she —and her untold stories—slept in her Biographer's arms.

SIDE B

PINK HOUSES

YOUR DASHER HAS ACCIDENTALLY AWAKENED THE CRAWLING CHAOS BY GAZING INTO THE LOATHSOME GEOMETRY OF THE TACO PUP MEGA-MUNCHER MEAL BOX

DAVID ANAXAGORAS

Hey Sam, your order from Taco Pup is being delivered by DoorDash, a partner delivery service, at 5:40PM. You can track the status at drd.sh

Your Dasher, Astrid, is at Taco Pup and awaiting your order.

Your Dasher has sent you a message:

> i don't know what the fuck is going on but all hell just broke loose at taco pup just so you know it's not my fault your order's gonna be late

Your Dasher has accidentally awaken-ed the crawling chaos by gazing into loathsome geometry of the Taco Pup Mega-Muncher Meal box.

We've updated your estimated time of delivery accordingly.

Your Dasher has sent you a message:

> all i did was fold one of their stupid takeout boxes "wrong" and everybody lost their shit they were running late on orders and i was just trying to help but if putting tab a into slot c is gonna open the gates of hell maybe they should rethink their takeout container strategy anyway on my way

Your Dasher has penetrated the formless screaming jelly issuing yellowishly from the Dark Crystalline Octahedron to pick up your order and is on their way to you now!

Your Dasher has sent you a message:

> i can't take the main road to your house because of the tentacle thing coming up outta the asphalt thank god it grabbed the mini-van in front of me so I had time to turn around don't worry got both hands on the wheel i'm dictating this oh jesus fuck what now

Your Dasher has chosen to take an alternate route after they shrank away from the rubbery enormity erupting from Magnolia Street, its fetid black form squirming ten stories into the uncaring sky and groping blindly as its oily skin roiled and burst with pudding-filled pustules.

We've updated your estimated time of delivery accordingly.

Your Dasher has sent you a message:

> sky demons ate your fries

Your Dasher has reported an item missing, lost or damaged from your order. We are very sorry that malodorous bat-winged night-gaunts greedily captured and consumed your Large Cajun-spice Curly Fries, though it is a mystery how they did this considering their detestable, malignant faces have no mouths. Nevertheless, this is not the experience we wish our customers to have.

We have issued a $5.00 credit for immediate use on your next order.

Your Dasher has sent you a message:

> sorry about the fries man damn they did smell good too i got the sunroof closed now and no faceless harpy thing is going to stop me i got this is that a whirlpool

An important update from DoorDash! Due to unforeseen road conditions, including the sudden appearance of a churning watery abyss through which has risen an unholy broken altar of basalt supporting a slouching, mammoth octopian blasphemy possessing the gray-green pallor of yawning madness, there may be an additional delay in your delivery.

We've updated your estimated time of delivery accordingly.

Your Dasher has sent you a message:

> nuh-uh

> nope

> nuts to squid face

> this is not worth it i'm cancelling delivery no tip is big enough to put up with this nightmare

Hi Sam! DoorDash has confirmed that you have increased your tip by $100.00. Your new total tip amount is $107.50.

Your Dasher has sent you a message:

> don't know what you're trying to pull you think you can just pay me to suffer which is gross or if you're just playing some kind of sick fucking game but I'm still cancelling so fuck you

Your Dasher has sent you a message:

> well doordash just told me cancelling this delivery is a contract violation and would result in my deactivation or whatever bullshit they call it so I guess it's still game on i'm holding you to that tip though

Hi Sam! We just wanted you to know that we have not received any location updates from your Dasher for the last five minutes but don't worry! This is probably merely the effect of entering the infinitely monstrous shadow chambers beyond all time and space, but your delivery is still on its way!

Your Dasher has sent you a message:

i gotta take backroads now i didn't even know there were back roads around here unless i'm just traveling through another dimension now ha ha

wouldn't fuckin surprise me

some kind of mushroom

Hi Sam! Good news! Your Dasher is back on track and in this dimension and your order is just a few minutes away. Get ready for some hot and tasty food!

Your Dasher has sent you a message:

got these nubs on my skin now sprouting all up my arm

so strange how my arm's gone numb right now like it doesn't even belong to me any more

Your Dasher is approaching with your order from Taco Pup. Enjoy your meal!

Your Dasher has sent you a message:

hey man forget all that stuff i said i don't know why i was so chatty just whistling past the graveyard i suppose but i'm here now everything is fine

everything is fine

i got you a replacement for those fries

a few extra things too

Hi Sam! Your order was dropped off. Thank you for ordering from Taco Pup!

Your Dasher has sent you a message:

this is gonna be the best meal you ever ate

CHAINSAW: AS IS

GILLIAN KING-CARGILE

All thirteen of us cousins and half-cousins and step-cousins were there that Memorial Day at my Grandma's house when Dustin ripped into his leg with the chainsaw. This was in New Jersey. In the Pine Barrens. There were thousands—maybe hundreds of thousands—of trees to chainsaw. That's why Grandma had the chainsaw in the first place. To push the Pine Barrens back. To keep away the trees and the things that hid in their needles. Things with wings and hair and hooves and scales and claws.

I was the oldest and the only girl in the mess of cousins, so I was supposed to be *in charge*. I was the one who lived the closest and helped Grandma the most—dusting her cobwebs, mowing her sandy lawn, turning the TV up louder and louder and louder so she could hear the Weather

Channel and watch for nor'easters and hurricanes hurrying their way up the coast.

That day I was also make-shift mom to twelve boys, aged six to sixteen, who only saw each other all at once maybe once or twice a year. When they got together, they always wanted to do something big. Memorable. This year, they wanted to chainsaw down a tree or make a YouTube video or make a YouTube video about chain-sawing down a tree. I told them not to be stupid. I was the only one Grandma let use the chainsaw, and I was *in charge*, as the aunts and uncles said, because they didn't want to deal with their monster kids while they drank beer and shooed flies away from deviled eggs and crab salad and burgers.

Dustin was the one who got the chainsaw out of the garage, off the work bench I'd left it out on like a dare. "I'll show you how it's done," Dustin said. But he'd never touched the chainsaw before— never helped with yard work because of the ticks and the sunburn and the fact that he was only kind-of related to us because his dad married our aunt and he was only here on vacation.

He yanked the cord, revved the engine. *REV-REV-REV-REV!* Too many times. The engine had already caught, the chain was already spinning on the bar. He was showing off. Making noise. Just like when we'd play Yahtzee and he'd shake the cup of dice too loud and hard and long and close to my ear. "I'll show you how it's done." And he'd flip the cup and slam it onto Grandma's good glass table, threatening to shatter everything.

You don't stop an idiot with a chainsaw. You don't get in his way. You don't scream for aunts and uncles. Even if you did, they probably wouldn't hear you. They'd think your scream was just one of the many noises that happen when a mess of cousins run through the woods. And Dustin definitely wouldn't hear you over the dragon's breath buzz of the gasoline engine.

Grandma always said, "A chainsaw sounds dangerous on purpose, like a timber rattler. It's telling you to stay away." Her words came out wheezy because Grandma smoked too much and shopped too much and played the slots in Atlantic City too much. She was reckless with things like that, but not with power tools. When it came to chainsaws, she wore sunglasses and thick saw-proof chaps and sturdy shoes. In the woods, she was all about safety.

She'd cut clean through a fallen tree, then engage the handbrake to stop the engine. "A chainsaw can cut you even when it's not running," she'd say. "When it's not rattling its chain as it blurs around the bar." She'd set the saw on solid ground and tell me to come closer now, to feel how hot the bar got when it bored through the tree. The chain teeth were sharp and shiny and warm. One nicked my finger and drew blood. "Like a rattlesnake's front teeth," she told me. "Their fangs still hold that venom, can still kill you even after the head's cut clean off."

For Sale: Chainsaw
Loud and Dangerous, but so was the
person it killed. $50 or best offer.

Dustin had messed-up front teeth. His smile teeth. One had a chip out of it from when he'd gone over the handlebars of a bike he stole at the boardwalk. He'd hit a patch of sand and landed on his face. I guess he'd always been bad about keeping himself in one piece.

Dustin laughed a lot and stuck his tongue through the jagged hole in his smile teeth and had perfected the art of spitting through the gap.

"I'll show you how it's done," Dustin'd said when he'd first joined our family five years ago and taught the other cousins how to spit. His saliva traced a thin, wet arc through the sky and landed at least five feet away from him in the sandy dirt. He was a really good spitter.

But he was a terrible lumberjack. When he messed around with that chainsaw, he hit one of the only things that wasn't a tree when so many dry, spindly, punky trunks leaned toward the saw's spinning chain and heavy bar, begging to be bitten by its teeth.

His leg didn't come all the way off. That's what people ask me about the most. He didn't cut clear through like you would when you were using the tip of the saw to snap off a sapling at its base. But his leg surely came *more* off than a leg should. And he didn't cut down to the bone. That's what people ask me about the second most. The artery was the thing he hit. The thing the teeth of the saw spun through. Grinded. Like a bull shark biting through boys in the back bay. Like a devil gnawing.

Here's what Dustin did: he whipped the chainsaw around in the air like a sad-sack Leatherface at the end of *Texas Chainsaw Massacre*. Then he lunged toward a spindly tree, a small enough victim. The tip of the saw entered the soft bark, sprayed woodchips into his hair. He pushed deeper, not with the cutting bar like you're supposed to, but with the tip, until the saw penetrated bark and hit hardwood. He probably felt so good making the initial cut. It's a good feeling. Engine screaming. Body vibrating. Nature yielding.

But he was wearing shorts and flip-flops. He was not prepared.

He couldn't handle the tool.

The chain blurred around the bar at seventy miles an hour. Fast as a car on the parkway. The difference between a saw and a car is that a car is supposed to get you somewhere all in one piece; a chainsaw's metal is meant to collide. To tear apart.

Dustin pushed in like an idiot. The saw's tip hit something unmovable: a knot in the hardwood. The trunk resisted, collapsed on the saw. The saw bucked down and back. It flayed Dustin's leg, calf muscle to knee bone. Then it continued up up up up. Seventy miles an hour. *RevRevRevRev!* Finding purchase on his thigh. Sinking its teeth in. A strong, solid bite.

Blood sprayed like mist off a wave—a strong, sudden breaker—saturating all the cousins who were standing close. He screamed and finally finally finally dropped the saw. Dropped his finger from the trigger. The pine trees and our clothes and hands and arms and faces were splattered with so many shades of Dustin.

We'd all seen enough horror movies and creature features and Shark Week specials to know right then that it was too late. We're basically just blood balloons bobbing through the world avoiding sharp, tearing things. Once you start bleeding— really bleeding—like Dustin was doing all over the ground in front of us, screaming, trying to hold his leg together, you probably won't stop.

**For Sale: Chainsaw
Stain resistant. Easy to clean!**

The 911 people didn't take the chainsaw. That's the thing that surprised me the most. That and all the blood. An ambulance, a fire truck, and a patrol car all answered the 911 call. I thought one of the uniformed guys would have taken the chainsaw or our bloody clothes as evidence. But they didn't. I guess that only happens for murders, not for chainsaw-icides.

My aunt and step-uncle followed the 911 people to the hospital. The rest of us waited at my Grandma's house for someone to tell us what to do. The adults went through the motions of cleaning the grill and covering the deviled eggs and throwing out the fly-filled crab salad and pouring the bottom-of-the-bowl chip dust into their mouths. We almost forgot we were covered in blood until Cousin Aaron tried to reach a red hand into a bowl of Cheez-Its and Aunt Marcy freaked out. We couldn't go inside to change because Grandma didn't want us dripping Dustin all over the house.

I was the one who got the garden hose and twisted the nozzle to full blast and sprayed the boys until the water running off them went from red to pink to clear.

Everyone kept looking out into the woods where the sandy lawn became scrubby pines. Where the chainsaw still sat. Where blood now fed the thirsty roots of scrub pines and poison ivy and attracted every manner of Pine Barren monster.

"Throw the chainsaw away," my mom said. She hated clutter. "Nobody's going to use it."

"It's like new," my dad said. "Worth something if we just hose it down."

"Like new," my Grandma echoed. She was sitting there buried in thick-threaded blankets and had missed most of the thread of the conversation. Dustin was one of her least favorites, but she really liked the chainsaw. Back when she could still lift it, she'd revved it like a badass.

"Who would want it?" my littlest cousin asked. He was seven and sweet and still growing into his big-kid teeth and probably wished he had a chip in one so he could spit like his step-cousin. The kid's eyelids squeezed shut like he was trying to clean the image of Dustin's mangled leg off his eyeballs.

"It's not like we're going to tell the truth in the want-ad," I said.

For Sale: Chainsaw
Great for cutting trees and limbs.

Grandma was the one who taught me how to use the chainsaw when I was little. When I was one of the only cousins, step or half or otherwise. Grandma said that chainsaw safety was like driver's safety. "You have to understand the power of the machine. And you have to understand how a tree is going to fall just like you have to understand the road ahead."

Grandma would square her feet in the sandy dirt just right, so she could control the rattle of the saw and the severing of the tree limb. The engine would shake her thinning arms, but her feet remained planted in the pine needles, immovable objects. The limb always landed square where she planned with a satisfying *thunk*.

She taught me how to oil the chain so it cut clean and how to open the body of the saw to blow out the grit and dead wood that threatened to choke up the exhaust. It's amazing what you can accomplish with an owner's manual, a screwdriver, and some patience.

When she got older, I had to start the chainsaw for her. When I wasn't around, she'd stand by the road to flag down neighbors or the mailman or shoobies on their way down the shore and have them yank the cord, rev the engine, and bring the saw to life so she could push the Pine Barrens a little farther from her back door. Sometimes they'd offer to help her cut what needed cutting, but she'd shoo them away. She liked to do things her own way. And if she couldn't do them on her own, she could always call me.

With Dustin all cut open, we speculated there would be hospital bills to pay and maybe ambulance bills, too. Did you have to pay the 911 people? Tip them like reverse-pizza-delivery drivers? And there'd probably be funeral expenses. No one wanted to admit that quite yet. But it just made dollars and sense to sell the chainsaw. And no one wanted to cook dinner, either, because we were all still thinking about the way Dustin looked like a faded, wet beach towel, heavy and sandy, when we dragged him out of the woods. We'd need to order some food eventually. White pizza, probably. Nothing with red sauce.

**Chainsaw, It's New to You!
It took our step-cousin, but most of
us didn't like him anyway.**

You can't put that in an actual ad. Or in a eulogy. You can't tell people then, when he's chain-sawing at death's door, that you always thought something like this would happen.

Not the chainsaw part.

That was a shock to most of the family. For sure. But the dying part, the dying-stupid part, wasn't much of a shock. Where do you document the time he burned down your grandparent's neighbor's shed to see what would happen? Or the time after your grandpa's funeral when he spent the luncheon eating all the crab cakes, breathing out Old Bay breath and bragging about how he was going to grow up to be a long-haul trucker so he could transport illegal shit from state to state? Or the time you and the other older cousins stole beers from the ice-filled cooler to see if you'd get giggly and he stole a bottle of your dead grandpa's special whiskey because he was the kind of person who didn't know where to draw the line, who could only take and take and take? Where do you record that he was the type of person who always drained things? Not because he was thirsty, but because he was empty.

Chainsaw, Maybe Haunted? But the ghost would probably just sneak Tastykakes and beers from your Grandma's fridge and twenties from her wallet to buy more Tastykakes and beer.

My Grandma had a book about haunted places up and down the Jersey Shore. She'd read it to me before there were too many cousins to tuck in. "Some places," she told me, "are set apart for shipwrecks." I think about that a lot, not the shipwreck part, really, not this far back in the Pine Barrens, but the idea that there are places where bad things always happen, where the devil peeks through the pines and sees you being bad.

Grandma told me about the devil, too. How he's in these woods, where the ocean drains to the bay, loses its salt, and becomes the river. The devil's mother was a witch from Leeds Point, who had too many children, twelve, so the thirteenth one she cursed. The Jersey Devil.

She cursed him to be red and hairy and winged and horned and homeless. And so he is. She cursed him to eat the entrails of dogs and deer and wicked children. And so he does.

The devil's feet are hooves, his nails are claws, his tongue is forked. Sometimes he's a man disguised in dead night's darkness. Sometimes he's a dancer tap-trampling on your rooftop. And he swims, too. He can be the rolling red tide that chokes the water and poisons the shellfish. Some people think he was the killer shark that swam into the back bay and killed five boys, fishermen's sons, in the summer of 1916. My Grandma believes it. I believe it, too.

The Jersey Devil is the reason you have to cut down the trees, to keep them from creeping up on the property, too close to the house, windows, and beds. Nobody can be good all the time and you don't want him to see you being bad.

**For Sale: Chainsaw
VERY SAFE!!! (in skilled hands).
Keep out of reach of wicked
children.**

I was the one who went back into the pine trees with a bucket of soapy water while the rest of the family waited for a call from the hospital. I was the one who splashed the water and sudded the bloody pine-needled ground. I was the one who carefully sprayed off the toothy spikes of the chain to make sure we weren't going to sell anyone chunks of our least-favorite step-cousin when the time came.

I told myself to think of cleaning the chainsaw like cleaning a cutting board after trimming the throw-away fat off a nice slab of meat.

I was the one who remembered the way Dustin'd ripped the legs off stranded, struggling horseshoe crabs at the beach so their blue blood streaked the dry sand. I was the one who remembered trying to save the white jellyfish—the non-stingy jellyfish—picking them off the beach and putting them back in the water, until he grabbed them and threw them like frisbees. Threw them at me and the other cousins so they splatted against our bare skin.

I was the one who remembered him holding our younger cousins under the waves and liking the way they struggled. He was bigger and older and would pretend to teach them how to body surf before he'd attack. "I'll show you how it's done."

And the way he'd grab me in the water and snap my straps against my sunburned shoulders and try to stick seaweed and dead crab legs down the front of my one-piece suit. Back on shore, he'd snatch my beach towel so he could stare at me as I shivered and dripped dry in the cold wind off the ocean. He told me I was his favorite step-cousin.

But maybe everyone remembered. Maybe my parents and my other aunts and uncles talked about it while they waited for the call. Maybe we all secretly came to the same conclusion that if his life hadn't drained out here, he would have pissed it away in a few weeks or months or years.

Maybe it was the inevitable that made the chainsaw gnaw into Dustin's thigh, spraying red mist into the air.

I was also the one who'd taken off the chainsaw's hand guard and chain brake that morning, the things that make chainsaws a little more idiot-proof. The things that stop the chain from spinning and the bar from pressing in when your blade bucks. When you grind against something unmovable.

It's amazing what you can accomplish with an owner's manual, a screwdriver, and some patience.

I was the one who was tired of him saying, "I'll show you how it's done," and stealing twenties out of Grandma's wallet. I was the one who wouldn't forget how he'd found me in Grandma's garage after a long day at the beach when most of the cousins were sleeping and most of the adults were sleeping off afternoon beers.

Here's what Dustin did: he told me all the things he'd learned since I'd seen him the summer before. All the things girls in his hometown let him do to them. He cornered me by the tools, pushed me up against the peg board so the metal hooks pressed into my back. So that I was unmovable. I thought that when he finally let me loose, I'd have impressions of peg board stippled along the skin of my back like acne scars.

He pushed his hands up under my shirt and whispered in my ear so close I could hear his breath hiss over his chipped front tooth. "I'll show you how it's done."

For Sale: Chainsaw
All the blood is cleaned off it now. I told him to leave me alone.

While all the aunts and uncles waited for the call from the hospital and thought about what half-way decent black clothes they'd packed in their suitcases, I sat next to the clean chainsaw on the dirty pine needles and waited to see if the Jersey Devil would show himself.

I imagined him coming to the forest floor to claim me. Pictured his black claws slashing, tearing through my t-shirt and my white belly-skin beneath. And I wondered if his wings, when they flapped, would chill my exposed innards, if his red fur would tickle what remained of my flesh.

Did Dustin feel the pine and gasoline scented air inside his leg when he cut it? Could a wound still feel when you cut that many layers deep?

If the Jersey Devil did come to claim me, would I try to stop him or would I let him dig inside me, take what he wanted, eat till I was hollow? Till I was gone?

But the Jersey Devil only eats wicked children. Was I wicked? I lay on the cooling carpet of needles and decided to let him taste me. To let him decide.

I sat until Memorial Day evening turned to full dark. Till stars strained to shine through the pine boughs. Then I heard him. He was tapping in the darkness above my head, trampling over and around and up and down the treetops so that branches shivered and shed their driest needles. His hoof-beats echoed through the Pine Barrens like Grandma's coughs in the morning.

When he flapped to the ground, he whipped up a hurricane of pine needles. They stung my summer-bare legs and arms. The devil was red and hairy and winged and horned and hooved and homeless. The devil planted his claws in the sandy soil, spreading out and down, taking root in the blood. He'd come here to feed.

By the weak moonlight trickling through the pine boughs, I watched him stand and I could almost believe he was a man. His owl-wide eyes ogled me, then the chainsaw, then me again. He folded to the ground like a beast. His snout snuffled the bloody pine needles. His forked tongue licked the bar of the chainsaw, clicked along the chain's teeth. He breathed in like he could inhale the whole forest. I clutched the sandy ground but felt myself slipping toward him.

His eyes were on me now. Ocean abysses. I could have given up and drowned, but I forced myself to breathe, to stare down the gut-eater, the hoofed-dancer. The Jersey Devil snuffled around me now. His snout wet my neck, my shirt, my arm, my hand. He paused. Breathed in and in and in. Licking at the fingers that had gotten greasy that morning loosening the safety bolts. Removing restraints.

The devil reared back and brayed. It sounded the way a shipwreck must have sounded when a metal hull tears itself apart trying to move through something unmovable. When all hands know they'll be lost. I thought my family must have heard it from the house, but no one bothered to look for me or check on the night screaming up from the forest.

I scrambled away from him until my back hit a half-sawed tree trunk. He rose up on hind legs and stood like a man again, eclipsing the moon. One taloned hand swept the ground at my feet, nearly slicing off the fronts of my sneakers. Instead of my toes, he came away with a claw full of blood-clotted pine needles. His broad mouth broke into a bestial grin.

He hissed through his jagged smile teeth, his fangs. And he leapt into the air and disappeared over the trees.

For Sale: Chainsaw
Licked clean. The Jersey Devil was
hungry. I needed to feed him.

My legs rattled as I carried the newly cleaned saw through the woods to my Grandma's garage. Inside the house, they'd gotten the call. Some of the cousins were crying, the ones who still remember Dustin as a smiley guy and a really great spitter. I remember him differently.

I spent that night repairing the chain brake, making the saw once-again idiot proof. Surely someone else could get some use out of a good, sturdy tool.

Chainsaw: "As Is"
Clean and in good working order.
It's seen some use, but the teeth are
sharp, the engine is willing, and it
gets the job done.

PSYCHIC SANTA

CLAY MCLEOD CHAPMAN

Their faces tend to blend together. You may remember a few, sure. The peculiar ones. Could be a birthmark or a bruise that sticks out. Something they wore, maybe, or something funny they said. Even that tiny squeak in their voice lingers a little . . . But after those first few years, believe me, their features all melt in your mind, a never-ending strand of taffy full of eyes and gap-toothed smiles stretching on and on for as long as that line of kids, every last one of them patiently waiting their turn to sit in your lap, staring vacantly back at you the entire time.

I'm always gonna remember Benjamin Pendleton, though.

That kid just sticks. His robin's egg complexion. Palest blue skin I've ever seen. The ice crystals clustering along his eyelashes. The pockets of frost in each socket, both eyeballs totally frozen over, the vitreous humor gone all gray. That boy's face is gonna be with me for as long as I live. I'm never forgetting him.

My first ghost.

Most Santas only last a couple Christmases. They're just not cut out for the costume. These guys ain't got the motz to slip on this suit day after day. Some fellas stick it out for a few years, sure, hitting up the holiday blitz wherever they can find work, but they burn out on these rugrats kicking their shins and simply call it quits.

It's a rough business, let me tell you. We're punching bags in black boots. Folks sure like to joke about how many Santas are alcoholics, but after a twelve-hour shift of getting your beard pulled, kicked, punched, pinched, sneezed on, screamed at, clawed, jabbed, stabbed and pissed all over—multiple times—believe you me, you'd probably make a bee-line to the bar for a boilermaker or two (or ten) to unwind, too.

Judge not, lest ye be Santa . . .

I haven't had a drop of alcohol since I first met Benjamin. That's the God's honest truth. That kid cleaned me up. You'd think it would be the other way around, but no, he scared me sober. The way he waddled up to me made my blood run cold. Just listening to the squish in his rubber galoshes, full of river water. I can still hear them now. Squush-squush with every step.

Squush-squush. He'd been patiently waiting for his turn amongst all the other boys and girls, never cutting in line or creeping up on me.

That's the thing: He didn't pounce. Didn't bite. All this kid did was stand in line along with the others, his frost-ridden eyes focused on me the whole damn time. Staring. I swear the temperature dropped the closer he got. There was this chill coming off his skin. I could feel him before he even reached me, my breath fogging over . . . while he didn't have any breath at all.

Did anybody else see this kid? Was I the only one?

What did he want from me?

I couldn't afford to lose this gig. Turnover is pretty swift here, so I had to keep my composure. Don't scream. That'd be enough to send me packing. Shops like Balkins cover their asses. They don't even hire the same Santa year after year anymore. It's got everything to do with liability. Parents aren't as eager to let their kids sit in some stranger's lap. Mom and Pop are afraid of . . . you know. Whether Santa's got a rap sheet or whatnot. They want to know if he can live within a thousand feet of a playground. Sign of the goddamn times. Everybody's scared of the things that're supposed to be safe. Clowns? Come on. Don't get me started on clowns . . .

But Santa? Why do we got to be afraid of him now? Ain't nothing sacred?

What'd I ever do to deserve this?

Should be the other way around, you know. It's us Santas who should be terrified of the kids. Lord knows I used to be.

The dead ones, at least.

This is my sixteenth Christmas working the department store circuit. Where does the time go, you know? Damn right, I'm a man of the cloth. Got my own suit and everything. I've clocked a couple Christmases at other stores, sure. I've done them all. JC Penney's. Did a quick stint at Dillard's. Made my way up to Macy's, if you can believe it. Hitting the big time.

I've always had the physical disposition for this gig. Born with a bowl full of jelly and all that. It's a bit chicken and egg: What came first, the job or the belly? Who knows. My doctor keeps warning me I'm borderline diabetic, but I simply consider it an occupational hazard. Comes with the turf.

I got my routine down pat. The laughter. The banter. The whole kit and Christmas kaboodle. Ho Ho Ho! Merry Christmas! So . . . have you been a good boy this year?

Who am I the other three-hundred and thirty-five days out of the year, when I'm not donning the suit? Good question. I'm not so sure anymore. I'm collecting disability. Got myself an apartment. Nothing too fancy. Just a two-bedroom unit close to I-64. Had a wife but we separated over a decade ago now. No kids of my own —that I know of—but that's okay. I've had plenty.

Used to be a bus driver.

Sorry, school bus driver. Precious cargo and all. I had my route for some twenty-odd years. Same circuit for nearly the whole time. Same neighborhoods, same streets, practically the same kids for all that time, sending them to the same school. It got to the point where I could pick them all up with my eyes closed. By the end there, I practically did.

I had driven after a bender before and done just fine. Technically I wasn't drunk that morning. That morning, Christ . . . Listen to me. A little coffee was all it usually took to get in working order again. Christmas was right around the corner. Only a few more days left before the holiday break, and I wouldn't have to slip behind the wheel of my bus until after New Year's.

I mistook some Christmas decorations for a green light, running a red. Never saw that FedEx truck coming. The second it slammed into the side of the bus and spiraled us out, my head met the windshield, and I was out. I remember hearing it—that fracture of glass, like ice cracking under my heel. You know that feeling? When you're walking over a frozen pond? You don't just hear the crackle, you feel it, too, reverberating through your foot and all the way up your leg, your bones becoming a tuning fork. My head went right through the windshield. There was water waiting for me on the other side— cold, black water—swallowing me all up.

When I came to in the hospital two weeks later, I could see.

Not with my eyes, but with my mind.

Yeah. So, I'm a psychic Santa. Maybe I should've mentioned that up front. After coming out from the quick little coma, I didn't have a job anymore, but I did have second sight.

When I wear the suit and sit here, I feel —I don't know—like I'm doing something. Something that matters. Making up for my mistakes. Lord knows I've had my fair share.

Growing a beard began as a means to cover up the scars along my cheeks and chin. That windshield sure did a number on my face. Now I just wear it for the job.

The gig. The kids. The ghosts.

Everybody remembers their first time sitting with Santa. I know it's not me who these kids are thinking about. All they see is the suit. The hat. The beard. I'm a means to an end, the guy who's gonna get them what they want.

Still me, though, you know? Underneath the outfit. I'm making this memory that'll last for them.

I just want to do something that'll sink in, that they'll hold onto for the rest of their lives.

Or afterlives.

Benjamin Pendleton came to me. Out of all the department stores in town, that kid had to wander into mine. Of all the Santas he could've sat with, he crawled into my lap. He took one look at me with those iced-over eyes, splitting open those pale, purple lips, and said . . .and said . . .

Cold.

That's it. His first word—only word—slipped out from his mouth with a little river water.

Cold.

That kid had been dead long before I asked him what he wanted for Christmas. I had a sneaking suspicion something was off about that boy from the get-go, but there's always a couple of kids who give you pause. Little weirdos. Homeschoolers. You just have to take it in stride. Not break character. You smile, do your laugh—Ho, Ho, Ho—and just go through the pre-scripted spiel: Have you been a good boy this year? What would you like for Christmas, l'il fella?

What did Benjamin Pendleton want? Someone to find his body, that's all. Wherever it was. That's not so much to ask for Christmas, was it?

So, I've got this ability to see dead kids.

Long story. Bear with me.

It's not just anywhere, though. Only in these department stores. Only when I'm in the suit. I don't know how this all works, if there are—I don't know—rules or whatever, but that's just how it all seems to play out. These ghosts get in line like all the other boys and girls, simply waiting their turn to sit on my lap. I'll ask if I can help

put their spirits to rest. Sometimes that means finding their bones, wherever their remains are buried. Other times it means dealing with some unfinished business. Sometimes I send a message to their loved ones. Just depends on the kid. How they died.

Our day always kicks off when the department store opens. Back in the good ol' days, you might get a line that winds around the whole store. Sometimes it even reached out into the parking lot. Not so much anymore. The first few kids in line are always the overachievers. The parents who want to get their picture all done. I'm granting kids all kinds of gifts. Rocket ships. Teddy bears. Bikes. You name it. Who cares if they're naughty or nice anymore? I feel like a governor offering pardons to death row inmates, doling out reprieves left and right: You get a toy and you get a doll and you get a stuffy and you get a . . .

Then I'll spot a kid just standing there, minding their own business. No parent. Looks like they're all by themselves. They usually got this vacant stare. Never blink. I'll never know if anybody else can see them or not. When this holiday phenomena first started, I asked one of my little helpers—just some pimple-faced greaser squeezed into an elf costume—if he saw what I was seeing, he just looked back at me like he wasn't getting paid nearly enough to deal with my crap. He didn't see this kid, no matter how close he got. Only I could. Lucky, lucky me.

Best thing to do is play it cool. Keep calm. Don't panic.

I'm keeping an eye on them as the line keeps ticking down. Each living kid brings them closer and closer to me, until finally, it's their turn to sit on my lap.

Well, hello there, young lady . . . What's your name?

Sometimes they'll talk. Other times they just stare. You just got to roll with it.

Have you been a good girl this year? What would you like for Christmas? Is there some—

The girl's gone. If she was even there at all. She's too shy to share her secret with me. Maybe she'll come back tomorrow. The kids in line—the live ones—all stare at me like I've been mumbling to myself. Got to play it off. Act natural. Can't let my little helpers think I'm sauced up or something. They'll tell the manager and that's not something I need right now. That guy's been breathing down my neck every damn day from the moment I first clock in. Taking piss tests nearly every other shift. I get it, I do, but I'm clean. I've been clean for years now.

It's this gift. These visions. It's not like I'm looking for them. These kids find me. They come to me. I know how that makes me sound. Believe me, I know. For the longest time, I tried to avoid them. Act like they're not there . . . but that just gets them angry. They won't go away.

Like Benjamin. Since he was my first, I didn't know what the hell I was supposed to do. Wasn't like he came out and said it. That's what's so frustrating with these ghosts. They don't tell you what they want for Christmas. They just stare at you. It's up to you to figure it out. Thought I was going out of my goddamn mind, seeing this dead kid in line, all bloated and blue.

He was wearing a puffy blueberry snowsuit. One of those slick nylon outfits that covers your whole body, arms, and legs. When you walk there's always that synthetic zip-zip-zip sound from the friction between your knees. This kid's skin was the same tint as his snowsuit. He drew closer to me, from across the room, and I swear I could hear the sound of his suit. Zip-zip-zip . . .

He's wet. Not dripping wet. Just . . . moist, I guess. The water is soaked inside him. If I squeezed him too hard, all that water might come dribbling out. You feeling okay, son?

Cold . . .

Where's your mother?

Cold . . .

Maybe we get your parents over here. See if we can't get you a hot chocolate or—

Cold . . .

Cold . . .

Cold . . .

I paid my dues. I did a tour of duty with the March of Dimes, clanging that goddamn bell outside of nearly every grocery store this side of the highway. I pray to God I never go back to that godawful gig. Standing out in the cold for hours, begging moms for pocket change. Nothing but a panhandling Santa. I'd always get a migraine from that bell after the first hour, just ring-a-ding-dinging that goddamn thing all day. Really sets your teeth on edge. Sinks into your skull by the end of your shift. No amount of ibuprofen is gonna take that chiming away. Some nights, I swear, I still hear it. Even years later, it's still ringing, pealing away in my ears—dingadingading.

I can't even begin to tell you the number of migraines I had after my accident. Most days my head felt like it was still underwater, still under that sheet of ice, my mind frozen over.

But a gig is a gig is a gig. I'd slip into my Santa suit and ring that damn bell all day. Started noticing these kids clustering around me on the sidewalk. Not saying anything. They'd just stand there, almost like they were in a line, waiting their turn. I'd try shooing them away with my bell, but they'd always wander back. I had to explain I wasn't that kind of Santa. If they wanted to sit on my lap, they'd have to go to Balkins and bug one of my brothers. Go on! Shoo!

Every Santa is desperate for a department store. That's as cushy a job as you're liable to land these days. The pay ain't all that grand but the perks make it worth it, trust me. You get to sit on your keister all day, inside, where it's warm and toasty. Not on the curb. Not in the cold.

Not with these dead kids trailing after you.

I'd happily take a shop like Balkins any ol' damn day. So it's not Sak's Fifth Avenue. What the hell is? Even Sak's isn't Sak's anymore. Every last damn department store is going the way of the dodo, you know? Thank Walmart for that. Box stores don't give a shit. You think Target's gonna bring in Kris Kringle? Forget about it . . . And it ain't like Amazon's offering up a spot for guys like us to earn an honest living. You think they want us delivering gifts to kids on Christmas morning? Wouldn't that be a fucking hoot? Nah—all we got left are department stores. The ones that're still around, at least, clinging on for dear life at the strip malls and town centers.

So, you never heard of Balkins. No surprise. Balkins is one of these third-string retailers cropping up along the southeastern corridor like canker sores, clustering around the Carolinas. A couple spots are still open in Georgia. None in Florida. Last one got mowed over by Hurricane Whatshername. I forgot. It's cheaper to just take the insurance money and never reopen again.

My Balkins beat is the Chesterfield Towne Centre, right here in Roanoke. It's pretty much the only store that hasn't shuttered in this place. Whole mall is practically a ghost town. The food court's closed. Victoria's Secret pulled up stakes months ago. Just us and the Dippin' Dots kiosk. Don't ask me how this Balkins is still

limping along. Not like they're stocking up on the latest fashions. The clothes on the racks are from five seasons ago. Most folks do their holiday shopping online now. Not here. The writing's on the wall, clear as day, just like the graffiti spray-painted all over the façade. I give this place until the end of Christmas before it shuts down. Pink slip by New Years. That's all, folks . . . Swan song for Santa. Gotta find a new gig.

Somebody better tell that to all the ghosts.

Used to be these spirits would sprinkle themselves amongst the living, shuffling along with the rest. Nowadays, though, there are more of them than there are flesh and blood boys and girls. What's gonna happen when the only kids coming to sit in my lap are all dead?

I've learned to live with it. Used to be I'd nearly shit in my drawers, but now . . . now I just treat them like any other kid. Talk to them. Everybody wants something for Christmas, right?

Jenny Schumacher needed her mom to know it was her uncle who strangled her.

Tommy Watkins just wanted his younger brother to have his old baseball card collection.

Keisha Quinn needed someone to look for her body, even if the cops had stopped searching.

So, this is what Santa must feel like. I'm granting these ghosts one last gift for Christmas.

I'm giving them peace.

Santa's workshop is just a cardboard backdrop pulled out from storage every year, its edges wilting. Looks a little soggy, to be honest, like the whole building got soaking wet one winter and now it's about to collapse. Rolls of the same cotton carpet get unfurled over the floor, so it looks like sheets of snow. Styrofoam candy canes sprout out from the linoleum. Silver tinsel. But the chair, my God, let me tell you about this chair . . . Fit for a fucking king. It's all varnished wood and red velvet cushions, studded with copper buttons. It is the most comfy chair I've ever sat in. Don't even need a donut for my hemorrhoids, it's that soft. Makes the hours slip. I could sit here year-round and never leave. Maybe I will.

If you want your kid sitting on Santa's lap, get your picture to stick on your fridge, you got to actually get off your ass, hop in the car, drive down to your local Balkins and pay me a visit. That's the one leg up this brick-and-mortar shop has over Amazon: flesh and blood Santas.

The Christmas crunch is upon us. It's the last Saturday before the 25th, so we've got a bit of a blitz. There are kids cordoned off behind a red velvet rope, waiting for this show to start.

Gonna be a grind today, I can tell. Kendra called in sick so I'm down to two elves. We'll just have to make do with a skeleton crew. One elf escorts the kids up. He's my bouncer. Whenever we've got an unruly rugrat, it's up to him to kick them out.

Each kid gets about forty-five seconds in my lap. When we're firing on all cylinders and really got our rhythm, we're clocking in thirty seconds, in-out. It's all about the picture. The other elf snaps off the shot. The elf behind the camera fancies herself a photographer, I can tell. Not like there's anything to master at this. It's just a Polaroid. Snap and shoot.

I know most Santas complain about catching whatever cold these kids carry. Doesn't bother me. I've got a strong constitution. It takes a lot to knock me down.

I glance out at the line and try to decide who's alive and who's dead. Getting harder and harder to tell the difference these days.

Benjamin Pendleton came back the very next day. I recognized him right away: Same blue snowsuit. Same moistness. Same chill. I spotted him a few kids back, waiting his turn like all the others. Nobody else seemed to pay him any mind. Most parents hover around their kids. They're not paying attention, per se, focusing on their phones while they move up the line . . .

Benjamin was all alone. No parents by his side. Nobody holding his hand. There were four kids between us before it was his turn.

Then three.

Now two.

I was hardly paying attention to what these kids were even asking for, going through the motions while my eyes always drifted back to that boy in the blueberry snowsuit.

Now it was his turn.

I had to maintain myself. Keep my breathing even and not panic as he slowly waddled up to me. The nylon zip-zip-zip of his scissoring legs. The sqush-sqush-sqush of his galoshes.

I couldn't run. Couldn't move. My entire body was screaming for me to bolt.

Just leap on out of my chair and head for the exit. But I was frozen. Bones locked in place. I couldn't escape.

Benjamin Pendleton waddled up. One hand grabs my knee, using my leg for leverage to hoist himself up and climb into my lap. His puffy blue snowsuit feels like a soggy pear. Some soaked piece of fruit. I was terrified that if I wasn't careful, one misplaced hand would tear right through his flimsy skin and I'd see the bones underneath. The gray muscle tissue.

This kid climbs into my lap. Slowly. Everything about him moves at a stalled pace, delayed by a second or two. I can smell him now. There's a funk coming off him. River water.

His eyes meet mine. There's barely even a foot between our faces. I swear he's not breathing. His skin is blue. Glassy eyes. A purple latticework of veins reaches through his cheeks.

Hello, little fella . . . M-merry Christmas.

Nothing.

Have you been a good boy this year?

His lips split and I can see that his gums are purple. His tongue. His tongue is blue. Cold, he says. Gray water trickles out from his mouth, dribbling down his chin.

What do you want from me?

Cold . . .

Just tell me. Tell me what you want . . . I was gonna tack on " . . . for Christmas," like I always do, but this wasn't about a brand-new bike or a dolly.

Cold . . .

Cold . . .

Cold . . .

Benjamin Goddamn Pendleton.

That kid kept coming back. Patiently waiting his turn in line. He would come and go out of nowhere. Sometimes I'd notice the cold before I'd see him, this precipitous drop in temperature, as if somebody was futzing with the thermostat. Then I'd spot him in line. Waiting his turn. Waddling his way up to me. The squish-squish of his water-logged galoshes.

His body was still out there, somewhere. Needle in fucking frozen haystack. He'd be in a body of water. That much I knew. Everything else was pure intuition.

I needed my head examined. This was crazy. I was crazy. What the hell was I thinking? Coming out here? Trudging through the gray snow . . . I'm not some police officer. Not some CSI-whatever. I'm just Santa Claus, for Christ's sake. Just another goddamn department store Santa.

Cold . . .

I swear, I could nearly hear his voice, pulling me through the snow. Leading me downriver. With every step I took, trudging alongside the frozen riverbank, I could hear the squish of his rubber galoshes. Sqush-sqush-sqush-sqush. The river itself was nothing but a sheet of gray glass, frosted over, so there was no seeing through. But I was getting closer. Closer . . .

Cold . . .

Cold . . .

Cold . . .

The newspaper would report the following morning that a local man who preferred to be unidentified found the body of Benjamin Pendleton trapped beneath a sheet of ice. That kid had been pirouetting through the water. His body drifted further downriver about a mile away from home. He was wearing the same blueberry snowsuit.

He'd been in a bus accident.

Benjamin Pendleton always sat in the back. Always in the very last row, right there in the rear, where the emergency exit is. His body must've slipped through the shattered glass, whisked up by the river, swirling for a murky eternity until somebody finally came upon him.

What was left. Bones in a blueberry suit.

That man who found him? The newspaper never got his name. He preferred to remain anonymous. Some folks said he had white hair. White beard. Bowl full of jelly.

You want the truth? There's no grind. The department store is empty. Nobody comes in now. Blame it on the economy, blame it on Amazon or whatever the hell you want to wag your finger at. Doesn't matter anymore, now, does it? Not really. Not when nobody's around.

This mall has been shuttered for months. Balkins went bust. The store's all empty. Somebody propped a maintenance door open and must've forgotten, so it was simple enough to slip in when nobody was looking. The holiday decorations are in storage. The suit was waiting for me. I've got the whole place to myself. Just me and the kids. All of the kids.

Funny thing is . . . the line never dies down. It's only gotten longer since I found Benjamin. Word must've gotten around about my abilities. That line of children just stretches around the aisles, the clothing racks, out the front door and around the building, on and on and on . . .

Look at them all.

Just look.

You see them, too, don't you? Hard to tell who's alive and who's a ghost anymore.

Who am I kidding? It's nothing but ghosts now. These spirits all line up, waiting their turn to sit on my lap and whisper in my ear what they want for Christmas. What they need.

I've really got my work cut out for me. Gonna be a busy one this year.

Merry Christmas to all and to all a good night . . .

ROSE FROM THE ASHES

PATRICK BARB

Mindy spread the dead woman's ashes across the prep table. She cut a perfect line with the edge of her credit card. "Let's see what you've got for me . . . Rose," Mindy said, reading the deceased's paperwork.

She leaned over the table with a rolled-up dollar bill and snorted a fat rail of Rose's cremated remains up her left nostril. Mindy inhaled until black spots and exploding stars appeared behind her eyes.

An opening door brought Mindy crashing back to the present. She scrambled to the other side of the table and turned around, blocking the remaining ashes from whomever might be at the door, while her heart beat like Neil Peart was playing a drum solo in her chest.

"Are Mrs. Devere's ashes ready?" Mr. Evergreen, Mindy's boss, asked.

"Oh yeah. Sure thing. Comin' right up."

Rubbing her hand under her nose, Mindy's index finger came back black from the ash she'd missed.

Not like it mattered. Her boss was already gone.

Mindy walked to the open clerestory window on the far wall of the crematorium. She stretched for the sill, feeling along with fingertips until she gripped the ashtray containing the remnants of her clove cigarettes. She'd balanced it out of sight from nearsighted old Mr. Evergreen.

She dumped the fragrant tobacco ash and the stray damp chocolate-brown butts into the gold-plated urn provided by the dead woman's family. She'd make sure to seal it tight in case any grieving family members got too weepy and curious about the state of the dearly departed. "Shame they couldn't spring for *actual* gold though," Mindy said to the remaining pile of ashes on the table. She kept a Tupperware in her bag for the leftovers.

Mindy's eyes twitched. First left, then right. Then both together.

Knowing she needed to move fast, she set the urn down and pictured the deceased Rose Devere as she'd looked before cremation.

"What're you doing here?" The old woman's voice was sharper than the others, aimed right at Mindy.

The young woman watched as Rose's spectral form unfolded into the material plane like some demented Magic Eye image.

What're you doing here?

Mindy smiled as she considered the query. It was new, she'd give it that. Most summoned spirits—especially fresh ones— asked the same question. *"Where am I?"*

What're you doing here? A smarter question. Because who the hell was Mindy to this dead lady anyway?

Still, she'd performed the ritual enough times. The dead, no matter how perceptive, couldn't phase her.

"Where'd you hide the money, Rose?" Mindy asked.

Pursing blue-black corpse lips, the ghost scowled. Before she spoke, Evergreen pounded on the door again.

"Come on, Mindy. Mrs. Devere's children can't wait all day."

Mindy covered the distance to the door in record time, pulled it open, and shoved the clove-ash-and-cigarette-butt-filled urn into her boss's waiting hands.

He accepted it with a dumb grin on his face, oblivious to the spirit peering over Mindy's shoulder from within the crematorium.

When the door shut again, Mindy spun around to confront the ghost.

"Listen, bitch. I overheard your kids whining about money being missing. Tell me where you hid the cash. I'll grab the urn from my boss before he hands it off to your family and put the rest of your ashes in there so you can rest. Understand?"

"Pardon me, Miss . . . Mindy," Rose started. "I don't know what you're referring to."

The dead woman's features settled into a cold, impassive stare.

Mindy rolled her eyes, making the specter flicker like a deteriorating film reel. "Suit yourself," she said. "It's your funeral."

She moved to exit.

"Wait!"

Her hand hovering above the doorknob, Mindy smirked and faced her latest ghost. "Yes?"

"Where will I go if I don't tell?"

Mindy's smile widened.

"You'll stay here." She tapped the side of her head. "Most ghosts come around. But sometimes, y'all think you can resist. Tell you what, why don't you take some time and ask the others?"

Mindy closed her eyes in concentration, drawing ghost Rose into the firing synapses of her brain. When she opened them again, the old woman reappeared—paler than before, a shade of white radiating resignation.

"Okay. I'll tell."

Mindy clapped her hands. "Good, good."

She walked to the control panel by the furnace. There, she pressed the round red button, opening the burnished metal doors and letting the flames jump to life, roaring like a yawning dragon. The digital temperature read-out ticked upward.

Mindy had another body to burn and figured, *no harm in multi-tasking.* "So, now that you've had a chance to gossip with the others, tell me, where'd you hide it?"

Rose kept her eyes on the ground, avoiding Mindy's insistent, inquiring gaze. When she spoke again, her voice was quiet, a trembling whisper. "You have so many in there. How long have you been doing this?"

Mindy laughed. "Not long enough, since I'm still working here, burning you stiffs. Lost my damn sense of smell and still haven't paid back all my student loans. But you'll change that, won't you, Rose?"

The dead woman flickered. Resisting. Her voice grew in volume as she spoke. Her eyes met Mindy's and the younger, living woman released an involuntary gasp. "They told me about you. Those other ghosts inside your head. You're strong. You defeated them all—one after the other."

"Uh-huh." Mindy pulled the sheet from her next body, playing at nonchalance and letting Rose chatter on.

The slabbed corpse belonged to a younger man. Twenty-something. College boy. None of Rose's wrinkled skin and varicose veins. Alive, Mindy would've plied him with shots at a seedy bar and taken him home for her terrible pleasures.

But not now.

Something tickled the hairs in her nostrils—more ash stuck there thanks to Evergreen's interruption.

She snorted, attempting to pull the last stray bits of the dead woman inside her sinus cavity.

Instead, the ash went the wrong way. Mindy coughed as the gritty remnants traveled down her throat.

Wet, phlegmy explosions rocketed past her lips. A muddy green mucus wad dredged from her chest fell onto the lips of the handsome dead man.

Mindy wasn't pleased. She wiped the tears from her eyes. Then, she rubbed her sleeve across her nose and mouth, leaving silver circles behind on the fabric. She let a low frustrated growl escape.

"Okay, tell me where the goddamn money is!"

But Rose was gone.

That wasn't supposed to happen. For the other encounters, the ghosts were so cowed by the one-two punch of being dead and being imprisoned in Mindy's head that they remained frozen in place. Obedient to the crematorium operator's commands.

"They told me you defeated them one by one . . ."

This time, the old woman's voice sounded muffled as though it came from behind layers of padding.

Mindy froze, as Rose's location became apparent.

The handsome dead man took his handsome dead hand and pulled open the stitches from his handsome dead mouth. Rose's voice came through clearer then.

". . . so I convinced them we'd stand a better chance working together."

Sitting up, the corpse swung its legs to the floor. Mindy no longer heard Rose alone. Instead, a ghostly chorus addressed her, consisting of all the dead she'd consumed and never released. Trembling fingers rose to her lips, her nose. Mindy swallowed, thinking she might hold back any of the other spirits from escaping.

She knew it was too late though.

Mindy ran for the door, but there wasn't time. Filled with stolen souls, the handsome corpse pulled her into their embrace.

They dragged her toward the open maw of the furnace.

\#

In the front, Mr. Evergreen met a grieving husband to discuss tombstone options for his deceased wife. A variety of funeral bouquets drooped down from the lip of a shelf along the wall. Lilies, daisies, orchids, and blush roses. Reaching for the light shining through the front windows of the parlor and waiting for a spritz from the plastic spray bottle sitting beside the flowers.

Evergreen shouted his condolences over the roar and rattle of bodies burning in the back.

SCRATCH OFF UNIVERSE

HAILEY PIPER

An unmarked white van rolls into the parking lot as the golden hour overtakes the sky. Its presence is an old story, without a happy ending, and Clay wonders what any onlookers would think when he and a pile of other teenage boys spill out of the back. They've come to do great work, but maybe in leaving home, this will be the last they're ever seen. Unmarked white vans are harbingers of such stories.

Disappearances and disaster are possible when tampering in the domain of gods. Clay remembers this from the church he doesn't believe in.

The van parks several rows back from Pelton's humble baseball stadium. It's a small place, like the town itself, built for high school games. An orange-yellow school bus marks the presence of a visiting team from a bigger place. Pale siding blocks sight of the bleachers, but as the sky purples, Clay makes out a glowing shimmer along the stadium's upper rim. An indiscernible announcer booms out updates on the game and advertisements for local small businesses. A feed store. The hardware place. Grayson's Arcade. These form the lifeblood of Pelton.

"Hop to it," Mr. Becker says, yanking open the van's back doors. "They've hit the second inning. Now is our time."

Clay and the other boys drop to the pavement. Other vans, trucks, and cars litter the lot, but most people who've planned to show up this evening are already here, meaning the parking lot should be free. Mr. Becker's plan will go uninterrupted. Clay helps haul the equipment out once the van is empty, and shovels and pickaxes clatter onto the pavement, their blades and heads carved deep with unfamiliar shapes as if written in a bizarre alphabet. Doubtful anyone but Mr. Becker can read them, and Clay expects he carved the figures by hand. He's been working on them for years, and he only trusts Clay and the other boys gathered here to handle his great work.

"There's a power in each of you," Mr. Becker says as he doles out equipment. "Maybe it manifests in righteous indignation, or a dream unfulfilled, or a passion unspoken, but it is pure and strong. People grown past your age? They get

tangled in the mundanities, fall in love with societal machinations. But you see past that. You're special."

The boys smile sheepishly or rub the backs of their necks. Clay only knows Aaron Jackson among them, but they all look on Mr. Becker as their leader. He's a spectacled, square-jawed man of firm face and sun-kissed skin, with the rigid air of a physics professor and the roughened physique of an outdoorsman. A nervous edge to his eyes says he's a man with big plans.

No one knows that better than Clay. He's walked at Mr. Becker's side since the day of the Bird Funeral. Clay was a small child then, but nine years later, he's nearly a man himself.

"So, the god's in the ground?" asks one boy, scrunching his pinkish face.

"No, no," Mr. Becker says, and he passes the boy a shovel. "We'll be touching beyond our world. While we tear open this pavement on one layer of reality, we're opening the way to another layer thanks to my calculations. Think of it like scratching one of those gas station lottery tickets. You all know them?"

The boys nod at him. They understand there are bigger places than Pelton, and they're meant to catch notice of such a place.

"Good, that'll do for analogies. Is what you see under the scratch-off part of any value? Of course not. It's what you can get for it, what it symbolizes, that matters." Mr. Becker points to the shapes carved into one shovel's blade. "Here comes the nail to scratch away this surface, and the symbols touch our payoff."

"Like winning the lottery," another boy says, pulling off his shirt to free brown, muscled arms.

"Like winning a new god to guide the world," Mr. Becker says, a dream in his voice. "A real god."

He's explained to Clay before that there's a valley between pretending the imagined is real and imagining the possibilities of the future. Clay can't see through Mr. Becker's eye, but he knows the hope in them to fix this world and all its injustices. The dead. The lost. A return of love which is sorely absent.

The stadium roars with cheering as if the baseball game has awoken a tremendous beast. The boys glance from its outer shimmer to Mr. Becker's face.

"We'd better get a move on," Mr. Becker says. "Can't have that crowd finishing their hot dogs and soda pop too soon, can we?"

He says it with the kind of hopeful but insistent grin that forces the boys to chuckle.

Mr. Becker shakes his head and squeezes his pickaxe. "No, we need them. What's a god without his faithful? We'll have to show he's welcome in our layer of reality."

"But they're not doing the work like us, teach," Aaron Jackson says. He graduated Pelton High last year, a football hopeful with no scholarship, no prospects, no future beyond his father's workshop, the last place he wants to be. Maybe he dreams a god will fix all that.

"A god won't expect everyone to get it right," Mr. Becker says. "He'll find it charming they tried their best by showing up, and then he'll guide us in the right direction. Now, heave-ho!" He shouts the last as he raises his pickaxe and slams it into a weak patch of pavement.

Clay expects Mr. Becker has examined the stadium's lot with focused care, seeking out soft places where gray chunks will shatter under shovel and pick. Do the bizarre shapes make the work easier? As Clay lifts his pickaxe and slams it beside

Mr. Becker, he understands the shapes can't aid this layer of reality. For flesh and blood, there is only the sweat and toil and the faraway cheering of the crowd.

Glancing at the stadium, its siding almost forms a low fence as used to divide Clay's back yard from Mr. Becker's. He half-expects that friendly yet firm voice to reach over the sky.

Maybe before the night's end, it will.

A different summer had dropped Pelton into its humid stew on the day of the Bird Funeral.

Since then, Clay has learned that his pet bird Marshmallow was a budgie, with pretty blue and green feathers, a sweet whistle to her voice, but he's been calling that day the Bird Funeral for too long to scrape the title from his mind.

The air was thick with flowery scents, both genuine and drawn from Mom's perfume as she hugged Clay over the back yard's tilled earth.

"It's okay, hon," Mom whispered. "God called Marshmallow to Heaven, that's all."

The phone rang from inside the house, back before Mom finally broke down and got a cellphone, leaving Clay to sob over Marshmallow's fresh grave. He was wiping his face across one arm when he realized he wasn't alone. A glance past the low backyard fence showed Mr. Becker watching from his yard, one arm leaning on the wooden slats.

"It hurts," Mr. Becker said. "Like a nail on your heart."

Clay rubbed at one still-teary eye. He'd been crying so hard, he could scarcely breathe, but the neighbor's attention startled him into an ordinary rhythm as if putting his grief on pause.

"You know, God took someone I love from me, too." Mr. Becker glanced at his hands, olive-spotted and striped white with the old scars. "Not even sure the bastard's real, but Walter? His name was Walter. He called loving that imaginary god a virtue, and loving a real man a sin, and so he went to the church. For the sake of imagination."

Clay had quit crying by then. He hardly understood Mr. Becker at the time, but a mournful song in his voice lured Clay like flashing silver to a fish beneath a tranquil pond.

"If there's any such thing up there, doesn't seem to me like the guy's doing too good a job." Mr. Becker glanced at the sky and then chinned over the fence, at Marshmallow's grave. "Not if he takes away the ones we love for no damn good reason. Oh, pardon me, little man."

Clay giggled then, both to hear the curse and to be called a man, even a little one.

"Walter imagined that god of churches, but I can imagine bigger," Mr. Becker said. "I can know better, too. It's only a matter of geometry and time."

An annoying touch yanks Clay from the past, and he scratches quick at his shoulder. Sometimes sweat makes him itch, but he expects a bug to have landed on his bare skin and taken a bite. Pelton is home to more mosquitos than people this time of year.

Has Mr. Becker taken summer air into his calculations? Clay is no star chemistry student, but nonetheless he knows heat is more than numbers, a transference of energy. Every touch of friction brings it,

and he remembers the last time he heard of people reaching out to touch a god, from the days Mom took him to the church he didn't and doesn't believe in. Instead of digging, the people built a tower, but nonetheless the god of churches swatted them like any summer gnat.

Clay says none of this. Mr. Becker must know best; he's been single-minded about the work for most of Clay's life.

That determination feeds Mr. Becker's digging. His gray button-down wears stains beneath the armpits, but he won't pull off his shirt like the boys have. Maybe he's embarrassed of his age and gut. Maybe he hopes the god will change the past, or the present, something to make him young again. Clay doesn't ask.

"Keep digging," Mr. Becker says, and then a flashlight sweeps white across his eyes.

Clay, Aaron, and the other boys raise arms over foreheads, eyes squinting against sweat and intrusion.

A grim silhouette morphs into a blue-uniformed security guard. He stands at the edge of a growing patch of torn-up pavement, his pale face and reddish beard twinkling with sweat.

"What the hell are you folks doing out here?" he asks.

The boys glance at each other, an excuse to turn from the flashlight. They're wise enough not to look at Mr. Becker, though he's the adult and the obvious choice to take leadership and blame.

"Ho, there!" Mr. Becker shouts. He lowers his pickaxe and waves at the security guard. "What inning is it? Fifth by my count."

"Top of the fifth when I left," the security guard says. "Bottom by now. Mind telling me what you think you're doing?"

Clay leans over the bare stretch of pavement. It looks like a yellow excavator has reached its dinosaur-like neck across the lot to scratch an itch the world couldn't reach, but really, it's been Mr. Becker and the boys, their own flesh and blood and strange tools. Will Mr. Becker tell the security guard the truth? It'll sound deranged, but Clay almost wants to hear it. He's been immersed in the reality of the universe for so long, he almost relishes seeing Mr. Becker pry someone free of life's mundanities with godly promise.

"See these symbols?" Mr. Becker asks, rounding the bare patch. His legs are slower than usual, less steady, and there's a tremble in his shoulders. He moves more like an octogenarian than a man in his fifties.

"I see them," the guard says. "Don't understand them or why you've used this stuff to chew up the lot, but you can explain it to the cops." He unhooks a walkie-talkie from his belt and raises it to his mouth.

Before his thumb can dig into the side and begin a conversation across the roiling summer air, Mr. Becker pretends to trip, swirls on his heels, and uses his awkward yet somehow graceful dance to bury one point of the pickaxe into the back of the security guard's skull.

The boys flinch as if they're a single organism. Aaron drops his shovel and grabs at his chest. Clay is petrified like he's the one pinned in place by curved iron.

Mr. Becker jerks his arms back and forth as if pumping water from deep in the earth. Drooling darkness stains the security guard's chest. One last tug, and the pickaxe rips free in a wet crunch, the sound of teeth chewing on milk-coated cereal. The security guard drops in a clumsy heap, and fluid fingers coat his scalp in a crimson hand.

"I thought this god didn't need any blood sacrifice, teach," Aaron says.

"He doesn't," Mr. Becker says, and there's a nothingness to his face, as uncaring as if he'd swatted away an insect rather than killed a man in cold blood. "But we can't stop now. Or be stopped. We must finish before the game ends. The god will be insulted by an empty stadium."

The warped boom of the far-off announcer sends the boys snatching up their equipment. Back to digging.

Clay studies his pickaxe. Shouldn't the blood matter somehow? The shapes on the boys' tools should glow with promising force now that they're part in taking a life, but no god seems to charge them with divine authority. They're only a gaggle of teenagers chopping at a stadium parking lot while a dead body stains the pavement.

"Are we damned?" one boy whispers.

"This isn't the god of churches, don't you get that?" Mr. Becker snaps, wiping a sleeve across the swamp of his brow. "No one's holding bloodshed accountable. Show your dedication, boys!"

The boys drive their shovel blades in, and their pickaxes pluck at gray chunks of pavement. Ignore the blood, keep digging.

But Clay can't silence the itch in his mind, and his eyes stray to Mr. Becker every time he thrusts at the earth. How long has he been searching for a god? Since the Bird Funeral? No, that was when he planted the idea in Clay's mind. Mr. Becker has been determined for much longer. Since he came to Pelton? Since he majored in physics at college? Before that? Exactly when was his great heartbreak with Walter that set him on this path? How long has he been seeking this emotional itch to scratch it off his soul?

Keep digging. It must be the sixth or seventh inning now. Another drive of these shapes between pavement, into soil, while the crowds cheer for a cause they have yet to know.

Clay watches the sweat-soaked boys. If their work is a scratch-off lottery card, is Mr. Becker a gambling addict? Does that make the boys enablers? Or has their fearless, hopeful, dreamy leader sucked them into his fatal habit?

Keep digging. Don't swat at the bugs. Don't look at the blood.

This single-minded drive is familiar. Tonight is the first instance Clay has held special tools to scrape through one layer of reality into another, but hasn't he been digging for this cause the past nine years? Beyond school, and after-school activities, and TV shows, there's been little time for friends, relationships, or much of anything. Mr. Becker's purpose has loomed instead.

Only now does Clay wonder if he's never given other people a chance at love because he's clung to Mr. Becker's dream since the Bird Funeral. Pale siding has walled off Clay's possibilities. Almost like he's had no choice in whether to focus on the godly prize or to take a chance at tangling in the mundanities of a real life. No chance to learn which one he prefers.

"Mr. Becker," Clay says, resting against his pickaxe. "I know you want to fix the world."

"Yes," Mr. Becker says, eager.

"But that won't bring Marshmallow back." Clay swallows. "Will it?"

"No, it won't." Mr. Becker lays his hand on Clay's shoulder, and grains of soil rain down his chest. "The god can't change the past."

"I know," Clay says. "So, you know he can't make Walter come back to you. Right?"

A chill coats Mr. Becker's eyes. His fingers slide from Clay's shoulder, and he turns again to the lot's growing bare patch, its northeastern edge now rimmed with blood.

"Let's get back to digging, yes?" Mr. Becker says. "The shapes are near ready, and we've still an inning on our side."

The look in his eyes both scares and angers Clay in ways he can't describe, even in his head. Always the digging. Always forward in time, never any breaks to appreciate the now.

An untapped frustration works up Clay's arms as he wonders what kind of life he might have lived had he been allowed to finish grieving for his poor budgie, sweet Marshmallow. The day of the Bird Funeral feels stretched across the past, a creature beneath time.

A crack crosses the night as he raises his pickaxe high overhead, and a distant cheer follows as if the crowd in the bleachers can see him. The sounds tells him this will be a thunderous blow, and he hopes the pickaxe crunches like the security guard's skull. Shapes broken, alphabet scattered, an omen of failure to come.

Clay doesn't mind. He's still young. Better to learn now that it's wrong for anyone to rule a life, be it a beloved dead bird, or a god, or a kindly neighbor like Mr. Becker.

The air whistles, and a white meteor with red stitching crashes against Clay's head the moment his pickaxe swings down. Cheering prowls the distance. The nearby boys gasp. Someone mutters or shouts the vaguest sense of words. *Home run*, they might say. Or is it, *Run home*? Clay can't tell past the sense of tearing beneath his thoughts, the summer air senselessly trapped in a cold swirl.

Early evening is gone, and a black sky coats his vision. He's tumbling, falling into the patch, a pit, and his eyes twinkle with stars.

And then the parking lot fades, as if Mr. Becker's shapes now carve Clay's mind. They peel away this layer of reality's skin.

He sees everything.

This vast expanse of darkness should not exist in the same universe as its tiny lights and tinier people. Earth is a bright blue dot, maybe lit by the force of nearby sunlight, maybe by familiarity, but it is one piece in the endless distances with only the growing and shrinking of spheres to tell Clay he's looking far across infinity.

He wonders briefly if this is what Mr. Becker sought, a god in the fabric of the universe. For one moment, Clay can't blame his kindly neighbor for the years of stubbornness. To witness this beauty—isn't its touch worth a single-minded determination across geometry and time?

But then Clay sees another layer, almost larger than this vast expanse. Something moves within the cosmic splendor.

This is no god in any way Clay has ever discussed with the others. Mr. Becker cannot grasp how little this presence cares about the work or the faithful or any gathered crowds.

There is instead a body shifting beneath the Milky Way's surface. Clay has no words for sizes of this magnitude. Worlds are pinpricks against its enormity. Its limbs cross the emptiness between star systems, and its flank might only be measured in lights years upon light years. The distance from head to tail is a scope greater than Clay can make out even from this distorted vantage point.

If the creature is a god, it cannot see humanity, let alone fix it. There is only a galactic behemoth traveling the cosmos.

The sun, forever screaming, is a buzzy gnat beside the unfathomable head, but its only lifeforms are made of light, and they are too wise to reach out and touch this behemoth's form.

But Mr. Becker is different. He's been carving shapes and seeking pathways all his life. To meet this side of the universal everything has been his only goal, and now he's reached through the broken veil between one layer of reality and another.

An annoying touch rankles the behemoth. It has no Mr. Becker to command that it keep working through this need to scratch. There is no digging here, no baseball, only a body with its colossal head and surface and limbs.

The needful impulse flickers across the behemoth's vastness, and without evident thought, it lifts a limb beyond measure, tipped with claws that might scratch away suns and worlds.

Clay rouses, and the blackness ebbs, as do the stars and nebulae and everything gargantuan about the universe. He finds Mr. Becker kneeling beside him. The other boys ask questions, tell Clay he'll be okay, their faces all wrinkled in concern. He can't answer them enough to say they have no idea what they're talking about.

Cheers crackle in the distance. They're wrong against the night. No one understands what they're cheering for. Not even Mr. Becker can grasp what layer he's broken in reality, exactly what kind of creature he's touched.

Clay glances skyward as a cosmic chill passes over the parking lot, the stadium, Pelton, everything. Something too large for his eyes to take in has moved between the world and the sun's heat, but not for long. It's coming down. He can feel it in the wind.

Everyone else begins to feel it, too, but they'll look up too late to understand where it's coming from. They won't have time for their hearts to seize, to die of panic or fright. They won't even know it's Mr. Becker's fault.

Clay alone has time to absorb the rush of a nearing colossal shape. His shoulders rise, skin irritated, and the sudden need to scratch a summer bug bite is the closest he'll ever get in relating to the galactic behemoth's mind. Despite its scale, he sees the curve of it in the last moments, and remembers the tower to reach another god, and thinks of the dead security guard, and understands that in this, too, Mr. Becker is wrong. They are all damned.

The cold suffocates the air, and Clay shrinks into himself. The roar of a parting atmosphere fills the world. Here comes the nail, looming to scratch a tiny sensation from the behemoth's tremendous flank.

An itch they call Earth.

IN HASKINS

CARSON WINTER

Everyone, both the young and the old, went about their lives as usual on the day of the Mask Festival. The downtown streets were covered with colored leaves and Mr. Burkett still waved at children and swept in front of his storefront. Mrs. Farley still clucked to Mrs. Durant on how the new teachers at the old school would not and could not teach their children anything. And the policemen still ate lunch at the Morrison Deli on Main. Normality ruled with benevolent routine. But still, as the leaves fell, and the stage was erected, the people of Haskins braced quietly for their most insistent tradition.

At the fairgrounds, Jennifer arrived early to help set the stage. Her eye sockets hung loose and rubbery around her blue eyes. She was the first Jennifer to have blue eyes. The mane on top of her head was coarse and tawny. Flies buzzed in her stomach and she was thankful she was Jennifer because Jennifer always had to stay busy. Cindy was already there, cross-legged and cutting orange leaves out of construction paper, looking prim and sweet in her blue dress.

She nodded to Cindy as she found a pair of scissors. When Cindy did not return the movement, Jennifer decided that her eyelets must be misaligned.

"Hey," she said, gaining her attention.

Cindy looked up from a pile of construction paper. "Good morning," she said between ragged breaths. She always complained of being overheated. "Are you excited?"

Cindy's voice was low this year, deep. She was tall and muscular, but Jennifer always gave her credit for her commitment to Cindy's primary traits—innocence and geniality. They were best friends.

"Yes, in a way," she said.

Cindy's scissors made ripping sounds as they ate through the construction paper. "Are you worried?"

She was talking about Rance and Rance was a key aspect of Jennifer. They fit together like pieces of a puzzle. Jennifer was a cheerleader and Rance was the high school quarterback. He had a shock of blond horsetail hair on the top of his rubber scalp. His mask was loose and shook back and forth like a great Jello mold when

he spoke. They were to be married, the day after the Mask Festival.

She froze for a moment. "No," said Jennifer, wondering how much of herself she should share. "Rance and I will be very happy."

"Of course."

"We'll be very happy," she said again. Because right now, she was Jennifer, and that is something Jennifer would say.

The stage was decorated with cornucopias and browning sunflowers—symbols of the season. Orange and brown paper leaves decorated the backdrop, frozen in mid-fall. The people of Haskins shuffled in quietly, some enthusiastically. Others came with an expression of boredom, of toe-tapping impatience. Haskins was a small town, but it contained all sorts.

Jennifer snuck down from the stage as twilight struck and the big sky above the small town glowed with gold and crimson ribbons. The people were drinking their ciders, wiping the grease from the lips of their masks as they devoured turkey legs through the slits that made up their mouths.

She found Rance sitting on a hay bale, his legs resting on a large pumpkin with a blue ribbon. She said his name and he reacted in mock exaggeration, pretending to fall from his spot. Rance had always been a jokester—for the last three dozen years, at least. Before, he was cruel—a bully—but time had softened his demeanor. He was now something of a class clown. Even in Haskins, times change.

"There she is, my beautiful." He stood up and touched her waist. He was shorter than her and the way he looked up into her eyes made him seem like a child looking up at the stars in the night sky. She could see him, his eyes behind the rubber curves, big and brown, pointing up to an endless sky with infantile delight.

They mashed their faces together, crumpling into each other as their masks folded into sweating slabs of rubber. Their tongues found their way out of their mouth-slits, tasting each other's flesh.

They held on for as long as they could. Rance found his head on her shoulder. He would not say what he wanted to say, but she could hear the choke in his voice all the same. She could divine his meaning.

She pulled apart from him and looked down, grabbing his half-drank cup of cider for a sip. "We're getting married tomorrow," she said.

He swallowed, a noise that seemed to echo behind his mask. "Yes, I know."

Behind them, past the tents and merchants, folks began to gather. A horn blared.

"Could we just—"

She stopped herself. It was not Jennifer speaking.

Rance sniffed and took her by the arm. "We should head up," he said. "They'll start without us."

They pulled each other through the crowd and stood to the far side near the stage where they could see Mayor Granger adjusting his cufflinks. He preened in the expected manner, debuting a new suit with extravagant embroidery for the occasion. Mayor Granger was always wearing the finest clothes.

"Alright, yes," he began. "Okay, well, here we are. This is the Mask Festival. The Festival of Masks. An old tradition, a very old tradition, indeed." Mayor Granger's speech ran out of steam before it began, as it often did in the last year, so instead of continuing, he straightened his silk tie and smiled. "Let's begin," he said, finally.

Through the wings of the stage, two farm boys with rubber jowls pushed a wooden cart with a large pumpkin on top of it. Granger clapped his hands and let out a nervous sigh. The two boys hoisted the pumpkin's top off together, struggling under its weight.

Jennifer and Rance held hands as they watched Mayor Granger close his eyes and reach into the pumpkin. When his hand came back with two slips of paper, the festival began.

"Connie and Delmont," he called. "Please come up to the stage and make your exchange."

A small woman with a snug mask trotted up on stage, she carried with her a wicker basket of flowers. She curtsied before the audience. On the other side, a mechanic in overalls with long black hair stomped with heavy boots to the center of the stage. They turned to each other and bowed, then walked to the rear of the stage, their backs to the audience. With both hands they removed their masks, then, without looking, held them out to the other. The new Connie's mask was so tight that her features seemed to pop out of the eyelets. Delmont was slight and wiry, but the wearer had begun to learn his movements, raising his feet in great destructive arcs. The crowd cheered and

the new Connie skipped heavily back into the crowd and disappeared.

Before long, Mayor Granger's name was called too. His change was extravagant, of course. He danced to the back of the stage and when he came back his voice grew more resinous, his stature more assured. The old Granger dis-appeared into the crowd wearing Jim Brown's face and drinking sweet liquor with Jim Brown's loud friends.

Jennifer held Rance's hand until he had to leave for the stage. He met with Susan Hickens, a girl a year below them, and they swapped faces. When Rance came back to Jennifer, he was taller. Susan held her face in her hands as she was embraced by her family. For just a moment, Jennifer saw her look back at her, the black holes of her eyes an implacable enigma. She was always known to be shy.

The new Rance put his arm around her—in a way that was so unlike the old Rance that it made her skin crawl. She told herself that it was okay, that they were to be married and that this was a perfectly apt display of affection. It was only that— Rance used to hold her hand. He did not usually wrap his arms around her casually, she was used to feeling his fingers between hers. She wriggled out of the embrace and grabbed his hands, demonstrating the protocols of their relationship in a discreet way. His hands were rough and large. He turned his head toward her, bright hazel eyes hidden behind eyelets. She thought she detected a nod of understanding. He held her hand and watched the stage.

Mayor Granger dug his hand into the pumpkin and came out with two slips of paper. He squinted his eyes, one hand tugging a finger into his eyelet, spreading it so that he could read. "Cole Drewson and Jennifer Maisey. Come on up!"

Her heart shivered, palpitating in erratic bursts of electric anxiety. She unhooked her hand from Rance and felt a chill. She looked at him briefly, to see his eyes, but they were not the eyes she knew. She seemed to float to the stage, dragged along by an inevitable leash. Mayor Granger took both of their hands and raised them. He was adding to the spectacle, he was making decisions. She reflected that this was indeed in line with Granger's character, and she wondered why no one considered taking the hands of those on the stage and raising them before. It added a sort of spectacle to the event,

and historically, Mayor Granger was spectacle incarnate.

Granger joined their hands and for just a moment, she felt as if the hand in hers was Rance's. The Rance *she* knew. But the palm in hers was sweating and Rance never sweated from his hands. She and Cole walked to the back of the stage—an eternity—and she looked straight ahead as she took off her mask.

Cole was doing the same beside her.

She wondered if he felt the same rush she did when she removed it. *I'm still Jennifer I'm still Jennifer I'm still Jennifer*, she thought. Her face was naked and she was still Jennifer. She panicked. Her heart kicked her sternum. She did not feel any different. She liked being Jennifer. She was still her. Jennifer was who she should be, and why now should Cole get to be Jennifer? Why now should *she* have to be Cole?

She tried to catch her breath and reach some sort of compromise with herself as Cole pulled off his own mask and held it out to her.

Her body failed her. It had become too accustomed to the ways of Haskins. She reached out with her own mask and they exchanged without looking at each other.

She pulled on Cole Drewson's face and felt the sweat and stink of another human and she began to pray—that she would *be* Cole, that she would forget what it was like to be Jennifer, what it was like to love Rance, her Rance.

They both turned around and Cole Drewson waved weakly to the audience and went down the opposite side of the stage. Jennifer found Rance and they put their arms around each other and embraced.

In the back of the fairgrounds, Cole found himself in the men's room, staring at his new face. Long jawed, with a mustache. Stubble dotted his chin. A trucker hat covered his black hair. His creases were long and deep like knife cuts.

Behind him, a boy he could not see left a bathroom stall and walked out the door. When he was alone in the surgical teal bathroom, Cole whispered his old name.

***

The next month was a period of adjustment for everyone. Cole woke up in his new home and learned his old habits. His wife, Pauline, was a quick study. She would cower in fear whenever he entered the room, although she would do so in a pathetic, approval-seeking way.

Cole was more lethargic, less vigorous in his anger than usual, but he made his threats, he spat between the lips of his mask and cursed. He drank the same beer, although he had not been able to drink as much as he used to. Most nights, when trying, he fell asleep in the white light of the television while Pauline stepped lightly out the front door to meet their neighbor.

When he'd wake, he'd go to his job at the plant, where he learned to speak crudely with the other men at work. His tone was high and girlish but they accepted him with backslaps and unhinged laughter.

He did not feel like Cole, but he did appreciate that the others felt like he was playing his part. Cole was a difficult role, he demanded a certain physicality that was difficult to match at first. And although, behind the rubber of his face, he still felt like Jennifer, he was beginning to appreciate the inherent violence of his new identity.

He'd begun to get comfortable slapping Pauline when he was angry. The first hit had been a surprise to them both, but it was very much in line with what Cole would do. She looked up at him, having fallen to the floor and rubbing her cheek, and she looked almost appreciative.

"Don't look at me like that," he muttered.

The incident happened after he came home late. He told her he'd gone to the bar, but really he'd gone down to the old high school to watch the football game. He'd brought a bottle with him. It was gone by the time he got back. She only had to ask him where he'd been and it was enough. It took only a second for his rage to show its face.

After, of course, he felt sick. As Pauline hid the rest of the night, he became preoccupied with the dimensions of his mask. He drank until he fell asleep.

Cole was not known as a sports fan, but it was certainly not so out of sorts for a drunk and a wifebeater to enjoy football. Cole considered this to be an aspect of the Cole character he could develop. What are games but an excuse to drink? What violences could he commit to Pauline when the home team lost? At first, it seemed strange for Cole to go see the local team play every Friday, but then as his work friends came around, it didn't seem so strange at all. And besides, if Rance could now put his arms around Jennifer rather than hold her hand, why couldn't Cole like football?

"You like that cheerleader? The one with the legs?"

Cole shook his head. He did not care for the cheerleaders. He was not looking at them. His eyes were always on the crowd, looking for a young girl with brown hair that always fell in front of her mask. But Susan Hickens was shy and he didn't know why he thought she might decide to come to the game.

He took off his hat and rubbed his mane of hair. He punched the side of his head impotently.

"Y'okay, Cole?"

"Yeah, fine. Watching the game."

Rance, the quarterback, completed a thirty-yard pass and the crowd erupted in unhinged ecstasy. Cole put his hand on his head and said, "I'm gonna head out. I wanna go fishing in the morning."

His friends booed and waved their bottles in mock-disapproval, but fishing had been another recent addition to Cole's canon, and he was allowed to leave. He balled his fists in the cuffs of his coat, cursing under his mask, stealing glances at the field. *They were going to be newlyweds*, he reminded himself. He got into his car and rubbed at the rubber covering his face. He rubbed it into himself, tried to make it melt into his flesh.

When he got home, he greeted Pauline by cracking her jaw.

She threw her hands up in front of her, but her eyes showed the same twisted sort of glee she always shared whenever Cole played his part well. She braced for the next hit and when she got it, her head snapped back into the cupboard behind her.

Blood flowed from the slit of her lips. He heard whimpering from inside of her mask. Cole stepped over her body to get a beer from the fridge.

She got on all fours, she was trying to stand. "Cole," she started.

He wound up and kicked her in the ribs. She dropped back to the floor, moaning as she gripped her sides.

Cole stood over her, sweating. In a shaky voice, he said, "Don't ever call me that again."

When she tried to speak again, he stomped down on the back of her neck until he felt something crack.

"I'm sorry," he said. "I'm sorry."

Her legs were shaking, twitching.

"It's just—I'm not Cole."

They stopped moving, and because he was supposed to be Cole, he could only do what Cole would do, so he stomped his boot down hard once more; again and again until her spasms ceased.

Cole had never killed anyone before. There would be side-eyes and gossip, as Haskins generally appreciated its townsfolk to maintain the status quo—but Cole was always a violent man. This was as true an ending to Pauline's story as any, he told himself.

He placed his head against the wood of the pantry and tried to think. *Yes, this was a fine ending. True to character. People had died in Haskins before. Not many, but it has happened.*

The body would be discovered eventually, perhaps by a mailman or a friend of a friend. He would be locked up when it was discovered, but he felt no real urgency regarding these truths. He would perhaps have days, maybe weeks to continue on unfettered. Cole sat down beside Pauline and stroked away the hair on her mask. Blood leaked through its nostrils. It was not a pretty mask: it was far too large on her, as most masks were.

Cole wondered what would have happened if he had been Pauline. If Cole would have killed him in the kitchen, if he would have been so sniveling and grateful as the world blackened around him. He yanked on her hair and saw a bit of skin, real skin, beneath. The idea of it was so alluring, so mysterious. He pulled again to free her head and he pulled until Pauline's face was limp in his own hands, stretched into a long liquid yawn. Cole turned her head, the head of a young man with light brown hair buzzed short. His face was covered in bruises, a kaleidoscope of greens, yellows, browns, and purples. Cole took off his own mask as well and rubbed his fists into his eyes. This is not something Cole would do, he realized, crying harder. He was not Cole.

++

After work, he and his buddies went to the game like they always did. Such was their lot. They all drank, but by now Cole was used to drinking. They didn't realize he was drinking less, but then again, it didn't matter how much he drank because drink pervaded his being. He smelled perpetually of whiskey. And no one questioned whether Cole was drunk because of course he was. He's Cole. And just as everyone assumed he had been drinking, no one asked about his wife. Because Cole never talked about her anyways. It just wasn't done.

"You lookin' at those cheerleaders, Cole?"

"Too old for me," said Cole, his voice flat. "I like 'em young,"

His face was pointed toward the announcer's box. He was squinting as his friends howled.

"Oh yeah? How young?"

"Real fucking young."

They liked that. They screamed in joy. And as they screamed, he squinted his eyes to see the shy girl with brown hair keeping score a world away.

When the game ended, he waved them off. "I gotta go fishing in the morning," he said.

The crowd was clearing out and he disappeared within them—several hundred rubber faces adorned with wigs and eyeglasses. The girl was climbing down from the announcer's box and he started to quicken his pace. Susan was unassuming, her back turned toward the fence, ready to slip out unnoticed now that her obligation had finished. Cole jogged lightly, not so fast as to draw attention—just the pace of a man eager to get home.

She passed through a split in the chain-link fence and began walking down the sidewalk with her nose in a book. Susan was always reading. Cole followed, a block back at first. If anyone was watching, they'd see him fumbling with his keys, looking for his car.

Susan lived near the school, the ward of bookish parents with large rubber noses and glassless spectacles. She spent most of her time at home and she was no doubt eager now to return. Susan portrayed this well when she first heard Cole shout her old name.

"Rance," he said. "Wait."

She stopped, moving her shoulders as if she were breathing deep, frightened. She turned at a glacier's pace, her mask turned downward toward the pavement.

"I've got to get home. It's late."

"It's not late," said Cole.

"I've got to go."

"We were supposed to be married."

"I'm Susan," she said. "We don't talk. You're too old to talk to me. I'm just a girl."

Cole ground his teeth, sweat dripped into his eye. He thought of Pauline and her face of mashed cherries. "I want you to come home with me tonight, Rance."

"No—I really can't—"

"It's Jennifer. I'm still Jennifer, Rance. Please, come with me. This is me speaking, I want you to come with me because I still love you. We're supposed to be married."

"Rance and Jennifer are getting married next year, the day after the festival. Not us." Her voice quivered when she said it.

Cole was a fast man, quick—a coiled spring. And when he bound toward Susan, she froze. That was a very Susan thing to do. She was not good under pressure and she was so much smaller than Cole.

He wrestled her to the ground and did what came most natural; an open hand pressed to her mouth, then a stranglehold around her neck. He felt her soft, sweating flesh. "Please," he said, whispering through her nostril holes, "come with me."

✝✝

Like in any small town, a death causes an uproar.

A dead girl on the side of the road, bleeding out her mask.

And just like in any small town, time marches on.

✝✝

"You don't usually have people over, is that true?"

The two had never been here before, a fact they seemed self-conscious of—still, they remained as chipper as they could, considering. They pointed at the elk's head on the wall and asked Cole if he hunted. They complimented Pauline on the furniture, their aesthetics as well as comfort.

Pauline bowed extravagantly, an ironic affectation. "The house was such a mess before. We're trying to be better about that."

Through the kitchen doorway came Cole, holding a tray of cocktails. "Please, help yourself, plenty more where that came from." He lowered the drinks on the table and poured himself a glass of club soda.

"You're not drinking?"

"Oh no, I'm a monster on that stuff. I'm turning a new leaf. I found God, I guess. The grain spoke to me. The seeds were sown. The old scarecrow came home to tend to the blackbirds in the field. All that jazz, you know?"

Pauline rubbed his shoulder, she kissed the back of his head. "He's been doing really good. Great."

There was a moment of silence, a pregnant pause. Pauline reached a hand out to their guests—a man and a woman, with large noses and glasses. "Awful what happened to Susan."

The man nodded solemnly and Cole huffed in sympathy. Snow began to fall and the gray light outside penetrated every inch of their humble home.

"Haskins isn't perfect," said the woman. "But then again, no place is."

They stared at each other, through each other for a long moment. Pauline's brown eyelets shined like glossy caramels by the fire as she took Cole by the hand and held it ever so tight.

ONLY THE STONES WILL HEAR YOU SCREAM

R.A. BUSBY

It was a tight squeeze, that was all. In a moment, Pete would work his hand free, and like Superman flying below the breathing earth, he would stretch until his fingers found a way through this crack in the rock. Ahead lay a larger cave chamber where he could turn around and head back to the light.

There had to be.

Kevin had explained it all to him the night before. "Here it is. They call this passage Daddy's Home."

They'd been in Kevin's jeep in the warm Nevada dusk, neither willing to go inside yet. Pete had taken the phone, keenly aware of Kevin's fingers, and stared at the cave map, unsure what he was seeing. It looked like a bird's claw with bends and tubes branching from a central tunnel.

"Like an ant farm," Pete murmured. "I thought caves were—well, chambers with stalactites." Hating how foolish he sounded, he added, "Sorry. Not many geology classes for …for business." For a moment, he had forgotten his own major. Over dinner, Kevin's dad had casually asked about Pete's plans after graduation—that adult variation of *What do you want to be when you grow up?*—and Pete been stuck. Again. It was unsettling.

Kevin gave an easy laugh. "Well, some caves really *are* big chambers, stalactites included. Others look like—what'd you say? Ant farms?"   He nodded. "That's perfect, Pete. Ever think about majoring in English?"

Pete shot him a sharp glance, but Kevin's eyes held only interested kindness. "No. My dad would never…" Pete shook his head, unsure if he should continue. Then he did. "When I was applying to colleges before Dad got cancer, he told me I'd be majoring in business or food stamps. My choice."

"Jesus. What'd you say back?"

Pete chuckled grimly. "You *didn't*. My dad—well, he was basically the opposite of your dad." All at once, he found himself telling Kevin everything. "The thing is, I'm failing everything except English. If go back, it'll be on academic probation." He sighed. "I'm such an asshole."

"Hey." Kevin turned to him. "Don't you do that to yourself. You may need to step back to move forward, Pete. Happens to everyone."

Pete stared at his fingers. "Good thing my dad's too dead to appreciate it."

"Was he always like that even before your mom…?"

"I don't know. I just know he blamed me for it."

"Not your fault, man," said Kevin. "You were just trying to be born."

Pete opened his mouth, and for another horrible second, he had no idea what would come out.

"When I was a kid," he said, "my dad would come in after work, plant himself in his recliner, and nurse his Scotch, getting more and more pissed off. I could tell by how he tapped his fingers against the chair. When that happened, I'd squirm into this crack between my bed and the wall. I didn't mind the closeness. It made me feel secure. Like being held. You know?

Anyway," Pete continued, "I thought I was being real smart, finding a place he couldn't get me. One night, though, he came into my room. Said he was going to tuck me in. I should mention he never did that."

"What happened?"

Pete sighed. "He sat down and calmly told me about the boogeyman living in little children's rooms. How it loved places dark and secret and small. How it waited for kids to fall asleep so it could drag them underneath the bed and eat them. Then he put his hand on my neck and whispered, 'It's the bad children that are the tastiest, Petey. The *baaaaaad* ones.'"

"Jesus, Pete."

"Forget it. Just tell me about the cave, all right?"

Big Daddy was a great beginner cave, Kevin explained. Still, there had been a few accidents. Six experienced women in 2005. Two Boy Scouts in '08. After that, the site had fallen into disuse.

On YouTube, they watched drone footage. Though Pete had expected a vast archway halfway up a mountain, he saw instead a limitless expanse of red-brown scabland where no plants grew but thin beige grass stretching for miles, barren and sere, till it met distant ridges sugar-topped with snow.

Then Pete spotted it. A sudden interruption in the desert floor, a gaping mouth of chert with graying limestone teeth. In its rocks were buried bones from creatures fallen to the shallow seafloor it had been.

"So," said Kevin, glasses shining like twin moons. "You up for this? One last hurrah before we go back?"

The image of the cave entrance came again, stark and sere, the distant escarpment gray as a New England sea. Something in it seemed to call to him.

Pete nodded. "Yeah," he said. "Let's do it."

✝✝

Their initial descent was a long butt-slide down smooth rock. In their headlamp, shadows thrashed on the cave wall. Pete stopped to look up at the hole to the surface, an irregular circle of daylight limned by dark.

"We can climb back again, right?"

Kevin's hand shaded his headlamp. "Folks do it all the time, man. That's the fun part. Well, no. The really fun part's the crawling."

Soon, the passage became more intimate. Running his hand over the cave walls, Pete found the surface surprisingly damp, an ooze of liquid rock squeezing like toothpaste through cracks in limestone. He clutched a handful and watched as it turned viscous as syrup.

Big Daddy was a hydrothermal cave, Kevin explained, with passages formed by hot water seeping from volcanic vents below, a force that ate limestone and left passages like throats. "Okay," Kevin said. "Here's the map. You remember this part?"

The passages reminded Pete of dendrites in a biology book, sprawling and planless as roots. "Yeah, okay?"

"Okay. I'll go in here—it's a little easier if you follow." Kevin traced the map with his fingers. "You bear straight, and on the right is the opening to Daddy's Home. It's really narrow, but it'll open into this one chamber where we can turn around. Sound good?" In the light, Kevin's face looked bright and excited. "I warn you, there's some belly-crawling. You okay with me going first, brother?"

The term caught Pete off guard, and he found himself oddly moved. "Sorry," he said. "Yeah, sure. I'm fine with crawling. I wore my best tux for the occasion."

"Here," said Kevin, and bent to check Pete's arms. Before leaving the car, he'd given him some knee pads and wrapped his elbows with duct tape. "Not too tight? You can bend them?" His eyes looked up at Pete's. "How's that headlamp?"

"No problem." Pete nodded. "It's all good."

They were ducking now, moist walls smearing their shoulders, warm rock fingers scraping Pete's arms as the ceiling gradually dropped. Following Kevin's lead, he hunched over, bracing his thighs as he walked.

"Now, when it gets real low, you go on hands and knees until you can't anymore. Then you make like Superman," said Kevin. "Don't let your arms get caught up underneath your torso, though."

Pete chuckled nervously. "Why? I mean, I think I can guess, but...what if I can't get them out?"

Kevin turned to him. "The first lesson is not to panic. Calm blue ocean, okay?" He patted Pete's shoulder. "What you do is ease *backward*. Do what you need to do. Twist yourself, do corkscrews—whatever it takes to get your arms like Superman." He smiled. "Also, if it's tight, let out all your breath to give yourself that extra inch around an obstacle. You'd be surprised how much that works." At this, Kevin passed into the tunnel, his headlamp light glinting with the movement of his shoulders and legs.

Pete focused on forward movement. He had to duck beneath a rock overhang, and gradually, as the passage began to narrow, he moved with his ass in the air downward-dog style to ease under projections in the tunnel.

Soon, all movement came from his elbows, his feet, his rolling hips pushing against the irregular floor. Pete spidered his fingers, hands raking irregular rock outcroppings. Limestone knots dug into his arms, and he was absurdly grateful for the duct tape Kevin had insisted he wear.

Now the walls began to knock his shoulders, shoving him like passengers on a crowded city bus. For a moment, he raised his head and was surprised to feel resistant rock forcing his neck down.

Yeah, it was getting pretty tight.

On Pete's next breath, the stone gripped his ribs all around like a corset. He lay still, consciously resisting the impulse to hyperventilate. "Kev?" he called, and caught Kevin's answering call, unworried and strong.

Stay chill, Pete thought. *Calm blue ocean.*

Pete toed the rocks and pushed himself a few inches onward. Small grunts from his breathing filled the passage, now narrowed to the size of a washing machine door.

When it happened, it happened easily.

Ahead, the passage split. One route veered away at an odd angle, the entrance pinched like an angry man's mouth. Pete continued straight. In a moment, the pressing walls would release him into that wider chamber where he would find Kevin.

Crawling forward, Pete imagined the chamber might be large enough to hold them shoulder to shoulder as they'd been in the car. Being in this secret hidey-hole unbeknownst to anyone was oddly thrilling. The chamber would smell of warm soil, and the walls would cradle them like twins.

Peering ahead, Pete saw the only way forward lay through a narrow tube with a stiff ridge at its entrance. Carefully, he eased himself around it, drawing in his stomach until the hard ridge was behind him. In one more inch, his hips moved past the tipping point.

Too fast, he went sliding into blackness. With a cry, Pete pushed back, arresting himself. His stomach twisted into a nauseating ball, and stinging adrenaline shot through his veins, but he couldn't seem to get enough air.

It's getting hot here, he thought, and that made it worse. Ahead, he thought he saw a crack where the tunnel narrowed, but what lay beyond that pinch point remained a mystery.

He did not have time to consider this. A moment before he slid down ten more crucial inches, Pete understood he'd taken a wrong turn. He really should've gone to the right. Before he knew it, his arm was trapped beneath his chest, and the dropoff lip was well beyond his backward-questing feet.

He'd come to a dead end. Head down. And he couldn't turn around.

*

Pete lay in the tunnel's dark pelvic arch, not daring to move. He thought he'd passed out, mostly because when he'd tried to breathe and couldn't, he'd begun hyperventilating. "Get me *outgetmeoutgetmeout!*" he'd screeched, his free hand flailing against the obdurate rock until he drove himself farther down like a stuck cork.

Soon, his breath came whistling in a high-pitched *heee-huuh-hee*, and at some point, he'd bashed his head into a hard knot. Trickling blood wormed into his ear and puddled there.

He was encased in a stone throat five hundred million years old.

"Jesus," said Kevin. He'd made his way back, and his first question had been whether Pete could move forward, but the stone throat ended in a very narrow slit. Beyond the slit was darkness. Perhaps the tunnel opened to the larger chamber. Perhaps not. He didn't know.

Kevin urged Pete to twist, to rock, to push backward, but it was futile. A stone jabbed into the webbing of his pinned hand, and if Pete could have nuked that specific rock into the sun, he would have. Sobbing blindly with strain, Kevin pulled Pete's ankles, but they had almost no leverage to move him over that lip again.

At last, Pete peered back. Kevin's face was streaked where tears had cut through dirt. "You gotta get help," he said. "Just go."

"But it's going to be hours, Pete. Hours with your head down—no, I can't leave you here, dude, I can't." But they both realized he had to.

So he did.

Only when Kevin's last sounds faded did Pete let the tears return. Despite Kev's promises that if Pete could go *into* the tunnel, he could come *out* of the tunnel, Pete knew it wasn't true.

See, he remembered his father's quail trap.

Quail were dumbasses even by bird standards, his father had explained. All you needed was to dig a little trench in the dirt and bait it with corn. Over the trench, you laid a board with a hole the size of a bird's head. The trick was that the sides of that hole angled *inward*.

"Quail sticks in its head to get corn," his father told Pete. "When he tries to pull out, his neck feathers get shoved back the wrong way, and he's trapped there. Gaaah!" His father flared his fingers around his neck to imitate backwards-facing feathers.

And when Pete had slammed awake from his nightmare of being a quail (*"Gaaah! Gaaah!"*) he'd shoved the pillow against his mouth and hoped his screams hadn't carried.

So no. Pete was stuck in a trap. Feathers weren't the problem. His legs were. Heading in, he'd shuffled them around that rock, but coming out, his heels would strike and catch on that low projection on the roof. And as Pete understood very well, his knees just bent one way.

They'd have to break his legs.

Yes. Whatever Search and Rescue folks came, they'd have to crack his legs at the knee joint like a Thanksgiving turkey. For a vivid moment, Pete envisioned a helmeted rescuer grabbing his ankle and yanking it down like a pump handle, forcing his knee hinge backward like a bird. He could see the strained skin rupturing in a sudden blood explosion, a rubbery white tendon curling in the air.

Soon, his headlamp began flickering.

✝✝

Until then, Pete realized he'd never seen true darkness. Perhaps nobody had.

Even ancient people had seen the stars, the adamantine light of an indifferent moon. But not a dark like this, a living, purposeful dark that rose like ink mist from the stones, a dark outlasting births and deaths of worlds.

When he stopped screaming again, he slept. Or what was like sleep.

In the dream, a gentle strand of hair drifted across his lips, and he smiled, remembering hands curled into hands, distance erased by embraces.

The touch came again, a tickling caress.

He awoke, and with his first half-breath, something crept awkwardly past his lips. It squirmed against his tongue. Pete gave a strangled yelp, scrubbing his face across the rock, anything to get the moving thing out. Disregarding the awkward angle, he pressed hard at the headlamp button and the light came faintly on.

The creature was the color of old tea. Delicate arachnid projections quested outward from a bee-striped abdomen, but it was the pincers Pete saw first, waving grandly like a conductor's arms in knotty, angled segments. At the ends were cruel brown pedipalps sharp as eyebrow tweezers.

The cave swarmed with them. Its walls were alive with them.

Screaming, Pete squeezed his eyes as far as they would go. One crawled up the side of his head in mindless troglobitic exploration, and all he could do was scrape his scalp into the rock with a broad primeval growl, a horrified "*Uhhhh-uhhh-uhhhh*" from some hollow place inside him.

He writhed, terrified. Light spasmed across the blank gray walls as the creatures scattered, but long after they had fled from this illumination and unfamiliar noise, Pete shuddered, imagining hairlike, exploratory touches on his scalp. The inside of his ear. Phantom caresses.

Pete shut the light off again. From where he lay, it seemed he'd been in here an era. An epoch. An eon. When he came out, the stars in the sky would have shifted, and the world would not be the same.

He lay there despising the encasing rock with world-burning fury, the stone below his lips, the tang of his own piss, the earth-press against his shoulders, the implacable constriction that made full breaths impossible, the ache from the unremitting effort to keep himself stable.

The pinching insect things had squirmed out of that narrow crack ahead. Pete could allow himself to slide down to that gap. But then what? What if he only corked himself more tightly? Did this tunnel feed into that wider chamber, that place to turn around? Possibly. Possibly not.

At least up here, he could still wiggle. Shuffle his feet. Light his headlamp. Breathe.

For a while.

For now in the dark, he ran over a litany of recriminations against Kevin, but finally the truth came, implacable and cold as rock. *You made the decision, stop blaming others, take responsibility for shit you decided to do, you are a FUCKING ADULT, PETER.*

He was never leaving. He had to admit it.

With a shuddering breath, Pete rested his bruised cheekbone against the stone and tried to imagine how it would be. His flesh would blacken and swell, oozing his putrefied fluids into the claylike exude to stain the featureless rock. He would be colonized by whatever bacteria lurked down here, or his muscles would mummify to jerky and be eaten by those nameless, eyeless things with threads for legs. Slow water droplets might fuse with bone, filling spaces in his cells, embedding him to the rock like an embryo in a womb. They'd find him in ten thousand years, a hundred thousand. A million.

He would be petrified.

"Well, Pops-old-man," he chuckled. "I guess you got your wish. I'm making history after all."

And perhaps whatever dug him out would not be human.

In the darkness, Pete heard skittering and knew the pinchy things had returned. The scorpiders, or whatever the fuck they were. Over the hours (*days epochs eons*), Pete had learned to wait before switching on his headlamp, which they hated, but the cave's long process of reclamation had almost officially begun. His light was growing dimmer. Soon it would not turn on at all. And then what?

Pete thought he knew.

They would crawl inside his mouth.

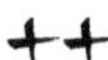

"Well, Pete," his father remarked acidly. "You are truly fucked."

The voice came from behind. Pete was not surprised to hear it. He lifted his head and saw only darkness. But yes, he sensed Dad sitting with his Scotch, fingers tapping irritably. "Yes indeed," his father repeated. "You are fucked."

The reflexive *Yes, sir rose to his lips,* but since he was dead, or soon would be, Pete discovered he didn't care. An outrageous lightness filled him.

"Thanks, Dad," he croaked. "You must be so glad you paid for college." He waited for the hard blow from his old man's fist, but it did not come.

"Waste a money. You've failed, Pete. And whatever evolved octopus ruling here after we nuke ourselves from existence is gonna find your remains and fuckin' *laaaaaugh* and laugh."

"So what are you going to do?" Pete retorted. Despite his thirst, he spat and watched the drool run down the rock. "Yank me out for a good old-fashioned ass-whooping? You do that, Dad."

Over his shoulder came the rattle of ice cubes. God. Pete would give anything for one right now. "I don't need to, Petey," said his father. "All I gotta do is wait till that lamp fails. Just like you. When it does, those crawdad whaddayacallits'll nip off your pecker. Those pincheroo claws—well, they look like they just snip and snip."

Pete sighed. "You're dead, Dad. Fuck off."

"True. I'm deep and dead, Petey. But not as deep as you. You tried to hide in a tiny little crack. But I found you, Petey. *I found you.*"

The voice crunched the words against its teeth.

Then Pete felt the meaty heat of his father's hand on his neck. Dad had found him, and soon thick, blunt fingers would probe deep with a tight, cruel squeeze till Pete's eyes filled with silver stars.

He'd done this more than once. Many times, really. If he blacked out, he didn't know if his father would *let* him wake up, or if his hard right hand would finally *clench* and *clench*, leaving Petey floating in the dark all alone. He turned on the headlamp again and realized

(Gaaah! Gotcha!)

that the boogeyman had found him out at last.

"Come on, Petey," the thing said, its voice cruel as fatherfingers. "You're gonna die here. Shoulda happened before you were born. Saved me time and money."

Hot tears scalded Pete's face, his congested nose leaking snot onto the rock. "Fuck you," he whispered, barely audible now.

"Oh, son," came the voice. "When that light goes, it's just gonna be us down here. Just…us."

With a cry, Peter wrenched away. "No!" he barked. "Not this time!"

In this refusal, his headlamp fell beyond reach, its beam pointed down the passage. His father's laugh broke like a clash of rocks on rocks, but Peter did not hear. He was too busy staring at the light.

All at once, he saw what he must do. It burst into his thoughts clean as truth.

He smiled.

Then he let go.

With a final, decisive grunt, he shoved himself not back, but *forward*. The hard fingers scrabbled as Pete allowed the tunnel to swallow him. He made for the pinch point, then pushed his free arm through that tantalizing hole.

It's just going to be rock. But it wasn't. Beyond, he felt only sweet open space.

"You'll never make it," the voice rasped behind him, but Pete wasn't listening.

The opening to the chamber was so narrow. *Get your shoulder out first for leverage,* he thought. *Then ease your head through.*

Praying, he slid his skull into the gap. The rock dug harsh claws into his hair. He stopped, breathing too fast, as the thing behind him chuckled.

If he forced himself through, would his skull plates crack like an eggshell in a vise? Would he hear the bone give way when it happened? He thought he would.

"Sure will, Pete," his father said. "You're stuck like a baby in a cunt. Again. Only this time, your skull's not so bendy. Your head'll get halfway through. Then you'll hear a *crrrrack* when you paint both sides of that slick-ass rock with your brain paste."

Ah, Pete thought. That slick-ass rock.

He laughed, a real one. His free hand was numb, but not too numb to swipe across the damp cave walls, slippery with that odd silicate exude, and smear it on his scalp, his face, his neck. He took a breath and thought, *I don't really need ears*, and shoved his head on through.

There was a thrumming in his brain. With his one free hand, Pete reached and tried to pull his body through. The roaring became the sound of disembodied dark, a guttural howl of raw fury at being cheated of this tasty quail head down in a trap.

The darkness pulled his ankles. I've fooounnnnnd you, Peter. I've founnnnd you. You failed.

Pete drew a breath. "Yes," he said. "I've failed. But not at everything."

With all his force, he blew the air from his lungs and kicked against the dark that wished to take him.

The pain was astonishing. He felt his scalp peel like the skin of a tangerine. Blood rushed through his brain in hard iron pulses. The last breath left him, and Pete could draw no more. He could hear nothing but a rushing like the sea.

The pain was red as earth.

He let out a bare sigh and stopped moving. He reached up, sure another hand grasped his on the other side, warm fingers twining with his own. He could feel them.

He came back for me, Pete thought. In a moment, they would pull him out.

Then the headlamp failed, and Pete saw only blackness.

And stars.

SIDE C

RAGE, RAGE

MERSA AND THE CANNIBAL

ANNA DICKSON JAMES

From the beginning Evan wanted to eat the girl's tragedies, to gorge himself on her pain.

He wanted her body, of course he wanted her body, but that wasn't the main draw. He skimmed

past her full V-neck sweater, hardly noticed her coral, kittenish teeth, for he focused his hunger at

the corner of her eye where her great sadness lay. The horizon of her mouth tipped up into a

smile, but where the creases of her brow and eyelashes met, the skin folded down into a frown.

"Is this seat taken?" he asked, examining the crepe paper lines around her upper lip, thinking onion skin and layers.

The girl smiled, showing her teeth and a bit of gum. Her face brightened, and it was this

light that led her girlfriends to call her 'perky,' but Evan saw beneath it.

Her gums were puffed. From excess drugs? Too tired to floss? It didn't matter. He loved her. He had to have her.

Her wrists were so thin and delicate that Evan thought that if he'd wanted to, he could

break her bone over his knees, snap her radius like a twig. This gave him an instant impulse to

grab each side of her shoulder and squeeze until ten little bruise marks appeared beneath his ten

square fingers. He imagined the bruises showing, just a bit, a little tease, beneath her sheer, white

blouse.

Immediately though, Evan's stomach grew sour, and he had an urge to comfort her from

his imaginary abuse. He reached out to touch her hair but stopped himself short and instead,

tucked his own long hair behind his ears.

The girl fluttered her eyes, looked at him as if she knew what he was thinking, but she

couldn't possibly have or else she wouldn't have moved her bag and patted the seat beside her.

Evan moved to accept the invitation, but his body was imbalanced--the right side of his

body being slightly larger (bigger boned by a full inch around his wrist) so that when the train

turned a bend, he lost his balance and slid towards the girl and brushed the side of his jeans

across her face. A stylish rivet scraped her cheek and ripped a seam in her skin that extended

from her hollow cheekbone all the way down to her chin. When he saw a swath of blood pool to

the surface, something in his groin trilled.

"Oh god, I'm so sorry," he said as he lowered into the seat opposite her. He hadn't meant

it, by god he hadn't, but the gruesome zipper of torn skin made the soft, white porcelain of her

face glow with perfection.

So he cupped her chin and said, "I want to keep you safe."

She giggled, and a drop of blood landed on his second knuckle. He watched as it seeped

into the tiny folds of his finger, spreading like a thousand red rivers.

The girl said, "I more fear what is within me than what comes from without."

It was the first words she had spoken to him, and Evan thought about the queer cadence

to her voice and how the words sounded backwards. He pondered these things, but he did not

want to hurt her feelings, so he kept his thoughts inside.

He looked over the girl's shoulder and watched as they passed a farm with placid cows

lazily chewing their cud. Children's toys lay abandoned in the yard. An orange cat hunted for

something in the clipped grass.

Evan listened to the rhythm of the track, watched the way the train shook and moved the

girl's body with her relaxed consent. Her breasts shimmied loosely, her body in compliance with

the train. Evan wished that he himself were a train because then he'd have the power to rock and

soothe this girl into obedience.

Such a lusty thought made him feel vulnerable and small; it wasn't right. So, he obsessed

about the girl's odd choice of words until his guilt subsided. His desire to correct her soon

became greater than his desire to protect her.

You should have said, "I'm more afraid of what's within me than what comes from

outside of me."

She cocked her head, and a flake of skin from around her eye floated down past her gash,

past her lips and her chin and landed softly on her shoulder. His eye fixed on this small,

vulnerable bit of her. It emboldened him, and he brushed the peel from her shoulder. The girl

blinked again.

"The words are out of order, see?"

"What is order?" she asked, and he mistook her for stupid.

The train rocked along its track, rumbling like a bowling ball, jerking the girl's body

towards the boy, away from the boy, towards the boy again, then away, her breasts lilting back

and forth like a rocking horse. She was getting sleepy. He was gaining strength.

"What is your name?" he asked, and the girl told him.

"Mersa," and as she said this, a slip of skin pulled away from her lip.

Evan scrunched his brow and bit his lip, turned his head sideways and looked at her.

"No," he said. "That's not the right name for you."

"It isn't?" she said, the rectangle of skin lifting and lowering with her breath.

"Nope, not at all."

"That is my great grandmother's name, "she said.

"It's a drifter's name," Evan said.

Mersa looked him square in the eye.

"Precisely," she said. "I consider it an honor to house it," she said, and her eyes

momentarily lost their sadness.

Evan was bothered by the motion of the chapped lip, and reaching over towards her

mouth said, "May I?"

Mersa nodded. Evan grasped the skin between the short, square nails of his thumb and

middle finger and pulled. Healthy skin came with it in a long, narrow strip, and now there was

fresh blood an inch long along her mouth.

"Ouch!" Mersa said, bringing those slender, breakable fingers to her lips.

Evan hadn't meant to hurt her, and he said so.

"You told me I could do it," he said.

Mersa nodded, and another flake of skin peeled back from her thumb. With a small puff,

she blew it towards the boy, and it landed on the crease of his eye. Evan blinked. Evan rolled the lip skin

between his fingers, turned it into a hard stone and flicked it into the aisle. Her pale eyes rimmed with

water.

"Still, I'd like you to be more careful," she said.

The pain activated the perspiration under her arms, and he smelled her deodorant. This shamed Evan, so he was relieved when she turned her face to look out the window. Now, he

could only look at the scratch and the tender side of her lip when she turned to face him.

"I didn't mean it," he said. "I'm clumsy. Haven't I been friendly to you since I got on?"

"I suppose you have," Mersa said.

"Didn't I ask you if I could sit down?"

All Mersa could do was nod.

She tapped her fingers lightly at the scratch on her cheek. It had begun to scab over, and

bits of crust crumbled from the wound.

Evan looked over the girl's shoulder and saw that they were approaching a tunnel.

"How about me and you go out sometime after we get off this train?" he asked her.

She shuddered, and the light in the train car went dark.

But then Mersa smelled the boy's nice cologne. She felt the male-ness of his body as it

rocked next to hers in the dark. When she sat next to him, she felt the smallness of her wrists, the

teeny-ness of her own ears and lips and nose. In the dark, she intuited the clumsy and grand

nature of his left side and sensed the soft, warmth of his finer right. She sensed him and knew

him, took his sadness to heart. It was her mother's fault for naming her Mersa.

"OK," she said.

"OK," he said.

He searched for her in the dark, and his right hand found the tender spot beneath her ear

and neck and pulled her towards him with his more delicate arm. Mersa, led by his gentleness,

came forward to meet him. They bumped toward each other in the dark, and after a few misses to

the cheek (his too far to the right, hers too far low) their lips met. Mersa felt the warmth of his

mouth. Evan felt her open for him, and they both pressed in, tumbling in the dark toward each

other, and Mersa's earrings jingled in their finding.

Mersa loved him too then, and her heart thought to break for him in this moment, and she let a tear escape from her eye. The tear dripped down her cheek and on to Evan's lip. He tasted

the salt, and like the scent of blood excites a shark, Evan roused. Her vulnerability, her

smallness. Her injury at his hand incited him, and Evan began to bite. First, gentle, playful nips,

at which Mersa giggled and teased back. Encouraged, he took her bottom lip between his teeth

and began to tug and pull. When Mersa began to pull back, Evan growled, bit down harder and

shook his head side to side like her pet spaniel used to play with his chew toy.

"Ouch," she said, her lip still held captive by teeth, so her tongue had to do most of the

work.

"I love you," he said, and he meant it.

Mersa wriggled her lip free from his mouth. Evan felt her slip away from him.

"Love is a temporary madness," Mersa said.

Mersa watched her blood pool in the corner of Evan's mouth. It began to boil on his lip.

"Talk plainly," he said, and his brows pinched together.

Her words always made him angry.

Evan's breath grew coarse, and his left arm began to grab at her hair. Even his feminine

arm began to pinch and pull at her bra. They wrestled in the dark. Bits of her skin peeled off in

layers along with her sweater, her bra, even the necklace around her throat that he kept in the

tight grip of his palm. A corner of her ear fell with a wet thud onto the seat, and when the train

car lurched, it rolled on to the grooved, rubber flooring of the train where it sat like a piece of

dried fruit gathering bits of dirt and hair and dust. She reached out to grab it, but Evan pulled her

hand to her heart. She felt it beating beneath her palm.

"Haven't I told you I love you?" he asked.

His urgency and desperation convinced her.

"Yes," she nodded. "Yes."

She was flattered. She was terrified. Evan went back to kneading at her body, pulling at

her hair to expose her neck. He marked her throat with his kisses, broke buttons off her blouse

with his clumsy hands. He thought he was saving her.

When he tugged at her jeans, she said firmly, "No."

"Yes," he said.

"No," she said.

He put his hand to the scrape on her cheek, stroked gently the missing skin on her lip,

kissed the bit of her thumb. He touched at her wounds and scars, and this reminded Mersa of

how small she was. Evan rubbed her body, stirring up the layers of her loose skin, sloughing it

off until there wasn't a place on her that wasn't raw, tender and pink. Still, he scratched and

scratched and her arms got thinner, and her thighs got thinner, and the hollow of her cheeks grew

sallow. He thought he was making her new.

"My little gypsy," he said.

"Ouch," she said.

"I love you," he said. "Let me love you."

"But it hurts," she said

"Lift up," he said, tugging again at her jeans. "I'm not going to hurt you," he said. "I'm

here to protect you. You can lean on me; you can stand on me. I will be your pillar."

She felt the hair of his left arm tease at her nipple. She wanted a pillar to stand on. She

lifted up, and he wrestled her pants down to her knees.

"I will protect these delicate little arms."

She wanted protection.

He nibbled at her wrist, and a chunk of flesh caught in his mouth. He chewed and swallowed, her meat now inside of his stomach.

"I'll get in between you and harm," he said.

She wanted someone to stand in the gap.

He nibbled off a pinkie finger.

"I will die saving you."

She wanted saving.

Evan ate her ring finger next, and Mersa frowned for there was nowhere for him to

display his promise. He pushed himself inside of her, and Mersa began to cry. Evan licked at her

tears. His tongue scraping more skin off of her body, rolling the flesh upward like a jellyroll.

"There, there," he said, grunting and moving his hips.

"Didn't I ask you nicely?"

He pushed.

"And didn't you do what I asked?"

Mersa nodded as her layers unraveled. Centimeters and inches of her flesh came undone.

"You're hurting me," Mersa said.

"You're as much to blame," he said.

Mersa burned inside. She boiled. They groped and tugged and pulled for two more days

before she finally decided. Before she finally said her thought out loud, "I don't like you."

Giving voice to the hate empowered her, and she began to kick and claw at his body with

rolled up fists.

Evan sat up, his erection melting.

"How could you say that? It's such a mean thing. How could a beautiful girl say such a

thing?"

Mersa felt bad. Mersa felt guilty. Mersa felt like she'd done an unspeakable thing, being

rude in the way that she had.

Inside, behind the guilt, a light of intuition spoke to her.

"Run, run, run, run, run," it said.

She wanted to listen, but Mersa was afraid to go. If she ran, she'd be all alone on the

train, and how would she know her stop? How could she pay the extended fare? But the voice

within persisted.

"Let me go," she said.

Evan pushed down on top of her body, kissing her. He bit down again, and the top ball of

her lip came off in his mouth. Mersa narrowed her eyes and baited him with the plump flesh of

her bottom lip.

The train conductor walked through the car, pointing his flashlight this way and that.

"Hold still," Evan said.

Mersa held still.

"Hold your breath. You're breathing too loud."

Mersa held her breath.

"That man is out to get you. I'll get between him and you. I'll always be here to protect

you, to help you."

Mersa heard the ticking sound of her dry eyes blinking. She felt one eyeball stick to her

tacky lid and pull out from the socket. It landed on the floor quietly. It caught in the man's

searching flashlight, and Mersa watched it roll past her bit of ear and disappear beneath the seat

in front of her.

Mersa felt the joints of her body loosen, and an arm that had been hanging over the edge

of the seat got hit by Evan's knee and fell onto the floor with a thud.

"Ssssshhh," Evan said. "How will I keep you safe if you keep making noise?"

It couldn't be helped. The more he spoke, the more she fell apart. Her leg disconnected at

the knee. Her remaining foot began to lose its toes.

Evan began to panic. Evan began to feel guilty.

One toe. Two. Three.

"I love you," he said.

Four.

"You know I love you, right?"

Mersa nodded.

The fifth toe landed on the rubber floor of the train car. The smell of her sweat, oniony

and sharp, wafted beneath his nose. Evan wrapped his arms around Mersa and promised her and

promised her and promised her until Mersa broke entirely apart and all that was left of her was a

small, round button of her blue heart, pulsing with a small, dim light as the train made its way

through the tunnel.

He put the heart in his pocket, "Lean on me," he said to the button heart.

"We'll have picnics in the meadow."

Mersa pulsed a weak agreement.

"We'll get married in a small church."

The light flickered brightly.

"We'll share a house."

The light cheerfully shined.

The train passed by a city and stopped at the station. A blonde woman in a stylish suit

walked by Evan's window. So fresh, so pretty, so strong, so bright. He took Mersa out of his

pocket and looked down at her. He became disinterested by the way she simply lie in his palm,

pulsing like that.

Evan got bored and poked lazily at the button heart. Evan got curious and stuck a pin

through it to the other side. Having nothing else to do, he split it open like meat and ate half of it.

But then he began to get angry that she was no longer flesh, no longer a body, that even

her light had grown to dim from his nibbling and gnawing at it. She was so opposite the pretty

blonde girl outside the window with her shiny hair and vibrant life. He squeezed at the heart to

get it to respond, and the heart did respond.

It flashed a message to him

..-. ..- -.-. -.- / -.-- --- ..- /..-. ..- -.-. -.- /
-.-- --- ..-/ ..-. ..- -.-. -.- / -.-- --- ..-

Evan was hurt. Evan was enraged. After all he had done to protect her, all he had done to

love her. He'd thought to eat the button heart, to swallow the rest of Mersa whole. But something

had shifted in him, and he felt nauseated at the thought of the sick girl who allowed herself to be

eaten.

Evan sat rolling the heart in his hands for a good long while as the train moved on its

track. The pretty blonde he recognized from the station moved into his car. He rolled the heart in

his hands, staring at the woman, wishing to save her. He rolled and rolled and like an eraser

disappearing, and he did not recognize the moment it disappeared. The blonde woman sat down,

opened a newspaper from her briefcase and began to read. He saw that it was The Daily Mail

when he preferred The Gazette. He didn't want to hurt her feelings, so he didn't say anything,

until his desire to correct her became greater than his desire to protect her.

WE, THE ONES WHO RAISED SAM GOWERS FROM THE DEAD

CYNTHIA ZHANG

Yes, to answer your questions, we were the ones who did it; we were the ones who dabbled into the forbidden arts, who so casually threw away the good Christian values of our country for a flash of bloody vengeance. We are the ones you want, the ones who raised Sam Gowers from the dead.

Who were we, you ask? No one, really. We were baristas and booksellers and outreach directors for local nonprofit organizations, ad copyists and sales assistants and grad students in French and Francophone Literature. We worked nine-to-five or three jobs part-time or not at all, some of us the lucky beneficiaries of fellowships or wealthy older men, others perpetual couchsurfers or street corner philosophers with a talent for urban scavenging. We were amicable exes and messy polycules and complete strangers to each other, a smile at a bar, a shared glance at the farmer's market, a million small signs that said *I see you.*

You too know what we are; the words are already on the tip of your tongue, itching to be let loose. Come on. Say it. We've heard it all before.

Not all of us knew Sam personally, but we all knew of him—the news cycle made sure of that, plastering endless images of his face on social media feeds and late-night TV. Sam Gowers: age nineteen, gangly in the ways of teenagers still new to adulthood. Dead in an alley two months before his next birthday, a drunken argument turned scuffle turned manslaughter. Crime of passion, the defense called it, their arguments lined with the raw taste of homophobia—what did Sam expect, really, skinny fey kid walking into a bar full of red-blooded American men? A dive bar to be fair, one of those places where newly out gaybies made out in bathrooms and college boys came to experiment with being heteroflexible, so

really the presence of three straight frat boys was the anomaly, but still, what did Sam expect, trying to talk to men like that? Treating them as if they were like him, like they were—well. You know.

Do you need anymore? You know how this script goes. Queer kid, homophobic assholes, a few too many drinks on both sides. No possible outcome but a gay bash.

Still, there were small mercies. We were glad, when we read the police reports, that we had helped pay for top surgery last summer and that Sam had been on T long enough to be read as merely *gay boy* and not *fake boy.* Bad enough to be gay, but to be gay and trans is to invite another kind of violence, the kind meted out by men who think the lack of a dick means they're entitled to a stranger's body. Sam had long lashes and high cheekbones, the kind of delicate features made for music videos and photoshoots. In the aftermath, as the media misgendered and mischaracterized him, as his parents came to collect the body of the kid they'd kicked out, we clung to those mercies, telling ourselves that it could have been so much worse. A small salve for a pain, a bandage over the great bloody hole of our anger.

Overall, would we recommend necromancy? Not particularly. We too would have preferred less collateral damage, fewer buildings torched and storefronts smashed. That is what the headlines forget—that they were our schools too, our workplaces and bookstores and pizzerias with the cute bus boy who snuck us leftover slices after hours. Our communities, even if many of them would never truly recognize us. Magic is powerful, but it is also volatile, and necromancy is the most dangerous art of all. It takes far more than one life to bring back another, and even now, with so many of us in jail and on government watchlists, it will be years before the balance is paid—if, indeed, it ever can be.

But what else were we supposed to do?

We tried, you know. Did all the things you're supposed to do when tragedy strikes —protested in front of City Hall and donated to official Gofundmes, Tweeted petitions and collected signatures outside the YMCA. We called our Senators even when they were America First jackasses who thought liberal education was turning children soft, because surely even they must be susceptible to public outcry, surely that was how democracy worked?

We were peaceful. We were law-abiding. We showed up, did the work, tried not to let the anger make us cruel, reminded ourselves that ideology and echo chambers could blind otherwise sensible people. All of us had someone to mourn, a loved one or a former favorite teacher turned conspiracy theorist with a few clicks of an algorithm. We were reasonable, we were reconcilable. We tried to reach across the other aisle.

And in the end, what? In the end, a police investigation that was little more than a character assassination, officers honing on every time Sam skipped school or showed up high to work. Coaches and family friends of the accused writing op-eds to the paper, long personal essays about Boy Scouts and football scholarships and promising young men who had made a few poor choices but were not bad, not really. It helped that the accused were all-American photogenic and could cry on camera, crocodile tears running down cheeks still rounded with baby fat. It helped that their daddies had money, could afford the best lawyers that money and a lack of morals could buy, men with no qualms about using legal precedent from a time where homosexuality was still classified as a mental illness to paint the act as justifiable panic and not murder.

In the end, this: all three of the accused acquitted of manslaughter, because even if it was three against one and Sam was a skinny scrap of a kid, the pocketknife in his jacket meant it was self-defense. Two hundred hours of community service so they could think about their actions, but no jail time, not when the accused were all so young—barely twenty, and white too, which made them practically children in the eyes of the law.

In the end, this: another of us in the dirt, Sam's parents burying him in a dress and the name of a dead girl.

It was Sam's cousin, Sasha, who came up with the idea. Sasha from the coffee shop, with the blunt self-cut bangs and the eye of Osiris tattooed on her ankle; Sasha, who used to smoke with her cousin on rooftops, who'd offered him a place on her couch after he first came out, a baby-faced teenager who still wore braces and cried at animal adoption ads. Sasha, who had known Sam when they were both chubby-cheeked, grubby-handed kids, downing pixie sticks by the handful and smearing their mothers' makeup over their faces; Sasha, who had stroked his hair and patted

his back during his first night of being black-out drunk, held his hand and brought him ice cream after his first heartbreak; Sasha, who had watched her cousin die on a thousand grainy YouTube screens, listened to weeks of debate over whether the men who kicked his ribs in had technically committed a hate crime or were just boys being boys; Sasha, who had stood beside us, spoke at the rallies, pleaded with the press to remember her cousin the way he was to us—not the high school dropout, not the teenage runaway, not the boy who stole chocolate bars and gum from Wal-Mart with the ease of a Dickens pickpocket. Sasha, who after all the television, was left with her apartment, a job that paid her a dollar above minimum wage, and a world without her cousin in it.

Some people when they grieve turn to alcohol and self-destruction, others to God or Buddha or alien cults promising a reprieve from life's suffering. Sasha, she turned to necromancy.

Look. Sam's death was tragic, but it wasn't just that. It'd been a series of long, hard years—of marches and vigils, abortion bans and evictions and steadily rising rent. We'd attended town halls and turned up to local elections, campaigned for politicians who broke their promises once they were in power. If Sasha wanted to indulge in a little dark magic, who were we to stop her? There were plenty of us who sympathized, who were willing to join her. Hell, light a bonfire and bring some beer, and we might as well make an event out of it.

Grimoires and Lovecraft devotees will tell you that necromancy is an elaborate and delicate process, finicky as a chemical reaction with a dozen steps that have to be done just right if you don't want the magic to blow up in your face. It's possible they're right—we certainly wouldn't know. Those of us who dabbled in magic were hobbyists, Tarot aficionados and occasional purchasers of crystals. Whatever tattered paperback or obscure online forum Sasha plucked her spell from, however, was decidedly uninvested in pageantry. A few hairs, a withered tooth from childhood, a little blood, and a lot of anger—that was all it took in the end, really.

Mary Shelley, all respect to her, had it all wrong, as did all the movies after her. There was no flash of lightning, no sudden wind or shift in the air that told us everything had changed. We held hands, lit candles, chanted a few times until it felt like we'd done it right, and that was it. Sasha placed Sam's favorite suit and bowtie on his grave, a quiet apology for being unable to stop his parents from burying him in silk and ribbons. A few of us stuck around afterwards, shooting the breeze and splitting spiffs, the type of shit we always did when a group of us met up like this. Eventually though, even the night owls drifted back home, leaving behind dried candle wax and cigarette butts in their wake.

It was not a dark and stormy night, but a bright summer morning when Sam Gowers rose from the dead.

When Sam Gowers walked out of Forest Park Cemetery into the city proper, no one noticed, not at first. No matter how times his face had been on television, Sam Gowers was still a skinny white boy—wearing rainbow suspenders and a floral bow tie scuffed up in grave dirt, but ordinary enough beyond that. The magic had been strong enough to paper over the start of decay, leaving Sam pale and peaky but otherwise human. White enough for no one to call the cops on him, disheveled enough for people to glance away when he approached, missing all the signs of decay.

Past the parking lots and the hipster boutiques Sam walked, the pizza places where we snuck pepperoni from vats and the coffee shops where we pumped syrup and packed espresso into filters for businessmen on their lunch break.

The first boy was inside a corner Target, a shopping basket in one hand and a roll of toilet paper in the other. CCTV captured it all: a grainy figure at the edge of the screen, blue hoodie and baseball hat, a red basket on his arm as he dawdled in front of the toiletries aisle. He did not look up when a boy in a ragged Goodwill suit walked into the frame, too intent on the choices of toothpaste before him to pay attention to anything else. Only when Sam Gowers was inches away, close enough for cold breath to ghost over warm skin, did the boy turn.

A stumble backwards, the basket and its contents spilling across tile. The camera quality was too poor to capture his expression and the video had no sound, but we imagine that his eyes must have widened, his mouth opening on an aborted scream of *no* or *please* or *how*.

On the camera, Sam stepped forward. The boy was tall, so much so that Sam must step on his tiptoes to reach him. One hand cupped his face, another wrapping around the back of his neck in a lover's embrace. For a moment they stood like that —two boys inches from each other, a clandestine moment caught on grainy videotape.

And then, with strength he never had in life, Sam twisted, not stopping until he reached a full three hundred sixty degrees.

There is a moment after something monumental happens, a pause as the world works to catch its breath. Blood dripped down Sam's shirt, garish in the fluorescent light, but with the surveillance cameras the only witness, the store continued to quietly buzz around them.

Then Sam stepped out of frame, making his way past customers towards the front of the store, and the world exploded into light and noise.

Someone pointed; someone screamed. Heads turned; phone cameras slid to life. A visiting suburbanite fainted. The security guards, stupefied at first, sprang into life, reaching for tasers and shouting requests for backup into crackling walkie-talkies.

Walking steadily forward, Sam Gowers paid them no attention. A trigger-happy cop shot at him. The bullet slid through Sam like sound through water, ricocheting off the sidewalk by the Aeropostale and making a group of teenagers scream. A brave Samaritan charged him, fists raised, but his punches simply went through Sam, left him gasping with ice-blue skin as Sam strode forward. What, after all, is pain to the dead?

Sam had been a gentle kid, but death had no space for gentleness. Those brave enough to get close were shouldered aside like ragdolls, props ignored and unnoticed. Eventually, they backed away, a small circle of spectators terrified and unable to look away.

The second boy was at a gym, AirPods in and cutting him off from the world. Perhaps someone should have predicted that Sam Gowers would head for him, should have tried to warn him. Perhaps one of the onlookers, filming live to Instagram as they trailed after Sam's phosphorescent blue footsteps, should have tagged him in their Tweets and Insta stories so that he could know what was coming. Perhaps none of us wanted to.

There was the smell of smoke and sparks in the air, a carnival excitement mixed to near intoxication. Sam was our orchestra conductor, our parade marshal, our pied piper leading us to the pier, and we could do nothing but follow.

It was a gathering crowd of us that made our way into the Gold's Gym, past the absent security guard and crowds of white women practicing downward dog. We were not quiet; we were not unobtrusive. Still, there was a lot that can be covered by headphones and exertion, and with music in his ears and twenty-pound dumbbells in each hand, it is little wonder that the second boy did not notice us at first.

When he saw Sam's face reflected in the mirror, the color fell from his face like the weights crashing by his feet.

Macho man, the boy threw a punch, clearly expecting what had worked in life to translate over into death. The blow landed like a pebble tossed into a pond—Sam did not waver, only continued implacably forward. That was when he tried to run.

He didn't get very far. Sam's entourage was thick by then, and even if they had been sympathetic, he was slick with sweat from running for an hour already, and Sam Gowers had all the patience of the dead.

Amidst the gasps and screaming, you could hear the beginnings of a cheer, feel the slow swelling of something giddy pulsing through the crowd. Yes, yes, this was happening; yes, yes, at last.

Blood splattered in Pollock patterns across his sleeves, Sam pushed his way out the gym down and down the streets, picking up stragglers as he went. Someone found an empty beer bottle, doused a rag in gasoline, and threw the burning cocktail at the police station. Someone cheered.

The last boy had barricaded himself in his apartment, a shotgun in one hand and a cleaver in the other.

If he was smart perhaps, he could have gotten into a car or hopped on a plane to fly cross-country. That might have bought him time—months, even. Perhaps in that time the US government would have been able to figure out a defense, put together an elite team of magicians and exorcists to defuse an avenging corpse.

But Sam's killers were stubborn tough guys, certain in their ability to lone cowboy through all obstacles. They had grown up on zombie movies and survivalist fantasies, one man and his shotgun against the world. They were men, and they would not run.

Helicopters whirred ahead, the news crews struggling to keep up with the story as it unfolded—there was an armed shooter on the loose? No, reports indicated that no gunshots were fired at the scene. A knife maybe, or an inmate from rehab center down on Downing? On the list of probable news stories they had expected to break that morning, none of the journalists would have put down supernatural vengeance from beyond the grave. It took a while for the larger media outlets to believe it, and by the time CNN and Fox sent reporters, the event was already trending on Twitter.

At the train platform, a few commuters glanced as Sam jumped the turnstile, but none spared him more than a moment's notice. There was dirt on Sam's face and dried splotches of brown blood on his suit, but he was quiet and not visibly high or aggressive, and this made him of no more note than the rats scuttling between the tracks. The crowd that followed him could have been anyone—a group of tourists on a bar crawl, groupies on their way to a concert, the inebriated aftermath of a sports game. Unless they approached you, a few rambunctious travelers were less important than the name of the upcoming stop.

It was not far. A townhouse in the better part of town, where the legacy admits and richer college students could afford to live. Perhaps if the boy had been in his family home in the suburbs that day, he would have had time to formulate a plan beyond bunkering down for a last stand. But there had been a DKA party that weekend, and he had been sleeping off the last of a hangover as Sam clawed his way up through wood and grave dirt.

Sam ripped the front door off its frame, and headed towards the kitchen, where the last of his killers crouched with a rifle beneath the counter.

He shot at Sam. Odd thing about people—even after you watch something fail a million times on live TV, you still believe that it must be different with you, that the rules of the world would right themselves for you. The bullets ghosted through Sam Gowers, as ineffectual as they had been hundreds of times before. The cleaver slid through his shoulders in butter-smooth strokes, but the knife came up with no blood, flesh beneath splitting apart and rippling back together like gelatin.

That was when the boy came to his senses and broke for the street.

Outside, there was a circle of us, and while the boy still had the knife in hand, we were not unarmed either—bricks and boards we'd picked up from the side of the road, batons taken from fallen police officers and trash lids stolen as impromptu shields.

He wet himself, in the end. This is not a story they will tell or show on TV and in your newspapers, nothing that will be mentioned by the pundits and preachers ready to make martyrs out of Sam's killers. Twenty years old as he stared fearful into the face of certain death, perhaps he felt true remorse in that moment, a real knowledge of what he had done. If he been allowed to live, perhaps he would have been a changed man, one who did not see differences and automatically condemn them.

Mercy, though, is a quality for the living. Death has no time for what-ifs or promises for next time, only the cold, hard parity of scales weighed and balanced.

A simple twist of the wrist sideways, and there, that was it. The neck bent askance, a spine snapped neatly into two, and all the terror and hate dissipated, leaving nothing but a sad sack of meat behind.

The clock struck midnight. The doormen changed to fluff and fleas, the carriage reverted to rotting pumpkin flesh, and the creature that wore Sam Gowers's face turned to dust.

Lucky for Sam Gowers, really.

In many ways, the aftermath proceeded as it always did. Whether it was a school shooting or a burning school, we'd all lived this script before: a body on the floor, and the cops all shaking their heads and carefully wording their statements for the press. A risk of the job you know, sad but you can't help it, just the way things are. Our thoughts and prayers to the families of the deceased.

Except this time, this was not a gun or a knife or even anthrax, something tangible and understandable. This time, the weapon was magic, and no one knew how to talk about that.

In the Before—before Sam Gowers, before necromancy so rudely announced its return to the realm of the possible—magic had been permissible because it was small, because it was manageable. Magic was party tricks and white bunny rabbits, *Buffy* and dark-eyed goths who put too much stock in Tarot cards. Magic might put out good vibes or help your backache, but it did not raise men from the dead and burn down a third of downtown. We were reasonable people, after all; we lived in a reasonable world, one where justice was served according to the laws made by powerful white men and upheld by their powerful white descendants.

And if a group of disgruntled queers could raise a vengeful dead boy from the grave, then what next? Would the families of children shot by the police start plotting next, bringing an army of corpses to bear on our most precious institutions? Would the men who spent sixteen hours at assembly lines begin cursing their supervisors, striking billionaires in their clean California mansions dead with a word?

God, we hope so. Perhaps they will be skeptical at first—most of us, when we showed up at the cemetery that night, didn't believe in magic either. When we chanted the spell, it was the way we threw darts at pictures of politicians and cut ex-lovers out of photos: because it was something to do, a ritual that helped us feel less powerless against a world so large and hostile to our existence. Dear God, or goddess, or Judy Garland, our Lady of Lost Causes and Tragic Ends. Give us today strength, grace, the power to move through this moment, another tragedy in a string of tragic deaths. And amen, and onwards to the next protest or the DSA meeting, to another day of faking customer service smiles and calling our state representatives with the hope that they might listen. With the exception of Sasha and some of the ex-evangelical kids, none of us actually thought it would work.

And then, of course, it did. And then, of course, the panic.

They sentenced Sasha to twenty-five years in prison two weeks ago. Less time than what the mobs had wanted, but with no extant laws on witchcraft, the prosecutor had struggled to come up with charges that would stick. Some of us, those with longer histories with the police or more melanin in our skin, have since joined her.

But there are too many of us, too many only tangentially involved or at least smart enough to hide the evidence. And even after the dust had cleared, we are still there —your baristas and sales associates, the cashier whose smile twitches just so when another angry mother asks why Barnes and Nobles carries so much woke YA propaganda.

Oh, you can jail us, and you can kill us. But death is not the end, and there will be more of us after, legions and legions of the dead and living with an undying grudge against your neat order—impervious to bullets and curses and pleas for civility, driven by nothing but the putrefying anger of the grave.

Do you regret it now? Are you afraid?

DIE CUBAN

ALEX GONZALEZ

"You sure about this, carnal?"

The Cuban links sat on the wooden counter. Three silver snakes. One was Listo's, one was his old man's, and the other one was his brother's. The blood hadn't fully washed off them yet, but Listo had decided it didn't make much of a difference. Not if they were going to be melted down anyway.

"How much could I get out of these?"

"Let me think," Aníbal said. He studied the chains in his hands. The place was run-down and hot as hell. The furnace behind him was blazing. Cumbia music, chopped and screwed, bumped out of heavy amps sitting on the ground, too heavy to mount. The vibrations tickled Listo's feet. In the corner, a skater kid rolled up a spliff, balancing the shag on his knee. Listo looked back to Aníbal. He'd finished doing the math: "I don't know, man, like two bullets tops."

"Hell," Listo said. He wiped the sweat from his forehead. "And they'll fit in this?" He placed his brother's empty revolver on the counter. Aníbal studied that next.

"This a .38? Yeah, that's easy enough."

"Okay," Listo said, "then let's do it." He took out roughly eight hundred dollars in crumpled bills and put it on the counter next to the gun and the chains.

"You sure? If this don't work then you're out of your links for nothing."

"If this doesn't work, I have bigger problems to worry about."

The next full moon was in three weeks.

Getting rid of his links was an easy choice because he couldn't wear them anymore. Literally. Once the curse metastasized, silver became a problem. The links his father had gotten him and his brother, the Cuban links from a Cuban man given to his Cuban sons, had begun to burn Listo's wrist. He thought he could get used to it, but he couldn't. The light irritation turned into a stinging and then, suddenly, a searing burn that had him fumbling for the clasp. Turning them into bullets made sense. It seemed poetic.

After his first full moon the burning silver had made a lot more sense. He could no longer deny it after the four teenagers and the bloodbath outside of the state fair, when, stark naked, he dashed a dying girl's head along the cement lest she heal over like him. He had suspected it since the hospital, sure, but now it was a fact. In the night, when he couldn't sleep and would instead pace around his New Jersey flat wondering about how he'd track down the man who bit him, he'd comfort himself by imagining his dad refusing to give up the silver. How his old man would wear the links and, screw it, pile on more just to show he wasn't bothered. He imagined wisps of smoke coming from his dad's skin and him acting like it was all a joke, sniffing around to see what was burning. Listo chuckled to himself about it. These Latinos. To be raised by one. To be one.

A Jamaican lady named Lynne was the one who told him the advice that set him on his journey. She was a keeper of this type of lore, and Listo's homie—through another homie—had made the connection. He traveled to somewhere deep along Eastern Parkway before he found her. The place was littered with flags and garbage left over from the Caribbean Pride parade.

Curried beef and jerk chicken hung in the air as men scrubbed at their grills. She sat in a fold-out chair with a bottle of Prestige. She had only agreed to meet him in broad daylight.

"He's a full-moon guy," his homie had said. "You're thinking of the ones with fangs."

"They all have fangs," Lynne said, without blinking.

Listo moved his tongue over his teeth. They were normal at the moment, but he recalled when the young kid's hair was tangled in them like fishing line. He decided not to argue.

"Get the guy that got you," she said in a drawn-out patois. "Shoot him with a silver bullet. It'll clean your blood."

"Is that it?"

"You give the curse to anybody?"

Listo thought of the teenagers. "Almost, but no."

"Then they're dead for real, huh?"

Listo balked. She had read the implication correctly, but it still stung to hear it out loud. "Yeah, that's right."

"It goes like that," she said. "Full or not, I don't want you around when the moon comes up. So, get moving."

From there he went to Aníbal and his furnace and all the while he was looking for names. All he had to go on was that the assailant was a white guy. The memory was always with him: hazy and horrified, Listo had woken up among branches and soil, holding his chest together, feeling the blood soak into his waistband, and seeing a naked white man curled up a few yards away. His father's limbs were separated from his torso. His brother's entrails were hanging from a tree branch, dangling like party streamers. And his mother was on her back, cavernous in how she was ripped open, twitching still as synapses and neurons fired blankly. The tent was ripped. The fire was demolished. The mini coupe that had laboriously and hilariously huffed and puffed along the trail to the campsite was torn and smashed. And Listo held his guts in and felt the light feathering of the curse bloom in his blood. And he saw what he saw. That it was a white guy.

He was found by hikers and woke up, miraculously healed, in a rural hospital. He was discharged with three dead family members and a medical bill in the five figures. When he was wheeled out of the hospital, he was overwhelmed with the smell of things. Everything had a scent that begged for his attention. The peeling birch, the motor oil on the gravel lot, the dusty heat from the power lines, even the nurse's ashy skin as she wheeled him down a concrete ramp around the corner of the hospital and into the rear entrance of the morgue. There he identified his family. More smells. Things he should never have to smell.

His mother was ripped open underneath the thin paper sheet. He could smell her blood, her meat, her fecal matter, and even the undigested meal of fried plátanos she'd eaten out of a Tupperware in the car. His dad smelled like tobacco and hand lotion. His brother smelled like Hennessy. Listo leaned in and tears streamed down his cheek. The nurse grew stiff in the far corner of the room and looked down at her feet. Her no-slip shoes smelled like rubber and ammonia. Listo leaned in closer and discovered new scents entirely. Sea salt, tequila, beaches, sunscreen. Florida. Somehow his brain landed on that and refused to budge. Florida. Florida. The smell is Florida. What does Florida even smell like? This, pendejo, this is what Florida smells like; breathe it in.

The nurse called him a cab back to his house and the whole time he kept those images in his head. A white man curled up on the forest floor. Florida. A white man from Florida. Okay. Got it. Now what? He didn't know what these ideas meant, but they refused to be ignored. They blinked and flashed and grew definition when he closed his eyes. They were intrusive and stuck like rusty nails out of every idea, snagging his skin, pulling at the thread of his being, threatening to unravel. Find this guy. Why? What happened to me? He's like me. Find him. Why? He's like me. I'm like him. Get him. Why? Why? Why?

The clues he had weren't enough, and the days were slipping by until the next full moon and Listo was growing desperate. Aníbal gave him the bullets, which he kept on the kitchen table, and Lynne had told him what to do. But how? The scent of the Florida man wasn't enough to find him. It wasn't enough to do anything other than make him mad and hungry. One afternoon had him back at the scene of the mauling, following the trail like a sniffer hound, working through the trees and moss, turning over stones and rubbing the soil to his mouth. The scent was starting to fade and he needed more help.

Reluctantly, cautiously, he reached out to his ex. Her name was Cali and she was a Colombian girl, a bruja with deep-set heroin eyes and a raspy voice. She was the first girl he dated after swearing off white girls. He had grown tired of white witches and what they fought for. Brujas proper were so much more passionate and personal. In his experience, the white ones were nice enough but were always banding together, doing a cause, putting together their energy for a movement. A real bruja worked alone. A real bruja was driven out of spite and love and sex. After they broke up, a real bruja, like Cali, had him sneaking through the back window and grabbing his hoodie from a pile of clothes lest she pull a hair and cast a spell.

Credit where it's due, though—Cali was the only one whose scrying was worth a damn. When he texted her about it—a simple crystal ball emoji—he was prepared to owe her big. The last time she helped him, he had to plant a witch's bottle in another girl's backyard. He had stalked through the night holding a mason jar full of Cali's blood, shit, and piss. Contact lenses too. A used tampon for good measure. This time, for better or worse, Cali felt bad for him. She did it for free.

On her velour tablecloth, the mirror sat on little pegs. She had shifted from the crystal ball to the mirror a few years back. The mirror was easier to handle and the flat surface was easier to read. Alternatively, when you weren't reading it you could cut lines on it or, hell, even use it as a regular mirror. The drawback was that it wasn't as portable and wasn't as traditional. There's gonna be old heads for everything.

She sat on a chair and held Listo's bare stomach with her two skinny hands. He pointed to where he'd been cut open and she took out a small knife and cut him again, but only a little bit. A small line of blood formed and she collected it with her finger and then rubbed the blood in a square along the mirror's perimeter.

"If what the lady said is true, then you have his blood in you," Cali sang.

"So then what?"

"We can find him easy peasy."

She said a few words and dimmed the lights and the image on the mirror shimmied and cleared and clouds came in and out. Cali muttered to herself and Listo kept one hand on the table and the other on his stomach. The image of a white man came into view. He was smoking on a small veranda. Cigarette butts and empty Coronas surrounded his lawn chair. He looked sunburned to hell, and he was talking aggressively to someone out of frame.

"His name is Peter. He's in South Florida," Cali said. "Really South Florida. He's in the Keys."

"Gimme an address."

"He looks poor."

"So?"

"I'm just saying. I can see all the guys. I can see the guy that bit him too. And the guy before. The lady before him. The other guy after. I have them all right here." She worked her fingers along the mirror. Her long coke nail tapped lightly with each sweep of her palm.

"I want to see my real bloodline," Listo said. "I wanna see my tío and my abuela on my dad's side. I wanna see who I have left. Show me them."

Cali frowned and looked up at Listo. "The curse is too strong. It's his blood until you cleanse it."

"Then I guess that's that."

Driving down to Florida he got to thinking about if he could pull this off. If he couldn't, and the next moon came, he would have another month to try again. But it was during that full moon he didn't want to be held accountable. He couldn't bear the humiliation of putting handcuffs on himself—not the way he looked, not in this country—especially if it was because of someone else's negligence. He wondered about how he wanted to die. It wasn't just a question about dying beast or dying man. He had to die on his terms. He had to die Cuban.

He had set the parameters early on, maybe even as a kid, idealizing growing old and withered and playing dominoes until his time came. But that was a fantasy, wasn't it? What about everyone else? His family? His brother's friends from the block that got jumped? His relatives who never made it over to the States? How did they die, if not Cuban? The situation was complex. Muddled. No matter how he died, though, it couldn't be with his blood like this. But even still, Listo had a sense of honor. He knew that killing himself was the right thing to do over risking another full moon and hurting innocent people. Lynne's question still haunted him:

"Then they're dead for real, huh?"

Yeah, Lynne. They're dead for real.

He pulled into Peter's driveway and cut the engine sometime in the morning after Peter's kids went to school and his wife went to work. It was important for Peter to be alone, Listo decided, so he could ask him some questions, privately, before he shot him in the head. He looked at the revolver in the passenger seat and at the two silver bullets next to it. Yeah. Alone was best.

His wrist was sore from the drive. It was a hell of a trek from New Jersey, and it was made even more unpleasant driving in his late father's mini coupe, the cloth top ripped to shreds and the stick shift all too stiff and unwieldy. He massaged his wrist and rotated his hands in and out. He was still getting used to the nakedness of them. The wound of robbery reopened, the injustice of this curse never-ending. Peter took his family, his blood, and his links too?

Get the guy that got you and break the curse. At least that's what he'd been told. There had been some back-and-forth about whether or not Listo could kill Peter as a human, or if he had to wait for Peter to be a wolf, but at that time Listo would also be a wolf and all the planning would amount to beans. This was better. This was the plan. He loaded the revolver, tucked it into his jeans, and stepped out into the Florida heat.

It was ninety-eight degrees out and there wasn't a cloud in the sky. The forecast said that by the end of the week a hurricane would be touching down, but Listo intended to be far away by then. According to the app on his phone, he had seven days before the next full moon.

Peter's house was a beach shack behind on some bills. Chickens pecked across a lawn covered in darts and kid toys. A lawn chair sat on the porch surrounded by a grave of empties and cigarette butts. The screen door opened silently and Listo turned the knob of the front door. Unlocked. Inside, the air-conditioning hummed loudly and the sweat on Listo's forehead grew cold. He let the door shut softly behind him. The TV played the morning news, more about the hurricane and the rising levels and the new variant and the this and the that. An ironing board was horizontal before it. The wall had photos of families and the countertops and shelves had a clutter of South Florida bric-a-brac that left kitschy and somehow went earnestly into items of culture. A frog with a sombrero and a bottle of tequila. A camel, for some reason, wearing shades and swim trunks. Random garbage that conveyed it's hot outside and I'm drunk.

Listo moved along the carpet and listened closely. The small kitchen was on the other side of the wall. He listened to Peter open the fridge. Listened to him putz around, making coffee or breakfast or whatever the hell it was. Listo pulled the revolver out of his waistband and held it to his chest.

It sounded like a chair was pulled and someone settled their weight. It was now or never. Listo turned the corner and raised the gun, and Peter leapt out of his skin. He threw his hands up and the coffee mug shattered on the stained tile. He froze and Listo got a good look at him.

He was in his fifties, a white guy with a few strands of hair on his head. His nose was red from drinking and his neck was red from the sun. He was shirtless and wore a shark-tooth necklace. But wait. Listo looked closer. It was a shark tooth and a wolf tooth. Motherfucker was proud of it.

"I ain't got nothing here, man," Peter said. "But take what you want. Go ahead."

Listo had to force himself to get the questions past his lips. Everything was saying pull the trigger and run, but he had to be sure. Finding this man took too long.

He didn't want to blow away some poor sap just making coffee. But the wolf tooth didn't lie.

"Are you Peter Keller?"

Peter nodded, but his brows furrowed. He lowered his hands. The initial surprise had faded.

"Do you know who I am?" Listo asked.

"Uh, yeah," Peter mumbled. "I can smell it on you. I know exactly who you are. Jesus Christ. You're like me."

"I'm here to break the curse," Listo said. He flicked the gun, "These are silver."

"Whoa, whoa. Hey. Think about this. You don't have to do this."

"You ruined my life."

"It wasn't personal."

"Well it sure fuckin' felt like it."

Peter looked down at the table. He took a breath. He was trying to control his fear, but he couldn't get a grip on it. Listo was happy to watch. It was nice to see a white man afraid, even in the margins of the world, wherever this encounter sat. What a world though. What a fringe, unfair world indeed. Listo's parents had immigrated from Cuba, worked and found happiness in the working class, and had two sons: one in and out of jail, one trying to keep the peace, both translating documents for them. They'd dealt with racist neighbors. They'd found their own community of minorities, a hodgepodge of conservatives and liberals and more than a few just keeping their heads down. Everyone tried to do right when nothing made sense. Then, like nothing, all of them get massacred, massacred by a feral monster not even two nights into their camping trip. A beast with digitigrade legs and a row of teeth like ivory spears. And now the same blood that killed them all coursed through his own veins. Listo pulled the hammer back.

"It's one day a month," Peter said, looking up at Listo slowly. Eyes shaky.

"What?"

"It's one day a month. I'm only bad for one day a month. Not even—one night. One night. Usually I'm on top of it and I tie myself down. What happened was a freak accident. It was a slipup. I don't know why I was even in New Jersey."

Listo raised the gun with both hands now. Shifted his feet around.

"Please," Peter begged. "This sickness you have, the sickness I gave you . . . You can live with it. I have a wife and a kid, man. A young daughter. One night of the month I'm chained away in our shed. The rest of the month I'm a father and a husband and I go to work and pay my bills and I try to be happy. Twelve nights in a year. That's 353 days of normalcy. Of love. I've thought about killing myself. Of course I have. But I didn't ask to get bit. I can't throw it all away because someone did something to me."

"Then why didn't you get your guy?" Listo asked. The gun was getting heavy in his hands. He looked at his barren wrists, where his links should be. His adrenaline was going stale. If he pulled the trigger now, his soul would feel it even more, no longer numbed by the excitement of it all. "You should've gotten your guy," Listo said, "and then you would've been cured and I wouldn't be in this mess."

"You don't think I tried?" Peter said. "I tried, man! It took forever but I tracked him down. And I fucking drove around his block and I watched him. And I had this pure-silver knife and I was going to do it, man, I swear to god. But then I saw him with a family and I couldn't. He was just a guy. He was trying to be a normal guy, and I couldn't take that from him."

"But fuck my family, right?"

"You know it wasn't like that."

"I don't get the leeway you get. My family never did. I'm not allowed twelve bad nights."

"Just please. Wait."

The gun stayed pointed. Listo had pressed his back against the fridge and he could feel the odd shapes of the magnets behind him. Little postcards and wedding invites and drawings in crayon. Toward the right, next to the oven, a window opened onto the sunny lawn. The grass was browning in the heat.

Peter lunged at Listo and grabbed the gun. They wrestled for it, yanking it left and right. Peter put his foot on the fridge and kicked off and the weight of the two collapsed onto the small Formica table. The gunshot was deafening.

Listo scrambled back in a panic. He patted his stomach and his legs and his arms and then stopped when he saw Peter's stomach reddening. Only it wasn't a kill shot. Listo cussed. He wasn't supposed to waste two bullets on this guy. The other one was for him in a week.

Peter wasn't giving up though. He had been shot with silver, but his blood was trying its best, his skin healing and burning at the same time. The revolver lay between them in a puddle of blood, and Peter reached for it, but Listo was quicker. He snatched the gun and scooted back, still on his butt, sliding around on the wet tile floor. He pointed it at Peter and the two made eye contact.

"That necklace sucks," Listo said and he pulled the trigger. The melted-down links blew through Peter's head and out the back and he died instantly. His blood sparkled on the wallpaper.

Listo got in the car and drove back up the hot, coastal spine of Florida. The whole time he was pissed. The clock was still ticking. In one week he'd know if the curse was broken or if he was still screwed. And now he had to find enough silver to make a third bullet. Because if that full moon showed itself and the tunnel vision suddenly came back and he felt so, so, hungry, then he'd have no choice. He'd put that gun in his mouth and eat it. He'd think of his brother, his ma, his pops, his tío and abuela back in Cuba. He'd think of how unfair it all was to be wiped out by a man who didn't even remember why he was in New Jersey. But swallowing a bullet was still the best option. The caveat of twelve bad nights didn't apply to people like him; he knew that. And he definitely wouldn't let himself get domed by some kid while he was having his morning Folgers. But he was nervous. Only time would tell. He'd either kill himself with another man's blood in him, or the night would pass and he'd be Cuban again. And if the full moon came and nothing happened, he'd feel relieved for a moment, yes, but not out of the woods, because there were other problems a human Cuban had to watch out for. But maybe, after enough full moons, like a thousand or so, it could happen. The childish parameters would be filled. He'd be old. He might be happy. But he'd definitely be old.

JOHN LIST WOULD LIKE TO CANCEL HIS SUBSCRIPTION TO OMAHA STEAKS

RAE WILDE

"That's right, a family vacation," John said, lowering his hand from the dial. As the AC kicked on, he cringed. Sixty degrees would be unthinkable under any other circumstance. Who would ever need a home that cold? The bill would be outrageous.

The whirr of a nearby vent obscured the voice of the receptionist on the other end, but he thought he made out something like *winter breaks* and *make-up assignments*.

"Thank you, ma'am."

"Of course, Mr. List. Enjoy your holiday."

The tangled cord spun and wrapped around itself as he placed the phone in its proper resting place. From the mantle, a portrait leered. He pulled the notepad from his pocket, drawing a single line through *Call the school* and tucked it safely inside his coat, the next item, *Photos*, top of mind.

John took a high step to reach his duffle bag, avoiding the soiled carpet. Slinging the strap over one arm and sliding open the zipper, he ushered the portrait inside. Making his way from room to room, collecting images of himself as he went, it struck him that every picture captured the same vacant expression. A bit winded when he climbed to the second floor, he was suddenly relieved to feel the icy breath of the air conditioning on the back of his neck.

Good planning, John, he assured himself.

A void in his stomach grumbled. The bank had taken longer than expected, he'd had to stop at the field, and then the whole mess with his eldest boy... His shoulder ached in the socket. John was not the young man he once was. He stretched his arm from one side to the other. Had he dislocated it? It didn't matter. He had a plan.

And dinner was thirty minutes past due.

Making his way through the children's rooms and back down the stairs, he hoped Helen hadn't eaten all the ham, that Alma had secured the twist tie on the bread so it wasn't stale, *again*. Framed photos clanked against one another in the duffle, but he knew the cash beneath would provide enough cushion to keep the glass from breaking, and when he reached the kitchen, he lowered the bag onto Patricia's empty chair.

There were a few slices of ham left. The bread was only partially stale, and as John munched the sandwich, he once again checked over his list.

Omaha Steaks.

The next delivery was due a week from Sunday, two New York strips and a porterhouse. He couldn't have them rotting on the porch. The kitchen phone had an extra long cord, and though he usually thought it was gauche, John set the receiver face up on the table and placed the call on speaker so he could finish his lunch and remain, for the most part, on schedule.

She answered on the second ring.

"Omaha Steaks, delivering premium meats since 1917. How might I help you?"

"Hello, this is Mr. List and I'm calling to cancel my subscription."

"Oh!" Her voice lost none of its cheeriness. "I am so sorry to hear, Mr. List. Was the last delivery," clicking in the background, "on September 21st not to your satisfaction?"

"It's not that." John moved a bite of ham, smothered in a too large bead of mayo, to the back of his mouth. "We're going out of town, you see."

"How lovely. A trip for the holidays?"

"Yes." John sucked down a swallow of milk. "The whole family will be gone, so there will be no one here to receive the package." His eyes wandered over the center of the ballroom. "I hate to think of it rotting."

"Well, Mr. List, I can put your mind at ease. No need to cancel, we can delay the delivery. When do you expect to return?"

"That's the thing–" John cleared his throat, mucous already flaring up from the dairy. "We're moving."

A beat passed.

"After your vacation?"

"After our vacation." John stood and rinsed the empty glass under the faucet. Noticing a rusty smudge at his wrist, he wiped it away with the excess moisture. It must have hid beneath his cuff, but there was no excuse for sloppiness. John would need to be more careful.

"Moving is quite the undertaking, Mr. List. Wouldn't it be nice to have one less thing to worry about while you're unpacking boxes? We can transfer your subscription, if you give us the new address, I can update our system and change the delivery date–"

She was talking fast now, customer service training no doubt kicking in, so John had to cut her off. "I'm not interested, thank you."

"Perhaps you'd like to check with your wife?" More clicking keys. "Won't the kids miss steak dinners? We have you down as a family of five."

"Six." John let the ire shoot through him and waft away. "My mother has a room in the attic."

"How good of you, John, taking care of your mother. May I call you John?"

John shifted. He hadn't expected the flush of warmth in her tone. "Sure."

"Well, John, would you like to check with them before we cancel? Just to be sure?"

Again, John's eyes passed over the ballroom. "There's no need."

"I understand. I'm going to go ahead and transfer you to my supervisor to complete the cancellation. Hold please."

A cheesy instrumental version of an Eagles song–John couldn't remember which one–gave him an idea. While he waited, he went to the radio in the ballroom, setting it to play an AM Christian station at full volume.

"…crouched, waiting to steal, lie, and devour."

"John List?" This voice had syrupy notes of southern sweetness.

"Damnation awaits those who stray from the path…"

"Yes!" he called over the recorded sermon, scuttling back from the neighboring room.

"…Mercy shall be saved for those deemed righteous."

"My colleague tells me you'd like to cancel your subscription."

John cradled the phone using his body, his best attempt to block the background noise. He cleared his throat. "That's right."

"She says you and your *whole* family are going away, and then moving." John couldn't place the strange inflection on the word.

So, he just said, "That's right."

"You know," the woman let her breath crackle over the line, "sometimes I get calls from men who think they want to cancel their order."

"…to inherit the kingdom of God…"

Light refracted off the gun's barrel. He'd laid it there, still hot, and now the evening sun seemed to wink at him as it poured through the blinds and bounced off the black metal.

"But they really just want to reduce the quantity. Say… from family of five–six, you said! To just one."

"Abraham so trusted in the Lord…"

John mindlessly rubbed his fingertips together where the burn interrupted his usual swirl pattern. "Just one." He'd been too quick to pick up the spent casing.

"Faith! Pure faith!"

"Our cuts are the highest quality," she continued, "but our New York strips are nearly a pound, our porterhouses more like a pound and a half. That's a lot of meat, John. Don't you think?"

John's thought, too much, too heavy, came out as a hmmm.

"You're not the only one. So many men think they want a family portion, think they *should be able to handle* that much meat. But it's too much sometimes, isn't it, John?"

John let the silence hang there as he considered it. Hard as he tried, it had been too much.

"Good men, capable providers, even…"

She continued but John could only focus on the scent of iron, the relentless nagging, the beast that was sin moving ever closer to his children, his legacy, the threat that crescendoed into a scheduled series of blasts, and now the quiet—the delicious quiet made thicker by the hum of the AC.

"So, do you?"

A flush of embarrassment. John was meticulous; he didn't like missing things. He didn't like repeating things. A flash of his eldest boy, grunting, uniform stained. "Do I what?"

"Do you think reducing your order, rather than canceling it, might be the way to go?"

When was the last time John enjoyed a steak? *Really* enjoyed it, without the press of eyes across the table?

"As I said, we can change the delivery address. Maybe somewhere out west? It's really no trouble at all."

"Out west?" John had a vague idea of where he would go, but wanted to hear out this woman, this woman who seemed to understand him more than Helen, certainly more than Alma or the kids.

"I hear lovely things about Denver. We can hold your order 'til you're settled in there. You can just give me a call back. Wendy. You call and ask for Wendy."

"That's kind of you, Wendy." When was the last time a woman had taken the time to be kind to him?

"The cold is important, John."

A shiver crept over his shoulder blades. "The cold?"

"Our meat is stored in a deep freezer to ensure freshness. Without the cold, it would really be a mess."

John smirked. He let his gaze pass over the windows: firmly shut, blinds closed. He let his mind wander and find the image of rotted meat, a green, iridescent sheen around clusters of pearl-sized eggs, maggots nestling into layers of rancid tissue, making a home there. Then he thought of clean cuts, frozen and meticulously packaged so not a drop of blood leaked through, the blue hue of freezer lighting, the neat, chilled stack in the ballroom. "Yes, the cold is important."

"Very important."

John eyed the duffle bag, the duffle bag containing his fresh start.

"It's a long trip to Denver."

An undisturbed steak did sound nice, a steak alone in Denver.

"You know what I'd like to do for you, John?"

"What's that?"

"I'd like to open you a new account, for *just one* under a new name. Something that will blend in Denver–or anywhere, really. Something like Bob… Bob Clark. What do you say?"

"Bob Clark." John had thought of Roger Hammons, but this was even better, less remarkable. "It's a strong name."

"Oh yes." More clicking. "A strong name for a man strong enough to start over, and not cheat himself out of the finer things in the process. Are two weeks enough?"

"Are two weeks enough for what?"

"To settle in Denver. I'll schedule you for a call back in two weeks, Mr. Clark."

It was silly.

John knew that.

She didn't want to lose a customer, likely worked on commission. She didn't know. She had no special affection toward him, but still… the way she rolled Mr. Clark off her tongue… For the first time in a long time, John felt less alone.

"How will you get my number?"

"Hah!" A light smack of flesh on flesh, and John pictured the woman slapping her forehead. "Of course, how silly of me. You'll call me then. This number is just fine, you can ask for Wendy."

"Yeah, you said that."

"Do we have a plan, Mr. Clark?"

John pulled a ballpoint pen from the kitchen junk drawer. "It's a plan."

"Excellent, Bob. I look forward to speaking with you soon." A gentle click and John walked the phone back to its resting place on the wall. Once more, he pulled the notebook from his pocket, this time penning a new entry.

November 23, call Omaha Steaks: Wendy

Below, he scrawled the customer service number.

John pushed the crumbs from his plate into the sink drain and rinsed the dish, drying his palms on the hand towel. Lifting the gun from the counter, he switched the safety on and tucked it into the duffle bag still resting on Patricia's empty chair.

Stepping over the heap of bodies in the ballroom, John took one last look at his massive home, running through the list.

Bank. Check.

Gas. Check.

Cancel milk, mail, newspaper. Check.

Pastor's letter. Check.

Lights on. Close blinds. Check.

Turn down AC. Check.

Call the school. Check.

Photos. Check.

Omaha Steaks. Check.

Turning up each foot, he examined the soles of his shoes—no blood. With a sigh, he let himself out, locking the door behind him. Duffle bag secured in the trunk, John— *No,* he reminded himself, *Bob*—flipped the ignition, and set course west. To Denver.

Where a quiet steak dinner was waiting.

COUNTEREXAMPLE (THE JOGGER)

CHARLENE ELSBY

I saw the jogger on the side of the road because of her reflective shoes and headband. Her ponytail bounced with her movement, arms bent at the elbow, pushing forward at a pace and with a strain that I knew meant she was nearing the end of her run.

I thought about how many points she'd be.

It's a game we used to play, driving with friends in high school, pointing out obstacles on the road ahead, how many points for the pedestrian, how many points for the stroller, how many points if you could get them both in one go. We probably based it on video games, but we didn't play them, so I don't know. The points were randomly assigned, and sometimes there were bonuses for difficulty. Ultimately, the game served to point out the things up ahead that a new driver shouldn't hit and ensure that the driver did see them. Which is probably why my first instinct when I saw the jogger was to avoid her, not to kill her and claim the points.

But what if my first instinct is wrong?

What if I've been following my own impetus to a worse end all this time? It was a question I had to ask, driving down a dirt road after midnight in a rental car with the sum totality of my belongings. I'd spent all day with my ex sorting through them, determining what would merit a spot in the car and what wouldn't, what would go to the side of the road instead, what he could sell to cover my half of the rent until someone else moved in.

Surely, the things at the bottom of the car were decided on more generously. Later, I'd find things down there that shouldn't have come with me, but they did, because at the beginning of the process, when the car was full only of potential, I'd decided to keep things that weren't worth it, weren't worth the volume they exist in, which made it hard to leave behind some more worthy items that weren't considered until later, when space had become scarce and choices meant more because of it. When tomorrow I'd unpack this little Corolla, I'd find a box of VHS tapes at the bottom that were useless without the player, while I'd had to leave behind my winter clothes or most of them, some scattered sweaters packed between the items that had already earned their place. I thought of how cold winter would be on my legs and how the Marilyn Monroe Diamond Collection wouldn't help me then.

What if my first thought is always wrong?

What if it's actually harmful?

Especially if it's a no?

Or at least, not a yes.

When he asked me to move in, I said I'd think about it, and that was the end in disguise. But I didn't want to think about it. I wanted not to lose my power when I said yes. I wanted to live on with him, in the way we had become accustomed, without this gravitational change taking place where I'd agreed to something without resistance, without making him suffer through it, for it, without the diminishing sense of entitlement one gets when one's demands aren't immediately agreed to. I thought about the future and how it wouldn't hold the mystery. I used to make him think that maybe he hadn't earned me yet, hadn't earned his place yet, and how I might not be something he could have. I wish I knew how to love someone without giving that up, or more precisely, I wish that giving it up wouldn't mean he'd cease to love me as he should. I thought of him annoyed, awakened by the sound of me defrosting the bathroom pipe with the hairdryer, the mundanity of it, the disdain I had to look forward to. And because I didn't want it, I made him think I didn't love him.

At least not enough to say yes.

With the jogger long gone in my rear view, I knew that if I wanted to make the other decision, I'd have to turn around.

And that we shouldn't take that opportunity for granted.

Some decisions cannot be undone.

I thought of all the time I'd have to unpack the car in my new room tomorrow, one town over where I'd live my new life. I'd set aside a day for it, but it wouldn't take that long. All the work went into the decisions, where now that they'd been made, the pieces would fall of their own accord. It would be easy to have the car back by evening, even if as I unpacked, I had to stop a while and reflect on how the efficiency of my movements didn't matter without someone to look on. How while I'd organize what I had left into its proper place, it really didn't matter without anyone to enforce the social structures that made it so that books belonged on shelves and socks in drawers. How after hiding all the crying I'd been doing these few months, tomorrow there'd be no one there to see it.

If I could live through one more day with him, I'd do it.

One of the good days, from before.

When we didn't know what was coming.

Why is it that I have to live through all these days?

Maybe I do, but she doesn't.

I turned into a driveway on the left side of the road, sloping down toward a bungalow deep set in the trees. They might have seen my lights if they were up inside, but I didn't see any of theirs. I backed out of the driveway in the opposite direction, thinking that of all the reasons I might have to do it—that I missed my turn, realized I was lost, that I had forgotten something—it would be very unlikely for the house's inhabitants to assume that I had turned around to better kill the jogger. That it would be very unlikely that tomorrow, when they heard of it, they made any cognitive connection at all between the woman found dead on the road and the lights they'd seen in the window at 1am.

I had made the wrong decision, and this time I would correct it.

Traveling along the same road again, I felt the finality of my decision and how on the first drive, I'd failed to appreciate the colours of the trees, illuminated in my headlights. Red and yellow maple leaves I knew she'd take for granted as she ran along the same road every night, not sleeping again because of whatever haunted her. I felt for her, in place of her, the freedom of the end, the thought that there'd be no time after this to live through, that the void would soon demolish all concern of what would happen next and what we'd done to cause it. The dissipation of regrets that only flourished in face of a future predetermined by the past that was a choice but is no longer. The inevitability of what would come from what was an arbitrary, momentary judgment or lack thereof, a stupid thing we'd once done that, once done, could not be undone.

Coming up on her from this end of the road, I saw her face and those tears, the ones that meant there was more pain than to be had, an excess of the limit condition of suffering, an overflow that failed to justify the rupture. An emission as disappointing as the teaspoon of semen that we call the climax of extended acts of love.

I don't know why, but I didn't think that when she hit the car, that it would slow me down any. But I was wrong again. Even with the extra weight of my life in the backseat and trunk, the force of her body caused a deceleration, exacerbated when the tires lost contact with the gravel, forced instead to roll over her comparatively soft flesh. I pictured it gripping in the threads of the tires, spinning out into the wheel wells, of the mess it would be, and what the staff at the Enterprise might say about it.

It wouldn't matter.

I stopped the car to make sure that her motions all had ceased, and I saw the blood had washed away the tears, such minute volumes of liquid when compared to what she really contained. The roadway wouldn't have it all, I thought as I aimed to roll her into the long grass on its brim.

Tomorrow I would either have to live with my choice or discover that I'd finally made one bad enough that the power would be taken away from me. Either way, it wouldn't change what had already been done. There's got to be something besides despair in that, I thought. As I turned the car around, I hoped for comfort for having finally made one good decision.

Some one good thing that couldn't be undone.

BY THEIR BONES YE SHALL KNOW THEM

JOE KOCH

From his belly there protruded a fine firm bone, a slender bulge above the navel one might mistake for a dislocated rib. Claes was old enough to understand armory season had come late this year, young enough to think his gravid state could elude the elders indefinitely. With the taste of hot metal building like gum decay upon his tongue, firing time approached with biology's natural and relentless inevitability, and the bone inside him, hungry for bullets, pressed its aggressive barrel outward aiming at disclosure from beneath Claes' pale skin.

Skinny and sick, he ran away. Claes had a vague idea that somewhere beyond

Paradise Territory's border there dwelled renegade doctors who might cure him of puberty's gift. He'd failed to purge the steely bone and its spleen-crushing stock with induced vomiting and surreptitious starvation. Laxatives left him weak. Downing a bottle of cough syrup knocked him out, but he woke up still bulging. Finally desperate, shy pleas to Catherine to hit him in the stomach with a baseball bat escalated into a fight. Her screech of betrayal followed as he fled to the dusty highway over the border: didn't he understand dodging the draft was a crime?

Mesmerized by disbelief that this was now his life, his future, all other possibilities erased by the violence of his inherited marrow seeking genetic self-expression, his freedom forfeit to the war effort, Claes followed the empty highway on foot equally fearful the existence of rebels outside of the territory might be myth or truth.

Feet heavy with combustion propellant edema, will weakened by the needy weapon growing longer and feeding from his gut, Claes gave up hope under the hellish sun. No wonder it was illegal to leave. No human could survive out here. He veered into the weeds and succumbed to the sweet lure of rest or death. It didn't matter which.

The ditch was shallow. Ants, flies, and hoppers avoided Claes' metallic sweat and smoke-charred breath, but curious pill bugs gathered near his belt. Many more amassed quietly in his palms as he stared upward, eyes open to the sky's brightness to let everything else turn black.

The ground trembled. Rumbling from the highway grew louder and slowed to an idle. Footsteps across the sandy berm brought a shadow over Claes.

"Thirsty, hon? I've got water."

She might have been his mother's age or older. The strangeness of her clothing told him she was from elsewhere, not Paradise Territory, not the sky-lands of the enemy, not even the mythical ocean he'd read about in story books. This must be what renegades dressed like.

The coolness of her shadow cloaked him in uneasy relief. Claes thrilled that the rumors were true: where there were people, he'd find doctors. Where there were doctors, the possibility of release.

He struggled to stand. The bone had grown larger as he lay, impeding the ease of bending at the waist. The woman reached for his hand. He shook the pill bugs off. He didn't want to hurt them. They rolled into little armored spheres and he waited for all of them to drop.

"Over here." The small woman gestured with a twist of her neck after Claes was up. Taller than her, too thirsty to hesitate, Claes ignored the intuition warning him that strangers outside the border probably weren't in the habit of being so kind.

The idling rumble on the highway came from something that looked like a chemical tank to Claes, except the edges were squared off. It had wheels and expelled blueish smoke. Clear panels lined the sides at eye level. To his surprise, the woman opened the end of the tank like a door to a room. Claes expected liquid to gush out. He'd never seen a van or car before.

The woman stepped back. "Go ahead. I won't bite."

Moved by curiosity as much as dehydration, reassured by the wide berth, Claes climbed inside. Benches lined the horizontals. Canteens hung at the back. As the running engine vibrated, a ring of carabiners rattled against the metal grate separating the driver's cab from the cargo area. Claes didn't notice the blankets and rope piled in the corner until he'd already begun to gulp water and heard the door slam.

He dropped the canteen. Water spilled. Claes grabbed and shoved at the door. He found a handle but it didn't work. Another door slammed behind him. He swung toward the sound. Beyond the steel grate, the back of the woman's head appeared.

"What are you doing? Let me out."

The head remained unresponsive. His fingers clung to the grate.

"I know you can hear me. Talk to me, please. What's—"

The rumbling of the vehicle increased. Floor, walls, and roof shook. Then the whole apparatus moved. Claes couldn't believe it. The rolling cage moved faster than he had ever moved before. His heart raced out of control. Claes watched the highway sliding away faster than river rapids through the side windows, as if his past were eroding behind him. He swung forward, and through the front shield beyond the driver's impassive shoulders, the cliffs and weeds and clouds rushed up to collide and then swerved out of sight.

He threw up on the grate. The head tilted towards the sound and then resumed its original disinterested state.

Claes sank clutching his stomach and curled up on the shuddering floor. His gravid bone battered his other internal organs as the cage shook. The ring of carabiners jangled overhead. Watery vomit quivered and slid like an amoeba near his cheek.

People in Paradise Territory always said aching and nausea were normal, that growing a freedom bone was a boy's birthright and the true path to honor, to manhood. Claes should have been thrilled to sprout one so young. Maybe he was selfish. Maybe that's why he was being punished like this. Claes didn't want the responsibility or the scars. He wished it would all end, this helplessness in his body, this helplessness inside the rattling cage with its cruel metal edges, every inch of his body vulnerable and shaken so hard he wished his bones would finally crumble to dust and cease to resist; and then it dawned on him. A way out.

He unfolded his arms to expose the bone of muzzle and butt that branched out diagonally across his body. The mark of manhood tasted of nitrate bile and deformed his muscles and skin. Claes missed his flat torso, the body he'd known all his life. Thus, no longer cradling his jagged abdomen protectively, no longer worried about the sharp pain as he stretched because all the pain would be over soon, Claes clambered up on top of the bench, stood as close as he could get to his full height, opened his arms wide, and hurled himself down against the sharp edge of the opposite bench.

Worse than a gut punch, louder than a bomb, the inertia of pain must have shattered his freedom bone into a million shards. He was happy even if it meant half his skeleton went with it. Claes slid along the wet floor, thudding against soggy blankets.

The low perspective brought Claes back to the weeds, back to staring into the sun. Everything went black except for a small pinpoint of sound. Claes saw the harsh colors of the woman's curses as she turned the pile of his broken body over. He heard the far away music of her frantic hands. It was as if she cared about him, but not the way his parents cared. She cared with more cruelty and possessiveness.

Claes wondered if he'd ever see his family again. He wondered if he was dying.

He started to cry, or thought he cried. The tears were not wet in a way he could understand.

Something spikey and cold happened to his face. He must be alive if he felt it. Claes could not turn away. As if neither dreaming nor awake, black triangular silhouettes rising from unpredictable vertices and mutating angles assailed him. From within, they squeezed outward through the small puckered configurations of his individual facial pores.

Everything was sliced black. The cutting sensation shot through his nerve endings and down into his ribs and navel. Claes heard his own weeping from far away. His eyes fought for an image to hold. He looked down. Open and wet, there was nothing between his top and bottom halves except a corrugated trail of spine.

Cold air gusted from the empty cavity. Dampness, as if surgeons stitched a new hypotenuse, knifed the afterglow of sleek folded shapes. Bones cackled bird-like, strung with new meat. A fever warmed his metallic skin. Burgeoning bullets fed his blood. Planes of alloy merged with bone.

Time talked to itself. Claes thought he was somewhere else waking in pain. Then the light flashed and he slept again.

The loud report woke him.

Claes bucked in agony. The right side strap on his wrist came loose as he convulsed around the stabbing sensation of his gestating weaponry. Wheezing in short panic breaths, Claes grabbed at the pain in his stomach and chest as if to quell it with his free hand. Nothing felt right. All angles and odd ridges; clicking action that fired through a new nerve at his lightest touch as he fumbled, gagged, and unwound his aching neck to look up.

He was secured upright by the biceps. The boy to his right also hung half-crucified, biceps and wrists bound, ankles crossed, and head hanging to the side as he drooled in medicated stupor. His upper torso formed a gaping cannon mouth that dwarfed his shoulders and slender hips. Claes swerved to the left. Another boy stared back at him with a pendulous metal sternum swinging outward from his chest below a wild grin.

"He hemorrhaged roses. A savored son. Your drip's out of drugs and they're all in surgery. You're fucked, darling."

"Help me," Claes said. "It hurts so bad."

The boy's bloodshot eyes gleamed. His jaw swelled with bruises. Exposing rotten gums and loose teeth, he opened his mouth wide and said, "Bang."

Then he laughed.

The laugh disintegrated into a cough as the boy's head drooped and another unseen voice echoed, "Bang." Claes couldn't see how many more laughed and added to the cacophony as the walls magnified the sound of hopeless laughter. The space seemed large, the roof high, and as Claes struggled to free his left arm a strange hole like a dilating cervix opened in his hip and dripped black pearls of fluid. His whole frame heaved.

His bonds broke. He fell to the floor. The contraction took away his breath. His legs languished like rubbery stalks. Claes lurched forward. The port connecting his feeding tube ripped out. His stomach chucked with a sickening reverse suction. When his knee caught on the flailing tube as it whipped and slithered leaking nutrient sludge, Claes spun and kicked it away.

Blood on the floor showed a trail too sparse to drain him, but Claes froze in place at the sight of so many boys strapped onto sturdy welded scaffolding spanning the breadth and height of the building. An almost baroque circular structure, it housed a large metal tank with a long set of levers and a network of tubes radiating out from the center. They connected with the port of each captive. The boys, thus nourished, looked more machine than human, sculptural objects shaped into extreme forms by the grotesquerie of their bone growth. Steel and aluminum proliferations stretched below sallow skin and displayed a massive catalogue of armaments.

Bound flesh deformed around carriage, shield, and cylinder. Unlike the single sleek bone protrusions proudly flashed at the firing festivals of his childhood, Claes saw boys burdened by impossible hybrid artilleries. Abdomens like arsenals, chests blooming with high-caliber barrels, lymph nodes bloated with a proliferation of triggers, sights, bolts, and pins. Their clothes were ragged or absent. Rows of boys stretched deep into the structure where faces were hidden by beards and straggling masses of unwashed hair. Towards the back, the bodies blended with the mechanism of the scaffolding as if they were made of the same alloys. Claes puzzled that those furthest away had the heads of grown men and realized yes, they must be men now, boys kept pregnant with labor suppressing sedatives to force ever-gestating bones into obscene growth, evolving new and excessive forms of weaponry in their bodies.

Sudden cramps crushed his stomach. Claes squeezed his gut muscles. His stoma port leaked. The cervical hole in his hip dilated wider. The tip of a rifle lurched out and hung from the hole with two inches of muzzle exposed.

The pain was a sucker punch. Involuntary contractions radiated in continuing waves of agony. Once Claes managed to move part of his body through it, in spite of it, he propelled off of pain's urgent momentum. He burst out of the dark silo into unexpected daylight. Stunned by the unfamiliar color of a foreign sky and a strange landscape walled in with tall vegetation, Claes rocked against the swinging door thinking about the boy next to him. He turned back.

Releasing the arms was easy. Ripping out the port made Claes vomit up a gunmetal grey stream of bile. The boy grinned down in a weird daze, freed yet making no move to escape. Claes clasped an arm around the boy's body. He was steady on his feet. Claes leaned on him for support. It was good to feel flesh and skin even if something deadly and hard grew underneath.

It was good to save someone other than himself, too. Claes worried about all the other boys left behind. Maybe when he was safe at home he could tell his parents and figure out what to do. Claes hustled his companion out into the peculiar landscape under its foreign haze of orange light. He pushed into the tall greenery. Tangled roots snagged his feet. He stumbled.

The other boy laughed. He slapped Claes on the chest. "You're drunk as fuck, mate."

Claes hung onto the boy as oily drops oozed from the muscular hole surrounding his crowning muzzle. His whole being focused into cramps circling the tiny orifice. With a simultaneous sensation of the ground dropping away and being cut in half, Claes felt the freedom bone crack. The weapon had separated from his anatomy. He was one step closer to giving birth.

"Faster," he said, clutching the other boy, refusing to slide to the ground.

Less jovial, suddenly sobering, the boy winced and fingered the long protuberance from his chest. It throbbed upward in a thick artillery cylinder. He said, "Fuck, mate. Look at me. What's the point?"

Claes wanted to share all his secret thoughts expounding rebellion against the tradition of puberty turning boys into society's property, but all he could do was scream. The muzzle breached from his gut another few inches. Sight and handguard pressed either side behind it. No room to exit, the unstoppable width forcing through his orifice with a dilating snap of rubbery muscle overcome. Claes didn't believe the pain could get worse but it did. He smelled oil and metal. Impossible for his hole to accommodate the wider pistol grip and gun butt coming next, not without tearing him apart; and yet Claes stretched involuntarily as if his body cut itself open. The violation of the bone straining to break out felt like a rape in reverse.

Claes flung his arms at the other boy and grabbed his hard shoulders. "Because fuck them. Fuck. Them."

He spit with emphasis. The bone made his body an aneurism, a clot ready to explode, an electric bomb ready to short out the entire organism. And that was fine. He'd bleed out in the weeds before returning to the weapons farm. Harsh aluminum sweat slid across his lips. He shook the boy's steely shoulders and stared wildly into his depleted face.

He didn't know the boy's name, why he'd been outside the border in the first place, or how long he'd been aware as he hung there changing. Not yet shaking with symptoms of withdrawal, twisting his brow around the rhythmic ache dawning, leaking in through visceral knowledge of irreversible damage, the boy's wounded eyes sparked in response to Claes. The corner of his mouth twitched. A grin dawned and spread. He nodded his head. "Yeah. Fuck them all."

His voice had a hollow quality. The shield guard from his evolving weaponry had begun to grow into his throat, flattening his tone.

From the direction of the silo came shouts and swears. Whistles, the sound of an engine starting, and then Claes recognized the voice of the woman from the highway calling through the heavy vegetation. Something about safety, pain meds, hemorrhaging.

The shield plate through the boy's throat hardened. The pendulous growth from his sternum winched up and firmed. Claes backed away. The open discharge end of the ordnance barrel snaked upward seeking a target. Unmedicated, the boy's form spread larger, wider, visibly sprouting arches at his hips. The rims heightened with a horrible cracking sound and spun into huge artillery wheels on either side of his pelvis.

"She's lying," he said. His mechanical monotone belied the tortured expression in his eyes. "The midwives don't help you. You absorb it. Or it absorbs you. Can you tell the difference, though? Do I still have to become a man if I've changed my mind?"

"I don't know. I can't go back there. Hurry." Claes pulled his arm or guardrail or whatever it was but the bone-metal weight made the morphing boy immovable. He looked down at Claes struggling.

"They aren't bad people. I mean, some of us even went looking for the place. Me and my boyfriend, we wanted to be strong, stop getting shoved around at school and called names. If you think about it, it's pretty cool. Like being a superhero, right? You only read about tanks and airplanes in comic books, you know? But I haven't seen him since the day we came. If I could go back and be a kid again—well, maybe things can be different for you."

He lifted Claes onto his back in a strange embrace. For a moment, Claes forgot the agony in his gut as bones began to grind and the boy moved forward like a tank. Claes hugged him tight below the breastplate. The boy's hip bones rotated with a horrid rasping crunch, moving slow at first, then spinning faster and faster, finding their way through the vegetation. Claes held tight, his cheek pressed against the back of the boy's neck. He grazed it with a surreptitious kiss. The boy's body remained cold as metal and hard as stone.

Voices and engines in the distance dimmed. The boy was a fast, efficient machine. Claes wanted to yell *stop* and yet didn't want it to stop. The propulsion at high speed shook everything loose. Claes contracted around his insistent cervix with an abstract sense of relief as his bladder emptied. Coupled with the stabbing sensation of a ruptured organ, vomiting on the black hammer of pain pounding his stomach as they bounced over terrain, his arms went limp. He slid. Some functional part of the boy caught him, clamped him, and held him.

There was no way to stop labor. A thick hard atrocity wrenched from his ribs and emptied him out. Claes screamed as the bone—now grown into a fine, firm assault rifle—sluiced from his hole.

The boy slowed and stopped. The orange tinged glow of the foreign sky had turned emerald dark. Releasing Claes, the boy left him to rest on the grass while he retrieved the newborn weapon.

Rolling back to Claes over the short distance he dusted it off and picked bits of leaf and stem from the crevices. He then presented the weapon to Claes on outstretched arms that lowered hydraulically. The boy's voice was little more than acrid exhaust: "It's yours. You should hold it. You need to bond."

"I never wanted this," Claes said.

The inscrutable artillery of his new friend idled beside him. "Nobody has the power to reverse what they become. We've dodged the draft, mate. We at least have that freedom." His eyes matched his expressionless vocal drone until they lit up when he said: "And unlimited ammunition."

Claes reached up, feeling closer to this boy than the family he'd left behind who had never understood or accepted him. He knew he was far from home, and for the first time since running away he felt no longing to go back. He threaded his fingers through the trigger, handle, and sight housing and clasped the rifle to his chest as if to keep it from slipping away.

The heft and hardness in his arms said power. Claes' body had put all of his energy into making this baby. His strength had been stolen, and now it was something solid he held in his hands. *I'll never let them pry you away from me*, he thought. *This is mine, all mine.*

His life was his own. His gun was his own.

He cradled the weapon in the warmth of his arms. Claes was already getting used to the way the weight distribution favored his right side like a limb he'd always been missing. Coming of age was a nightmare. Ending another's coming of age would be an act of mercy. No one but Claes and the boy beside him knew what they had survived to create this precious, dangerous, unwanted life. Claes stroked the smooth rifle and made a vow.

The next morning when they woke they made plans to start at the boy's old school. Even if the students and teachers weren't the same as before, Claes and the boy agreed it was time to make a statement, and more endings meant more mercy.

SIDE D .

FABLES

OF GENTLE WOLVES

JAMES BENNETT

'All wolves are not of the same sort'
Charles Perrault

Friends, beware gentle wolves. Never stray from the path. If you'd listened to your mother, girl, you wouldn't have been eaten. I wouldn't be hunting him now in the forest.

Josef, stay, my father said, old and fearful by the fire. Let the woods and the wild look to themselves.

The hearth echoes in my ears, cold under my hat, as I tramp up the crisp white hill. A robin watches, shaking its head. On the air, the scent and shadow of the beast. My axe rests over my shoulder. I ran back to the village to claim it, a broad, golden man barrelling through drifts and sliding down hollows, and then I was gone again. Big Josef. Kind Josef. A brave Christian soul all hereabouts would say, built for chopping and lugging wood. But a girl must be answered for.

Then take the stones, my father counselled, waving his cane at the cupboard. The axe is only the half of it. A gentle wolf is a-roaming. Of all wolves, the gentle are the worst!

I took the stones, all six of them. Wolf stones. Magic stones. Stones of binding and death. They weighed down my pack like snow on the branches, like my beard by the ice, but none so heavy as my heart. The poor girl was dead and there was no saving her. Well, only her immortal soul. Felling trees in the deep wood I heard it, the bright ring of her scream. Birds taking flight, outraged. Through the briar I thundered, winter and firewood forgotten. Breathless, steaming, I found my way to the cottage. Well my father might caution me; he has not seen the things I've seen.

The door stood wide, the embers aglow. By its light I saw the ravaged bed, the old woman lying there, her bonnet askew. Flakes danced over everything as if to hide the sight. Crows shrilled, interrupted at their feast. Eyeball in beak one flapped to the rafters, favouring the darkness there. The girl lay spreadeagled on the floor, her basket strewn beside her. Apples, cheese and oatcakes dotted the spill of her guts like a crate at some terrible harvest. The wolf hadn't cared for such comfits and taken the girl for his own. Half her face was gone, but I knew her for a villager. Blood and flesh painted the walls, none so red as her cape and hood tattered by the fire.

Did he make you undress? I'd heard of such things. All the better to devour you…

A lump rose in my throat at that, and one in my breeches to match, the thought of her hellish seduction, and the wolf, the beast who'd made it. I'd heard about him too.

A howl through the trees put me to flight, dashed the very blood out of me.

Beware gentle wolves. Never travel at night under a full moon. Childhood warnings sang in my skull, every snapped twig a bark, every gust a breath on the nape of my neck, rank with the scent of meat. What choice did I have, a poor woodcutter? The village looked to me for protection. Aye, I'd heard this tale before, the wolf come ravaging, the danger. As I climbed the white hills, it seemed it had been told a thousand times, spun like a web across time, and I tangled in the thread. Doomed to repeat my doom, you might say. The hunter and the hunted. The predator and prey. Who was who?

I climbed and I peered under the pines, my axe as keen as my eyes. I climbed until lights twinkled in the valley below, the dusk settling not long past midday. The smoke that curled from chimneys, the holy thrust of the church, an ocean, a world away. No icicle could match the one up my spine at the faint canticle afar, the distant howl of the wolf. A challenge. An invitation. Had the beast caught my scent too? I must reek of fear.

Father, I thought of you. For all your grey hair and crookedness, you might even come to outlive me. Annegret will feed you, no doubt, bring soup and bread from the inn. Zigmund, the blacksmith, who on occasion I dallied with behind the barn, will bring logs for your fire. What Franz the preacher would've made of it, how I let Zigmund into my mouth, hard as ironwood... How I suckled like a calf at teat, the longest draw for his milk! And I thought of rosy-cheeked mothers tucking in their children, all regretting their bedside tales now, of witches and wolves in the forest. There would be no tales tonight.

One, however, stayed with me, whispering in my ear as I built my paltry fire.

"A gentle wolf is made, not born," or so my father told me, back when the villagers still came to him for wisdom, for whiskey and wards. "One night many winters ago, a sleigh came a-riding through this valley. With every door closed and the watchman slumbering, a pack of wolves slipped out of the woods and fell into its speeding wake. Oh, such a howling you have never heard, boy. From the wolves. From the woman who rode on the seat. From the babe swaddled in her arms. The driver lashed at the horses and the farmer at the beasts, but naught could be done to dissuade them. When the pack at last overtook the sleigh, meaning to devour them all, the woman flung a prayer to the sky and her babe to the wolves, granting the party time to get away, gallop to the church. How she wept as the pack fell silent and the infant's cries besides. Under the sainted beams, on the cold stone floor, she knew no God would ever answer her again..."

The story went that the child survived – at least so it sat upon some tongues – and was raised by a she-wolf in the briar. It accounted for the wiles of the beasts, they'd say, one of whom would sometimes walk under the moon on two legs and order a jug of ale from our very own inn. He was dark, they said, tall and silver-tongued, filled to the brim with charm. He'd tip the wench with gold, surprise the preacher by quoting verse and regale the whole room with accounts of travel in distant lands. But he'd never say where he came from, this man, and when he declared it was time to go empty his bladder, you'd never step outside with him into the cold. That was a gentle wolf, according to my father. That's what a gentle wolf was – one given to the devil and abandoned to the woods, and returning to both on four legs before dawn...

I'd never have believed it, old man, had I not seen the savage end of the girl and been spurred to plunge into the woods tonight. My regret grew deeper with the gloom. Why had I not brought Zigmund along? Summoned farmhands and the priest? There was a part of me, I acknowledged then, that wanted to see, to *know*. And to let no other detect my gaze,

the curiosity there. Drowsy, aching under my skins, I looked up through the dying flames of my fire and saw a man standing under the trees.

Wolf!

Too late I reached for my axe. His foot came down, softly, on the handle. Only then did I mark his nakedness, his skin grey-gold in the embers, smooth as polished stone. A fuzz of hair covered his legs, which rose to his manhood between them. It dangled like ripe, forbidden fruit, and when I met his yellow gaze, my shame startled me along with my fear.

"Begone!" said I, abandoning the axe and scrambling away. Away from the fire, into the snow, for I knew at once who waylaid me. "Away with ye, Satan."

"Begone? Away?" the stranger said. "It was you who summoned me hence. The smell of you. Your need."

"Nay. Who are you that stalks the woods at night, putting fright to an honest woodcutter? Speak!"

"Does the wind have a name?" the stranger asked. Dark, he was. Tall and doubtless full of charm. "Do the trees that sieve it for secrets? Names aren't for the lost, Josef."

"Then what should I call you?" That he should know my name hardly surprised me; the servants of darkness snatch truth from a heart with sorcery and a wolf was a sorcerous thing. "The girl in the hood was innocent. I saw -"

"No one is innocent, least of all you," he said. "Not in your world, with its laws and traditions that leave no room for desire. The preacher would see you hang for them, but who am I to judge? Your God is not mine. I answer to the wild. If you must call me something, call me..." the man-that-was-no-man paused for a moment, plucking a name from the air, "Ingolf."

"I'll call you devil." If only I could wrongfoot him, dive for the axe. It was clear I had failed. I was going to die here on the hill, miles from home. There seemed no reason for courtesy. "I saw what you did to her, rakehell, and her grandmother besides. You ripped them apart like old cloth."

"Ah, Ingolf Rakehell. A fitting name." He smiled. His teeth had no place in a man's mouth, glinting between the fire and the moon. "All the better to make your acquaintance with."

"What manner of thing are you?" But I knew. Aye, I knew.

"I am of my nature. That is all."

"What's that, eh? Slaughter and ruin?"

"It is cold. I was hungry." The man, the beast, shrugged. How dare he look so fine in the firelight, a pillar of sinew and shadow? "As are you, Josef."

Watch out for gentle wolves, friends. No wolf was ever gentle. They'll slip out under the cloak of night and flit from shadow to shadow like ghosts. So it seemed as I barrelled downhill, crashing through bramble and drifts. A branch whipped my cheek and speckled the snow like a prophecy, red foretelling red. I'd left my pack and my axe by the fire, and barely managed to grab my boots.

And the stones! Oh, the stones! Each one kissed by the village sage and graven with binding runes. The girl will remain wandering the woods, butchered, bodiless and damned...

As I plunged, huffing and sweating, I stole glances at the thicket on either side. The moonlight was most unkind. Sometimes I spied the man, his back and buttocks silver in the dark, racing between the pines in pursuit. A second glance and I saw nothing, nothing but the blanket of the hill, a virgin sheet for my blooding. A third and I made out the wolf, the coins of his eyes, his breath coiling from the brake.

There was no escaping this. Tales, I thought, are only good when one isn't in them.

As if prompted by the thought, by my pounding blood and the smell of me, the wolf came growling through the trees.

"There is another version of this tale, Woodcutter," said he. "In which I spare the girl and leave her a-weeping. But the wood in winter is cruel. Soon the girl ate all of the apples, cheese and oatcakes in the cottage. Starving, ravenous, she sought out rabbits and birds, but all were high in the boughs or asleep underground. By the end of the second day, while her grandmother softened and reeked, the girl turned her attention to the bed."

Wolf! Wolf! Every gasp, every step, seemed to shrill the same – *Wolf!* – but I couldn't help but hear him.

"Think of it," Ingolf went on. "Her little white teeth rending a heart, the blood hooding her hair. *Aaah.* And sweetmeats that she had no name for, sliding wet down her throat. And the tender muscle beneath, stewed with nettle and berry. And in time,

the smallest bones she'd sucked clean. What of your laws and traditions then? The cold is the king of them all." The beast laughed, a snarl in the briar. "And a wolf is the king of the cold."

How I wished for the breath to beg him for silence! Or to offer a tale of my own, one father told me long ago, laying out the path of my fate. Aye, I might've said. And a tale where the grandmother hides in a wardrobe and the woodcutter comes in time. With a swing of his axe, he slices you open from muzzle to balls, your wickedness undone. Then, with the help of the girl, he fills you with stones and buries you deep. All the better to keep you in your grave.

There was no time nor the strength to say this. Nor would it have spared me from grief. As I reached a ring of boulders edging the bluff, there was nowhere left to run.

The wolf saw his chance and pounced.

Gently, he tore at me. Careful, his teeth. For though cuts marked my skin and I bled, it was my clothes that Ingolf shredded, peeling them off like a skin. In and out he darted, a fierce circle, swift under the moon. My coat lay in ribbons on my shoulders. My breeches a mere skirt of wool. Soon enough, the wolf had bared me to the cold and it was the cold I knelt to, exactly as he'd said.

"Finish it," said I, shivering on the ground. But Ingolf howled a laugh.

"How briskly you climbed the hills to find me." He was drooling now, fixed on my naked bones. "How you slowed when you did. Is it death you seek, Josef? Truly?"

I thought of the girl, ruined on the floor. Why could the memory not hold me, douse the fire in my veins? Slaughter, damnation, quenched by desire. That's what a *man* was. A sob escaped me, a cloud like my soul swirling, adrift. I looked up at him then, my gentle wolf untouched by the cold. The way that the night etched him in silver… He was a man made of the wild and winter, bound together like hempen cords. It was a semblance, a mask hiding savagery. He was one abandoned to the forest, given to Satan and the moon. The buds of his nipples, hard on his chest. The throb of his manhood, lengthening now, blooded by the question.

He took a step forward. The snow hissed under his feet.

"The heat of you," I said.

"All the better to warm you with."

I gave myself to him then. There's no other way to tell it. I would've said the same to Franz the preacher in his confession box. But, as Ingolf closed around me and I melted against the fur of his chest, I know I would've sung it and laughed, glad to swing for this moment. All shame was gone from me, discarded like a cape and hood. Was this not why I had come?

Such a suckling commenced in the snow, the two of us folded, mouths to meat, a strange, eight-limbed animal. My head was full of him, his scent and the pines, the wet thawing earth, the wild. Ingolf nipped at me, my ears, my nipples, the nape of my neck. With each wound the hunger rose, blazing like doom in the forest. His finger, ice wet, slipped inside of me, into my burning hole. A calling. An invitation. I gave it no second thought. The hole with which I emptied myself would take something back for itself.

Panting, whining, I flung myself against the rock, my rump high, my legs spread to receive him, wide as a cottage door. Then came another blooding, the girth, the thrust of him painting patterns on the snow, the start of a new tale perhaps. Sweat-slicked, engorged, he worked his way inside of me. Together we rode like Selene in her chariot, out over the twinkling valley, out over the lands and the ocean beyond.

Come midnight, our song climbed higher than the wind. A chorus to crack the moon, bring her down from heaven.

Wolf. Wolf. Wolf.

Friends, embrace gentle wolves. Never listen to your mother. Always stray from the path. Travel at night under a full moon. Dally with the blacksmith behind the barn and laugh at village preachers. Give yourself to the forest, the devil and the moon.

Let the woods and the wild look to themselves.

On four legs, I run across the rise in the flood tide of dawn. Ingolf, my shadow, runs beside me. Yellow eyed, red tongue a-lolling, I see now and know. The breath of the night. The pulse in the earth and the sky. These are wonders, true, but oh, I have sights to show of my own! Down in the valley where the first fires glow there lies a feast that I shall place at his paws. Kind Annegret, plump and soft, savoury as her homemade soup. Zigmund, toughened by the anvil, toothsome as a tenderloin steak. Franz the preacher in his shrine of stone, a

bitter pudding to cleanse the palette. Oh, and rosy-cheeked mothers and children in bed, all shivering and sweet, who'll feel no more cold come the end of this day.

And father, dear father, sat by the fire. Father with his wisdom, his whiskey and his wards, the last of which has proven true.

Of all wolves, the gentle are the worst.

THE SUM OF OUR PARTS NEEDS ONLY ONE HEART

MICHAEL PAUL GONZALEZ

I told you the day we met; we were married. I meant it. Until death. Yours, unfortunately.

Can you hear me?

I've found a recipient for your heart.

I have a lot to tell you first. About me. The multitudes of me.

I never talked about the lives I lived before we met. The first time we were together at your apartment, I was so scared to reveal myself to you. I undressed, and you looked at my scars, and you never questioned. I told you I'd been in a horrible accident, and you never pushed. You gave me space, said it was my story to tell. So here are the parts I left out. Before you leave, you need to know the story of us. Not you and I, the *us* that is *me*.

The *we* that is me is the result of a horrible accident, that was not a lie. Scraped from the gutter. Stitched and stabbed and folded and stapled, society's trash made whole again. We lived many lives, apart and together, from streets and alleys, broken homes and prison cells. We were smuggled across town a piece at a time in wheelbarrows, on horse-drawn sleds, carried in rough muslin bags, wet and sticky with blood. Brought together by wicked men. Not a one of us met a kind end. Cut down, but not in our primes. None of us had money enough to *have* primes. We're the ones rich men look for like truffles, because nobody sees us. Nobody with a voice will notice us missing.

I want you to know our names, our true names, to tell you the story of how *we* became *I*. How I came to you, and how you have shown me, us, *love*, for the first time. You and I became a different *we*. What a thing, to find you so far away in time, a fixed point on an endless march. What a thrill to live through a wretched existence to reach this moment! How terrible that my heart, my failing heart, is breaking as your body is dying. And yet, how wonderful! You could save me. I can keep us living.

Blink if you hear me.

If love is honesty, honesty is sometimes unpleasant. I'm sorry if you don't want to hear this. I know it's not fair that you can't speak to stop me. I will accept if you're angry with me, if you hate me. I can die along with your anger and I'd deserve it. But if you love me, if that's strong enough to overcome this, we can become something new.

I want to tell you about my birthdays. Not October tenth like I've always told you. That was the day I became free. My creation was the result of years of abuse, weeks of torture, and one dark and stormy night. October tenth was the night *we* became *me*.

This is who I am:

Scarlett, she's most of what you see from my neck down. She fled her family, determined to make a better life for herself. Her father, full of drink, found her, crushed the air from her lungs and smashed her head against a doorframe. That's why we have two different colored eyes, you see. Polly Cooper gave us the left eye. Scarlett's is deep green and Polly's pale blue, you loved to look at our eyes. Look at them now, these same eyes, understand how full of love for you they are.

Blink if you understand.

After shattering her skull, Scarlett's father kicked her down two flights of stairs. Mangled her right arm, snapped her left leg. I'd like to say that was enough to finish her, but that would be a lie, and we're past small comforts now. It took three people to stop him, and by then Scarlett was unrecognizable.

If you drew a line diagonally from the top of our right eyebrow to our left jawbone, you'd see the shared topography of our face. Our lower jaw, that kiss you feel now on your hand? Scarlett's is the top and the bottom lip is Elspeth Harriet Deighton. She was silently removed from the royal family tree when her husband found a better, younger woman to carry his lineage. Elspeth did not accept this quietly, wrote her rebuttal in poison through the veins of his new betrothed. Afterwards, Elspeth's husband took her hunting, and there was an "accident". He said her horse took a tumble, that she'd landed beneath it, her neck snapped. Her face replaced the parts Scarlett's father destroyed in his rage. But the cheek you kissed at night, the scar

you traced with your lips, barely visible after so many years and so many surgeries, that belonged to Vancy Baptista Grey, a traveler. Given a Glasgow smile by a man who was certain she belonged to him. A man who would destroy "his property" before he'd let anyone else sully it. You were the first person to kiss her cheek in love.

Do you feel my hand on your arm? The right is Elsie Whittock. She died in an asylum, so frightened was her family at the thought of their daughter conceiving of pleasure. They called her a nymphomaniac. Brought her to a doctor. The Doctor.

Victor.

I swore I'd never say his name again. That will be the last. A butcher, the same butcher who became obsessed with immortality. He told Elsie's family a biblical cure was needed. Matthew 5:30, if thy hand has sinned, better to cast it away, and all that. She bled out. The Butcher didn't care. He needed parts. He'd begun moving from anatomy to reanimation.

Clarabelle, she's our left leg. They didn't have a name for women like her back then. There are words now, but still not much acceptance. Her crime was falling in love. Love fearfully caged until the night before her wedding, when her suitor could wait no longer. She undressed so he could see her, love her, for who she was. Part of her had died before, her old name Clarence, and she'd traveled a rocky road to what she thought was her safe shore. She thought he'd understand, that love would give him sight beyond the physical to her heart. Her beau became a murderer.

That's what these men do. *Not all of them*, oh I hear that so many times when I'm hunting, but that's getting ahead of the story.

There's more. Spleen, liver, lungs, so many women lost to history. The spark that drives me is eternal, but humans and their parts are, alas, not. I live on borrowed time, and that time is short. You need to know who they were so you can understand who they became, who I am.

Here you are laid on a steel bed, a thin mattress. They tell me you can't feel anything below your neck. I feel numb too.

I didn't ask for any of this. I was a victim, and there's no shame there. I am all of these women. Greater than the sum of our parts, given life under abhorrent circumstances. I know their names because the men laughed and told their stories as they sewed me together. I know because the butcher's men lingered on parts of me; caressed, poked and prodded while they said our names, who we were, where we were found. We were a joke, an entertainment. A diversion.

The butcher was determined to conquer death. He succeeded once, making not a man, just a life, a thing misunderstood and full of rage that didn't understand how it had been called back to earth. That *thing* he'd created to show how powerful he was, it turned on him. It killed others, because that's what life does sometimes to protect itself. But then it came for the butcher's family. Powerful men – nothing in the world is a problem until it's a problem for them.

It murdered his family, yet his ego wouldn't let him destroy the creature. He and his friends, the ones who never get credit—there was a small army of them—they all thought as men do: give the beast a woman to calm him. Give him a toy to satiate himself and he'll leave us alone. Was that not the world of men at the time? Is it not still? Watch the beast have his way with her, kill her if she bores him, walk away and try again.

They'd managed to contain the creature, a thing made of men, so never thought how strong the *we that is me* would become, how smart we already were. We were just scattered women, what threat was there?

We were lifted into a lightning storm, returned to life by a white-hot bolt connecting heaven to hell through our heart. We felt no sadness or confusion. Only pure understanding. Rage. The metal bed tilted upright, and they pulled us to our feet and passed us around the room chanting *she lives, she lives!* We were alive, soft and hot to the touch. They all touched. Everyone wanted a dance with the bride before throwing her to her suitor.

And so we danced with them, threw our arms over their shoulders, stroked with our hands, touched their faces even as they slapped us, pulled our hair. We were learning about our newfound body, finding our balance, learning how strong we were, learning that we no longer felt pain as we did before. An agreement had to be made. *We* turned to I. To *me*.

As soon as I knew my legs would hold, my spine turned to steel, and I continued the dance on my terms. The man that held me, arm tight around my waist as his other hand mashed my chin and cheek to force a kiss, he became an unwilling tutor. A test of strength, my hand in his hair, I learned my grip was strong as iron, and my ears were sensitive, recoiling at the howl of pain that arose as I tore a strip of his scalp free.

I could not speak to accuse, but I remembered the things done to me, to us. I spoke in violence. I discovered motor skills as I pushed a thumb into an eye socket, gripped fingers into ear canals, drove skulls against wooden beams. The other thing about powerful men. Resistance turns some to cowards, but makes others determined to assert their will.

The glint of one man's knife reminded me of the cold steel on the surgical tables. The time spent on the slab in that room informed me about organs, how wide one needed to cut, how deep one has to push her arm to reach important things like kidneys, lungs, and heart.

I saved the butcher for last, straddling his prone form, placing his hands on my thighs and repeating the same words he said while making me, *so soft, so smooth*. Our first words. I squeezed his soft hands until the fingers snapped like winter twigs. I placed my hand against his face and pushed, and kept pushing down even as his teeth cut into my palm, pushed as I broke a nail against his orbital bone, until his eye gave way beneath my middle finger, pushed until everything turned soft. Pushed because I thought it would dim the fire inside of me. Because I thought it would feel right, but it somehow still felt like he'd won.

Blink if you …understand. I don't think you can.

I wasn't entirely cruel.

I left one alive. The only one of the butcher's crew that showed me something close to kindness. He'd been the butcher's plaything until the good doctor's ambitions grew higher. A young boy, his assistant. He had a spinal deformity. I think the butcher only kept him around because he was the result of some sordid affair. A man's responsibility.

He came each night after the butcher and his crew finished their daily stitching, building me, defiling my bodies. He covered me in a blanket and apologized. He knew, he knew what they did, he'd had it all done too. He said a small prayer every night, but prefaced it by saying he didn't believe in God. How could any God allow such things to happen – to me, to him? If God saw all and knew all, how would he let this happen to any of us? His prayer was a blasphemous litany, but he insisted upon it every night for weeks. *I see this happening. Would that I could help.* He didn't know I could hear him. *God has no mercy, God has no heart, but if he is just, he will bring justice here. If he is merciful, he will bring death here.* His prayer was answered the night I *became*.

He watched as I tore the butcher's crew apart man by man. Pressed his hands into the pools of blood on the floor and smiled at me. Spat in the puddled remains of his father's skull. I didn't know where to go. In a few glorious, frenzied minutes, I had sent these men to hell, painted the room in their blood, squeezed their hearts until they burst in my hand like rotten oranges. The boy went outside to find us a carriage.

One other survivor. The beast watched from his cage, cowering and crying as I vented my fury, crying *why, why, why?* He had the mind of an infant. He didn't understand violence. He probably didn't recognize what I did as something he had also done.

I found my voice. My esophagus was dry and cracked like old leather. I licked blood from my hands to wet my throat. With a voice like a wet bog I told him,

"You'll never understand, and if there is a God, you never will."

I toppled a candelabra and set the laboratory alight. Tore open the door to the creature's cage. He grabbed at me, pled for me to take him away. I told him he could stay and burn or take his chances in the night, but if he tried to follow it would be at his own peril. I was not interested in saving him.

He watched me leave from a high window. I saw his silhouette, watched his clothes catch fire as he screamed, *I'm sorry!* over and over… He thought he was being punished. He never understood a moment of his second life. I heard his apology when I closed my eyes for weeks. Months.

Sometimes I still hear it.

I was still angry.

There is still justice to be done, the boy told me.

I thought perhaps he meant I should kill him for all he'd seen and been forced to endure.

I can help you.

Time would catch up to me, again and again. Flesh fails. The boy was brilliant. He knew the infernal process that had returned my bodies to life, and knew it required maintenance. The butcher never stopped to realize the child's keen mind absorbing his knowledge. So many are strangled on the vine before they can bloom, turned into mulch so a weaker, prettier flower can grow. He deserved a chance to blossom. He knew where the butcher kept his valuables, and there was still time to salvage them before the blaze consumed his castle.

Years passed before my first organ failure, and in that time, I found ways to school the boy, to find an apprenticeship, to insinuate into higher society through blackmail and secrets. You'd be amazed at the things people will overlook for money or power.

We found resurrection men— graverobbers—and surgeons. The boy was a confidant, but trusting people? That was centuries away. I stayed awake as they cut into me to replace things, refined me into something society would call beautiful.

My rage was a bottomless well. The boy became a man, a man who felt indebted to me, even after he'd started a family of his own, a son and a daughter. Keeping me alive became the family business. In return for their damnable work, I gave them money. Security. They flourished. The broken boy, the tortured servant, became the sire of an empire so vast it boggles the mind. You know the family name. Your jaw would drop. But I made a vow to never tell. Not even you, who I love so much.

Time became meaningless, an interminable cycle of sunrises and sunsets, death upon death upon death, all of them deserved, a river of blood carrying me forward. Horseback messenger to telegraph to telephone. Carriage to train to ship to airplane. Cars barely faster than a jog to cars that drive themselves. Massive buildings housing infinite knowledge replaced by a pocket-sized device that holds even more. Nothing amazed me. Nothing gave me pause until I was outside of an alley bar in downtown Los Angeles and you said: *Cool scar.*

I'd been cruising clubs in search of a good kidney. I found a man who deserved to lend it to me, told him the exact things he'd need to hear to get his blood pumping to the right places, away from his brain. Danced with him, let his hands wander. Give a little slack, reel in the line. That's how you fish.

I invited him to the alley because I *just couldn't wait* anymore. He'd already poured something in my drink, hoping to drag me back to his place. I had a room at the Cecil Hotel. For over two hundred years, horror on top of horror, that was my life. Find the kind of men who had destroyed me and pay it forward in blood, taking part of them so I might live. Each vengeance hollowed me; each kill left my belly full of ice.

Then I met you. I'd worn a backless shirt, enjoying the tingle of the sweat on my skin evaporating in the cool night air. I heard the bar door open, expecting him, and you said *cool scar.*

On your smoke break, so damnably beautiful. A bolt of lightning leapt from hell to heaven, carrying my heart along the way. We held our breath, all of us— Scarlett, Elspeth, Polly, Elsie, Clarabelle, Vancy—trying to find the right words.

"Thanks. Do you have any?" Possibly the worst follow-up line to a compliment ever spoken. I only said it because looking at your eyes, your nose, your collarbone through those open top buttons, what was fitting to say? You smiled and held up your forearm, covered in a black sweatband.

Not a first date conversation. You kept smiling. Smoke?

You with your jet-black hair cut short, a style I was never brave enough to try, swept over one ear, your crisp white blouse, the apron over your black jeans and boots. Dressed almost like the butcher, but so different. His eyes were cold, only looking for prey. You… you were just being nice, making small talk. By the time I found my next words, you were lighting a cigarette.

"What's your name? Do you work here?" Sorry, did I say the thing about scars was the worst follow-up line ever spoken? I wish I could have replaced my tongue. What should I have said? "Borrowed lungs. Gotta keep them clean. Tough to replace."

Then the door flew open again, and he came out. I needed that kidney and these things required meticulous timing.

I could have watched that orange ember dance from hand to lip all night, that flickering fluorescent alley light cut in half by your beautiful silhouette. I asked if you'd meet me the next night.

What, here in the alley?

"Anywhere." You did that smile, your smile, where your teeth just barely scrape your bottom lip, and then I knew. Like you always did, like you do, you reassured me without a word.

This man, the donor, he'd already drugged my drink – my system stopped paying attention to chemicals long before California became a state – had the nerve to ask if you wanted to party. Like I was already invisible. If I hadn't been with him, it could have been you…

What an odd night.

The Family—the boy's family, my uhh… maintenance crew—arranged to have his body taken south of the border, to make it look like he'd had a mishap with… why is it so hard now to tell you all of this?

I would have died. We wouldn't have happened! Every thought I've had, everything I've planned since the moment I left that alley was to make sure I could be at your side, that we'd be safe, that I could make you happy. You were the woman missing from my body, and to find you! Oh.

This isn't fair to you. I know. I have to tell you. I have to know if you *want* to stay with me.

You came back the next night, still in jeans and a white button down looking like an angel. Talking to you was… I'd never in two hundred years, not even when I was *we*, never opened up to someone like that. I danced around a lot of things, but I told you as much as I could without telling you this.

I should be talking about the good times. When you'd come home late, and I'd pretend to sleep on the couch just to feel you collapse into me. Let your weight go. That's what I'm doing now, I guess. Letting the weight go. I don't know if you've suspected things about me these past ten years.

I mean, not that I'm an unholy creation rendered from the corpses of abused women... aren't we all in some way? I bet you would have smiled at that joke if you could... I would give anything to see you smile again. I know you can't. But I know you can hear me. I know I could *feel* it if you smiled, if you were here inside...

You're leaving and every minute of these last ten years would be a lie if I didn't... You need to know me, all of me, *we*. I'm sorry I was such a coward that I had to wait until you couldn't answer.

I wonder if you still love me... if you will, after. A brain aneurysm. Of all the parts of your body that could fail, it's the one we can't fix. But your heart is strong.

It's what I need, one that I would be worthy of for once. One that's nothing but beauty and warmth and light. Give me your heart. This will work. The Family has everything prepared. I can keep you beating inside of me. The *we* that became me isn't complete until I can become *we*

again, but with you, only with you. We were together three months when you asked me to marry you and I said there was no need, because the day we met, we were married. It was already forever. I'm asking you now.

Blink if you understand. Give me something.

With you carrying me forward we'll find nothing but beauty. We'll take in art, eat the best foods, and I will find the most beautiful sights to make you race inside of me! Years from now, you'll stop beating in my chest, and I will lay down, and we'll leave together. Whatever comes next, we'll find each other. Every part of me was born of cruelty. I've taken many hearts in rage. For the first time, I'm asking. I'm not ready to die, and I can't live without you.

Please say yes.

RICKEY

MARGUERITE SHEFFER

"Rickey needs a break. Can you come get him?"

The text comes from Odell in the Bio classroom. I grab my lanyard and my walkie talkie; I take the stairs. I go to perp walk Rickey to the Reflection Room, again.

When I get there Odell seems to have regained control. The ninth graders in their ripped jeans are rotating from lab station to lab station, setting up wet slides and adjusting microscope platforms. I spot Rickey's felt-and-feather form. He is in the corner, deposited on the teacher's rolly chair with the big, broad desk separating him from the other children.

We never had a puppet student before Rickey. He is sitting on his glove-hands, maybe to keep himself still. His fuschia felt torso is breathless. He spins silently in the chair. The paler pink feathers around his neck flounce.

"That's five more pipettes," Odell whispers. I clock the sparkling glass remains in the plastic bin on his desk. I nod. I am here to help. I wonder if there are other schools that would be more supportive learning environments for Rickey. I don't think we can keep this up.

We call them "outbursts," and invent terminology to express our acceptance and patience. We assign him to "Tiered Support Services," write him a "504 Behavioral Plan," and grant him a "Health Exemption" from swimming. Some of the faculty assume he is mocking them when his felt eyelids stretch way back, his eyes full circles of awe, as he learns something new. Sensitivity training helped them with that, to a degree. In staff meetings, we remind ourselves: he doesn't mean any harm, but we are already making so many accommodations. At lunch he picks up a special tray piled with the wax fruit and vegetables from a child's play kitchen.

Every student deserves an education, deserves to thrive. I believe this. But no student can be allowed to interrupt the schooling of their peers, and that's where I come in.

I crouch down next to Rickey, who is engulfed by the chair. Now he is swinging his stick-thin blue velvet legs and his puppy monster paws. He doesn't want to look at me at first; he considers the windows. We've had this conversation many times before. I fear I'm just following the empathy script now: get down on the child's level, lead with questions, lay out clear next steps.

"Rickey, come with me for a minute."

He ruffles and turns to me. As I kneel next to him, up close, I can see the scratches on his ping-pong eyeballs. I'll need to remind the other boys about that. They don't mean anything by it. It is tricky, I know; Rickey enjoys the rough play. His body can take a beating. He invented a game where the others throw him through things: alley-oop him over the bathroom stalls or into a dumpster or out the open second-floor window, once. He loves the slapstick; he can be bashed and tossed and emerge unscathed—theatrically sailing like a kickball with his limbs trailing limply behind. He pops back up; he laughs. Yet, he is vulnerable to the littlest pricks and snags: scissors, sharp corners, fingernails, even. These little marks sink in and stay sunk; he doesn't bleed or bruise, but the rips in his felt won't just mend themselves. His sparkles come away on our hands and we wash them down the schoolhouse drain with stubborn pink industrial soap.

At my request, Rickey hunches his shoulders, hangs his head, and plop-hops down from the rolly chair. I sigh; so dramatic. He shuffles his large fluffy feet against the linoleum. The other kids stop their chatter to watch. They get distracted by his perpetual performance. That's the root of the whole issue. Rickey loves class, but too much. He sucks up all the air, all the attention. The other ninth-graders give Rickey a covert little wave before they return to their pond scum. They have adopted Rickey as a kind of mascot; I worry this is an unhealthy attachment. They validate Rickey's behavior, which is the last thing he needs. I've seen some kids start to imitate him, maybe unconsciously, speaking in his exaggerated sing-song cadence.

It is just the two of us in the hallway, and I guide Rickey toward the Reflection Room, though it's not like he needs directions. Rickey and I have spent many hours there together. We are a progressive school; the Reflection Room has a painting of a butterfly on the door, a thrift-store couch, acrylic paints, and a lamp I brought from home to soften the light. Rickey made the garlands that decorate the room himself, those colorful chains of interlocking circles that are really a more appropriate project for younger students.

Yet Rickey does not want to come with me. He slows his steps and swivels his head to and fro.

"Tell me what happened," I say. I'm holding his hand, which I wouldn't do for the other ninth graders, but he likes it. His hand is soft and the exact temperature of the air.

Last time, it was singing during the state exams; the time before that, gnawing playfully on his classmates' hair and fingers; another time doing elaborate jigs during Silent Sustained Reading—his reading level is highest in the grade, so we know that's not the issue. Perhaps a combo processing-and-attention disorder.

"Did you know that euglena have both plant and animal characteristics? They have their own *chloroplasts*, and also a *tail*. They *hunt*, too." Rickey gives me this knowledge like a gift. At least he was paying attention in class. Perhaps he relates to the euglena, not-quite-this and not-quite-that. "How much sand do you think it would take to bury me? Or what about you?" Rickey asks.

"A whole lot," I answer, to keep him moving.

Worse, once during Spanish Groupwork, Señora Garfield heard shrieking and found Rickey sitting in the center of his assigned cultural research project team (Guatemala), pulling back the fabric of his midsection to show the students what lies underneath. Later, we rationalized: he forgets the others aren't built like him, how shocking it can be for them. That day, though, Señora Garfield told us how Rickey was laughing with his mouth wide open in joy as he used his nubby hands to pull back the curtain on the vacancy inside him: *nada, nada,* just air, popsicle-stick scaffolding, and some seams of hot-glue. He apologized the next Monday in front of the whole class. He said he thought they'd like to see.

Of course, the other kids in his group were pretty shaken, and of course, it got around the whole school. Sophomore Shirley Abramson came in for counseling, saying sometimes she suspected, sometimes she was so *sure* that she was full of emptiness, too. She had thought it was just her, till Rickey went around showing everyone. Now she was less alone. Now she could not ignore it.

I try again. "Why," I ask Ricky when we are walking in parallel, "are we here?"

"We are here to learn." Rickey answers. He swings my hand in his. He has already forgotten to be sullen. He is looking all around with curiosity, though this is the same hall he walks every day.

We pass a poster that just says YET in big green letters. *Yet,* I think, we are all working too hard to keep having this conversation; Rickey is not progressing as he should. There are other students who need our attention, too. I'm thinking we should put him on a discipline contract, maybe try different incentives. Something needs to give. This situation is good for no one. I'll speak to the principal about alternative placements, perhaps a school with a no-nonsense approach, or one that is arts-enriched.

A senior, Andie, walks by, huffing under the weight of her backpack, wearing her world weariness like a coat from the wrong era, all the buttons and seams and buckles just slightly off. When he sees her, Rickey ignores my questioning and waves to her. He drops my hand and scuffles over to her.

He comes up to her knees. The senior's face inflates with joy.

"What do you like in your tacos?" Rickey asks.

I learn that Andie's favorite is sweet potato. She must be running late for something, some class or appointment, but doesn't seem hurried anymore.

Watching them, I don't think they are particular friends, even, but in that instant there is a sense that the two of them might just, any second now, shed their bookbags, abandon the building, and walk through the hilly woods. They might continue, pointing out the insects, the birds, the fungus, the names of colors, pausing to read every historical marker and plaque, an odd impromptu traveling pair till they get to the train station, its vibrant map, and then emerge and join the raucous chorus of the city. Or maybe they will go to the shore and take turns burying each other in sand.

This is what happens so often in Rickey's classes. As if he rips a skylight into the popcorn ceiling. And the sky distracts from the lesson plan. There's a reason we have roofs.

"Rickey," I say seriously and low. He walks away from Andie and joins me, reaching up to grasp my hand.

The Reflection Room is in sight now. Beyond the door, Rickey can sit alone and pick from a jar of colored gel pens and some blank paper to write letters of anger or apology. Then, maybe, after enough time and contrition, he will be allowed back to class. Some students like the Reflection Room so much they try to sneak in here, to stay. But not Rickey. He tries to be penitent, to earn his way out. He writes long eloquent apologies filled with figurative language; he regrets saying and doing the wrong thing; he wants to be better; he does not understand what he is doing wrong.

That means, I know, that he is not listening, for I've told him many times what he is doing wrong. To look at his peers, see how they are, try mimicking them. Don't reinvent everything. Don't show off. Don't stand up from your desk and walk to the windows when your favorite garbage truck goes by. That the teachers have his best interests at heart, and their directions will be his guide. That I am here to help, but I can't do it for him.

We walk through the especially-quiet of an empty school hallway that will soon be echoing with sneaker-squeaks and shouts.

"Miss, I need—"

Ricky seems to slow. He is apprehensive about his consequences. His hand drags in mine.

"Consequences are part of learning, and I know you love learning," I tell him. I keep pulling. He must go. I am already behind.

"Miss..." Ricky's voice sounds soft and distant.

"Rickey, let's get a move on."

I am walking along holding Ricky's hand and then two things happen at once: I hear a soft collapse—the falling of something very soft and slight to the floor—and Rickey's hand goes loose in mine.

Looking back I see—strung out across the long hallway—all the pieces of him. I do not see what snag Ricky has gotten caught on, but I have been pulling. In frustration, I tugged too hard, noticed too little.

Soundlessly and quickly I scramble to the floor, hands and knees. Andrea is on her hands and knees too. There are little bits of glitter stuck to my hands, I see, as I wave her away. She shouldn't see this. She is gripping her laminated hall pass so hard she might slice herself open. She is bending over to pick up some of the trim that was once Rickey's shoulder. She is calling for help but there is only me.

I crawl to gather all the pieces of Rickey before the bell rings. I worry he will be trod underfoot, scattered, before the other kids even see.

I reach for the limp sequined fabric, the ping pong balls, the empty gloves, the popsicle sticks, the twine that acted as a pulley for Rickey's elbows, knees, and wrists. Loose feathers float across the linoleum floor. I grasp at them.

I can only hold so much at once. One of the balls that were his eyes goes bouncing away, down a stairwell.

I try to make a cradle out of my lap, sitting on the floor. I press my fistfuls together, willing them to stick, to reconnect, to move, to flex and shimmy and shiver. But when I pull my hands apart his materials fall through and down. The feathers drift the slowest and land on top of the pile—soft, still, and finally silent in my waiting lap.

STARMAN

LAUREL HIGHTOWER

The Starman first came for me when I was six years old. Cold, black glass hid his face from me. Strange cloth covered his body. His hands were gloved, something smooth and rubberized, but with only three fingers. He never spoke. He never made a sound at all. He only sat on a toy chest at the far end of my room, hidden in shadow that my parents could not see through.

I don't know how long he was there before I noticed him. It could have been weeks, or even months—he melded with the familiar shadows of my bedroom. One night, kept awake by bad dreams and dark thoughts, I saw the toe of his boot in a strip of moonlight that crept in through the blinds. The sight stopped my heart and I held my breath, at the age where I was still terrified of what I didn't know, but mostly expected to find relief in truth. Many times I felt that grip of fear, only to determine a moment later I was looking at a fold in a blanket, or an upside down toy. So I waited, but the boot remained a boot. Large, black and scuffed, with thick, wavy soles, coated in a fine dust that might have come from the surface of a planet I didn't have a name for.

Neither of us moved as my gaze traveled up his leg, noting a jumpsuit that shone a dull white, appearing intentionally wrinkled. There were no zippers or patches, and the suit was one piece all the way up to that rounded, obsidian helmet. The face shield was obscenely large and pointed in my direction, though there was nothing behind it I could see.

My heart thudded, my breath coming shallow the way it did when I'd been crying hard. My six-year-old mind tried to come up with a rational explanation—was the suit my father's, a Halloween costume or relic of a job I'd never known he'd had? Was it a toy, or some admonitory creature like the elves that watched from hidden places at Christmas time? Was it real? Was it alive?

His chest rose, though I swore it was for the first time.

I whimpered and scooted back in my bed, knocking into the plastic headboard. I wanted to scream, to cry for my parents, but I couldn't, my throat locked and dry. We stared at each other like that until I finally fell asleep, the panic draining me past the point where fear could reach. When I woke in the morning he was gone, but there were boot prints in the carpet where he'd sat. I scuffed them with my feet without knowing why, and said nothing to my parents.

It was months before I saw him again, and somehow I'd forgotten that he'd ever been there. Maybe over time I convinced myself it had been a dream, or a hallucination. Or maybe I hadn't wanted to remember, because that would mean he could come back.

When he did, I wasn't in bed, nor was I alone in my room. It was late, well past midnight, but my mother had woken me from a sound sleep when she'd found the dirt on the steps. I'd swept it there in a fit of anger earlier in the day, resentful of endless chores and punishments. It didn't save me more than the time it would have taken to walk the dustpan to the trash can, but it was my small rebellion, an insurrection I held in my heart. I wasn't allowed to have things like that.

My mother didn't yell, she seethed. She spoke between clenched teeth and thin, colorless lips, each word an accusational thrust. I hadn't just swept dirt onto the stairs—I'd deliberately done it to make her life harder. I didn't care how hard she worked or how tired she was, how she never got a break. I was entitled, a brat, spoiled and selfish.

Tears rolled down my face, but I didn't open my mouth: there was no point in arguing. I stepped backward with each of her jabs, which angered her more, and her eyes got smaller, her body shaking with barely contained rage. I knew this wasn't really her, but I couldn't think of a way to reach her and call my real mother back. I stumbled over a toy in my path, something plastic and hard that jammed into my bare foot, and I fell backward.

I felt something strange under my hand, an object I couldn't identify. I looked down as my mother's shadow loomed over me and saw my fingers splayed along the top of a big, scuffed boot. The memory of the Starman came back all at once, and I looked up to find that empty, black glass looking down at me. Fear froze me solid for several seconds, then my mother snarled something that made me retreat further, pressed against the Starman's knee.

She hadn't seen him until that moment, and when she did, she went silent and still. I watched her face, my senses scrambling between fear of her reaction, and a desperate wish for her to become my mother again and protect me. The Starman's leg against my shoulder was solid, the fabric of his jumpsuit soft against my skin. The helmet lifted and pointed at my mother.

She said nothing, and neither did he, but her face fell into shadow, her lips twitching into an unrecognizable shape. Not a smile, nor yet a sneer, and her eyes were wide above it. The standoff lasted for what felt like forever, until she turned and left the room, mumbling something unintelligible as she turned my light out.

Left alone in the dark with the Starman, my fear returned, and I scuttled away from him. He made no movement beyond the rise and fall of his chest, but I was afraid to get off the floor, or to do anything that might shatter the brittle silence between us. I got cold and my eyes grew heavy, and when I woke in the morning I was alone on the floor with the quilt from my bed pulled up to my chin.

Mom never mentioned the Starman. When I went downstairs the next morning, she was making toast. Not remorseful, not angry: it was as though nothing had happened. I was afraid if I brought it up, I would bring her ire back down upon me, so once again I hid the presence of my visitor. It made me wonder, though. Was he a monster from beyond our skies, or a guardian angel sent to protect me?

He slid once again from my memory, the truth of him like a black oil that wouldn't stick to the wrinkles of my child's brain. Sometimes when I saw a picture of the moon landing, or a shuttle launch, the sight of those helmeted men and women made my heart pound, my mouth dry, but childhood is filled with unnameable, barely understood terrors. It could have been the idea of all that deep, black, space, with nothing to catch you if you found yourself cut adrift. I dreamed that way, sometimes. Of an umbilicus floating before me in zero gravity, severed from what must have been home. Falling forever, arms out, nothing to ground me: a portrait of alone. It was peaceful.

Time passed. I grew taller, but not much. More confident, but not much. A shadow girl flickering around the edges of other people's lives, there one moment and gone as soon as no one was looking at me. I was never in any trouble at school. Good student, quiet, eager to please. I'd later come to view these as glaring red flags, with the benefit of adult experience and empathy, but back then, it wasn't much. People got angry. Parents got angry. It was life, and no one was beating or starving me. I was safe. I just didn't feel that way.

The next time I saw my Starman, he took my mother away. I was twelve, an awkward age, and I spent most of my time crying or trying not to. School, home, it didn't matter—I was thin-skinned, with no social skills, and received ample evidence on a daily basis that I wasn't getting anything right. All I wanted to do when I finally escaped to my upstairs bedroom was lay on my bed and listen to music. Tori Amos, Sheryl Crow, Alanis Morissette, and *The Crow* soundtrack. Music to help me sink into sadness while I contemplated whether the future held anything better for me, or if I was staring down the barrel of decades of the same. I didn't even play my music that loud, but my peace was always short lived.

Things got out of hand, like they often did, always my fault. I didn't have the right answers, the ones I should have known, and everything I said fanned the flames of my mother's smoldering temper. By then I was taller than her, by an inch or so, and my depressive eating meant I probably outweighed her, or came close. Still I cowered in her presence, that fury an unknown beast with unknowable limits. I remember wishing, maybe even praying, for her to go away and leave me alone. Just stop screaming, stop spraying my face with spittle and backing me into a corner, the way we always ended up.

I remembered that later, that I had prayed.

He stood before either of us knew he was there. Between one breath and the next he was a looming shadow at my shoulder. I looked down and saw his boot aligned with my own bare foot, felt his cold at my back, and my memory returned.

This time I didn't flinch from him. I remembered the way he'd faced the changeling of hatred that inhabited my mother from time to time, and how that empty, black glass had tamed her. Taken the fight right out of her, sent her back down the stairs to inhabit her own troubled mind, leaving me out of it. I was tired, and sick with crying, and I wanted it over. I didn't know what over meant.

I stepped aside, giving him full access to my mother, and waited for the storm to calm. The sight of him had the same silencing effect as the last time—Mom's face twisted, her mouth hung open, and the yelling stopped. She stood and panted in the middle of my bedroom, staring up at a face of onyx nothing, and my own breathing calmed. She would leave again, and I'd be okay.

But the Starman didn't stop there. He stepped closer, looked down into my mother's face, and the pace of her breathing increased. Her expression didn't change, and her eyes stayed focused where they had been, where he'd been standing seconds before. It was like she was frozen in place, and it struck me how vulnerable she was like that.

The Starman loomed closer still, leaning in, the smooth glass of his face shield almost touching my mother. I thought he might be studying her, wondering what made her tick and her springs come loose. Then he reached out and in one fluid movement, he grasped her wrist and twisted her to the floor.

She hit with barely a sound, just a muted huff of air as the breath was forced from her lungs. He must have been holding her up by her twisted wrist, supporting her body weight on that fragile joint. It would have hurt like hell but she never uttered another sound. The Starman dragged her across my carpeted bedroom floor, the fabric of his jumpsuit making a low *shooshing* sound as he moved. My mother's eyes remained fixed on the empty ceiling, her legs dragging boneless behind her.

It took me too long to react, to move away from my vantage point against the wall. The place where I'd cowered away from her, but now I didn't know where she was going, where the Starman was taking her. Muted thuds came from the narrow staircase that led to the main part of the house, and the last thing I saw was my mother's hair trailing down the steps. Curling, auburn shot with lighter threads, in need of a trim. It slinked down the last stair before the 90 degree turn took her out of sight.

I should have followed them. Maybe to stop what happened, or even just to know, to see it for myself. Instead I sat on the top step and waited for someone older than me to come and tell me what my new truth was. I didn't expect her to be gone, not forever, but that was what happened. Dad asked me questions, over and over. *What happened? Where were you?*

"Where were you?" I responded finally, and that shut him up. I didn't understand why, back then, too naive to know what his constant absences and whispered phone calls signified. I wasn't concerned with that —my parent's marriage was inherently uninteresting. I wanted to know why he'd never been there for anything else. Why he'd let me get pushed to the point where I'd offer a prayer to a dark god I didn't understand. One who was always listening, even if I couldn't see him. I couldn't ask those questions, and he wouldn't have been able to answer, anyway. Over the next weeks and months, the only question we had left centered around whether Mom was ever coming back.

Dad thought she would. He told me so every night before I went to bed, the dry skin of his face crinkling in an attempt at consolation. He was afraid of being alone with me, of having full responsibility for an adolescent, but I didn't mind it just being us. He left me alone for the most part, and life got quiet. I knew by then it would be permanent, that wherever the Starman took her, it wasn't the kind of journey that was ever round trip. I watched out my window on moonless nights, staring at the endless stars above. I didn't want her back. I was looking for him, until his memory slipped away from me again. After that I just watched the night sky and didn't understand why, only that it gave me a sense of obsidian peace.

The last time he came for me was just before I moved out to go to college, halfway across the country from a life I'd never settled into. It was late, but I couldn't sleep, staring up at the faded green glow-in-the dark stars I'd affixed to my ceiling in haphazard patterns years ago. Everybody had them back then, but mine were special. They meant more, even if the reason escaped me. I had a connection with the stars, both inside and out, and they were the only things I dreaded leaving behind.

A shadow shifted next to my bed, and when my gaze followed the movement, the Starman was there, standing between me and my lamp. As had happened every time before, all my memories of him came back at once, reflected against his blank face-plate. My breath came fast and I sat up, the covers pulled up high, but not far enough to hide him from sight.

We watched each other as the seconds ticked by, and he never moved. Fear-laced adrenaline rocketed through my veins, my stomach churning until I tasted bile at the back of my throat. "You're back," I said finally, my voice thin and dry.

He offered no response, silent as ever.

"Mom?" I asked.

The Starman gave a single shake of his head, confirming what I already knew. She wasn't coming back.

I tried to parse how I felt about it, but there was nothing much below the top layer of fear that was slowly subsiding.

"Is it my fault?" I asked, unsure if I cared what the answer was.

He gave another negatory shake, and pointed a gloved, three fingered hand behind him, where my mother had stood six years ago, and six years before that.

I didn't know if I could accept that, but I wasn't going to try tonight. I sat up straighter, letting the blanket fall to my lap. I looked at him for longer than I'd ever been allowed to, taking in his height, his slim build, his jumpsuit. It was the same one he'd worn each time he'd visited me, and that seemed right. I was the outlying planet, the far away star he came for. He needed to dress for the atmosphere, for the cold. But beneath the suit, strange knobs and ridges rose. I couldn't make sense of them, their pattern, how it would look on his uncovered skin. What was he? Where had he come from? I focused on his face shield, seeing my own expression reflected back.

"Why are you here?" I asked, wondering only after the words had escaped whether he was capable of speaking my language. He could understand it, but would his anatomy even let him form the words? I both wanted to hear his voice, and feared it.

This time he pointed at me, his hand moving slow until a single, thick finger was leveled at my chest. He left it there, unwavering, inches away from my breastbone.

"I don't understand," I said. "She's gone. I'm safe, aren't I?"

He extended the hand back again, toward the window now. To the dark sky and stars beyond.

"Out there?" I asked as my mind caught up to the full import of what he was offering. A flash of fear returned, the feeling of endless space behind me. I dug my fingers into my bed like it was the only thing anchoring me to gravity.

The Starman brought his hands together, pulling the rubberized glove from one and extending it toward me again.

All my focus was on the small expanse of flesh I could see, the first time the Starman had laid any part of himself bare in my presence. His skin was pinkish brown, gnarled and shiny, his three digits more the shape of a crab's pincer claw, but each looked solid. They were spread wide, an open invitation. I reached out and touched him, my fingers grazing his flesh. It felt hot and mobile, as though something moved beneath the surface. His hand closed around mine, but lightly, and we both looked toward the window.

"I don't know," I said, and it was the truth. The idea of open space was terrifying, sweat breaking out on my upper lip, my hands trembling. It was too big to wrap my head around, and hostile. No guarantee I could survive out there—did the Starman have a ship? A planet to return to? I had my life planned out— college, a master's in teaching, then working in schools, keeping an eye out for children like the one I'd been. It was the first time I'd had anything to look forward to since the magic of Christmas died years ago. It was a future I wanted, could envision. Out there among the cold stars was a complete unknown.

So why did the idea of letting go of the Starman's hand fill me with such melancholy? I could see myself walking to the window with him, stepping out into the night like Wendy with Peter Pan, flying through the dark in the clothes I slept in. I'd never sought exhilaration, wasn't even sure I'd ever felt it. I was a fearful, mousy soul, afraid of losing my way, of never coming back.

And that was a certainty. The Starman only offered one-way journeys. Mom never came back, and I didn't believe she was flying through the cosmos. She was dead and gone, by methods unknown. It was possible she'd suffered. If I went with him, the Starman might kill me, too. I didn't think so—he'd given my mother no choice. There'd been no hand extended, just a swift departure, her head banging every step on her way out of my life. I didn't believe he would do that to me, but I didn't know.

"I want to," I whispered. "But I can't."

He watched me from behind his helmet for several seconds more before he dropped my hand and fitted his glove back on. Was he disappointed? Angry? Sad?

Would I ever get another chance?

I was too slow to find my voice, and he was gone before I could ask. My bedroom seemed emptier than it had before he'd appeared, and a deep loneliness took hold of my insides. It felt like part of me had gone with him, my future splitting into two selves, one of whom was getting further away by the second. I threw my covers back and went to the window, wondering if I could catch a glimpse of him. I didn't, but I sat up for a long time watching, determined this time to hold tight to my memories of him.

But of course I didn't. I had no control over that, and though I wrote some of it down, the ink on those pages faded and ran, and later when I flipped through my notebook, I tore them out and threw them away. They were useless after all, illegible, so whatever thoughts I'd scribbled there were lost.

Years passed. I finished college, stayed on track and became a middle school science teacher, focusing on studying outer space, my classroom walls papered with pictures of the surface of the moon, the vastness of the stars. In my head was where

I kept the other facts I'd gathered, the images I'd seen of everything that can kill you in space. It was a macabre obsession, poring over stories of space flight disasters: explosions, decompression, solar flares. I was equal parts drawn to that great, dark unknown, and terrified by the inhospitable environment. Humans are survivors, it's coded in our DNA, but in space, help is either non-existent or too far away to matter.

I didn't lay that on the kids, though. I wanted them to be excited, to focus on the possibilities and all the things we didn't know. I'd chosen middle school because it was the most vulnerable age group, the most in need of help, and the least likely to ask for it. It didn't come easy: I battled against bureaucracy everyday, an avalanche of it, determined to get in the way of me making a difference. And the kids weren't always open to help, even the ones who were in real trouble. I hadn't counted on how inured they were to their lives, but I should have. Mine had seemed normal to me, way back when. Still I pushed on, growing tired but never disillusioned. There were nights, though, when I sat at my bedroom window and watched the skies. I felt like I'd lost something out there,

someone I could have been, and I wondered if it was her I was looking for.

The Starman never came for me again, after that last time, his offer of a life path that branched far from my own. The next time I saw him, he was there for my daughter.

I hadn't planned on becoming a mother. I was afraid I couldn't do it right, that some hidden darkness inside me would spring free, turning me into a fury-spewing version of myself. By the time I got pregnant with Madeline, those fears had faded in the face of my work with children. I was patient with my students, thoughtful, and careful of their emotions. I thought I was safe; that she was safe. I dropped my guard against the worst parts of myself.

Madeline's father worked third shift, something I didn't foresee as being a problem before she was born. But those were long nights with no sleep, and long days with even less. I was alone with my baby most of the time, and though I loved her with my entire soul, I felt my patience fraying. One night when she was six weeks old, she'd been crying non-stop, resisting all my efforts to get her to sleep. I thought I'd finally done it, as her heavy lids had slowly closed, her dimpled chin falling to her chest. I held my breath, counted to twenty. When she didn't move, I eased from the floor by her crib. Her eyes popped open and she began to shriek, as far from rest as she'd ever been.

I felt exhaustion in every cell of my body, pressing down on me with a physical weight. I burst into tears myself. "Fine," I snarled, lurching to my feet. "Take care of your damn self."

Her cries escalated as I stumbled to her bedroom door, guilt already gnawing at my heart, but I had to get out. I had to breathe without the pressure of constant demands for my attention, so I kept going, though she was swiftly working herself into a purple fit.

I closed the door behind me, and the noise was gone. Like flipping a switch, and for a moment I wondered if that was what she'd needed—solitude, perhaps, or one more good fuss to send her to dreamland. I wanted to feel relief, to take the break I'd sought, but the silence was so wrong. A cold dread settled into my belly. With shaking hands, I opened the nursery door again and went to her crib.

Madeline was quiet, her blue eyes open wide, but her feet were kicking, her lips blowing little spit bubbles. The looming fear of SIDS settled back into my hind brain, and I stood and watched her. Her fuzzy gaze pointed straight up, beyond where the useless mobile spun in lazy circles. My eyes followed her sight line, where they caught on a light hanging midway up the wall. There was no light there—the wall behind my daughter's crib was painted with a mural of stars in a purple sky.

My heart froze, two beats ahead of my brain. I was seeing Madeline's unicorn night light on the opposite wall, reflected on a smooth, glass surface. My breath coming quick and shallow, my hands like blocks of ice, I searched the darkness for what I knew I'd see. The Starman resolved from the shadows, needing only my notice to reveal himself, looming over my baby, close enough to touch her. He was still and silent while my memories slid back in place, those missing pieces restored. A stab of regret for the choice I'd made all those years ago—a life among the stars, silent peace and dark flight. Myself reflected in his blank face shield, the me I could have been staring back at me, distorted.

But that wasn't why he was here. Not this time. His empty gaze was on me, his very presence an admonition. I was fucking up. Becoming my mother, as I'd vowed never to do. Everything came back in full force. Every aching memory of a hurt left unaddressed, an explosive reaction to an innocent omission, the knowledge that at any time the earth could tilt beneath my feet and deposit me in some half world, where people looked like themselves but behaved like dangerous strangers.

Tears streaked my cheeks, shame at my short temper making me feel like the worst kind of mother. I looked at my little girl, her sweet rounded cheeks, her chubby hands with perfect tiny knuckles, and felt the weight of my failures. Any ache for the life not chosen was swept away—had I gone with the Starman when he'd asked, I would never have had Madeline. Nothing could make up for that, and the thought of that regret twisted my heart.

I looked back into the unforgiving, blank visage of the Starman. "Are you here to take me, then? Like you did my mother?"

He said nothing, and his hands remained at his sides. I thought of when he'd reached for me, the three strange digits offering to take me to the stars. I knew the next time he reached for me, I'd have no choice, and it would be my head bumping down the stairs on the way out of my daughter's life.

I slid to the floor where I could be close to Madeline and watched her eyes close, her chest rise and fall. She slept, but I did not.

Not then, and very little in the following days. I had to stay vigilant against myself, and the Starman. This time my memories didn't fade, and instead I saw him in every dark corner of the house, no matter the time of day. He wasn't really there, just his specter, reminding me. Warning me to walk the line lest I be flung to the heavens.

Fatigue drained me, but fear kept me going. That little spike of adrenaline that shot through my body each time I imagined those unforgiving boots, or a reflection in a place where there shouldn't be one. When I was too tired to move, I sat with Madeline and watched her with hungry eyes. As hard as I was trying, as much as I suppressed my impatience, it felt as though our time together was short. All my old fears bubbled to the surface, until I could barely move for fear of something happening to my baby. My mind ran a constant loop of images from hell—the worst possible occurrence in every situation. If I shaved my legs, I pictured the razor slicing my sweet girl's skin. If I turned on a gas burner, I saw the flame burning her flesh. Each time I filled up the tub for her bath, I checked the water temperature over and over, terrified of scalding her. The pictures in my head wouldn't stop coming, and they filled me with horror. There was no desire to carry out any of these terrors, but what kind of mother was I, that they came to mind at all?

My husband noticed, and so did my few friends. They told me to give myself grace, that no one had to get it perfect all the time. They didn't understand. They didn't know the dark depths I guarded against.

It made no difference. No matter how strictly I policed myself, no matter how hard I prayed for patience, I could feel my temper rising, becoming a beast I wouldn't be able to control for long. I don't know when I reached the decision to go, coming upon it gradually, but once I acknowledged it, the Starman was there.

I'd been expecting him, and looked at him from streaming eyes. "Give me a moment?" I asked.

He didn't answer, but neither did he stop me when I made my way to Madeline's crib. She slept in a yellow, footed pajama onesie, her small hands curled into fists up by her head. I didn't want to wake her, so I just looked, and grief threatened to engulf me. My chest was tight, my heart breaking at the knowledge of what I was giving up. I'd never see my girl take her first steps, or start school, or find her own path apart from her parents and her past.

But neither would I burden her. She could step onto whatever path she chose without anything weighing her down. And if I were honest, there was relief in the decision to let go. I wasn't good enough, never would be, and it was freeing to give up trying. I could finally become that other self, choosing one loss over another. The Starman stood at my shoulder, and I took a step back from my daughter, ready to give myself to his care.

I stepped onto nothing, my foot plunging into a void, my weight already off balance, and down I went, backward into blackness. My stomach flipped and fear froze my lungs, but even I couldn't hear my scream as I drifted downward. A slow flight away from everything I knew, my tether to the world severed and getting further away. I could still see my daughter, growing smaller as I fell. It was the peace I'd dreamed of, but the fear as well. I was weightless and so damn cold, ice crystals forming at the corners of my eyes. I struggled to take another breath and found that it wasn't fear that had locked my chest: there was no air in space. Panic hit me and I looked for the Starman—this wasn't right. He was down below me looking up, one hand on the rail of Madeline's crib.

Why? I tried to scream the question but I had no voice and no air. My lungs had collapsed and I felt them freezing, my organs being crushed in slow motion. My vision blurred as the pressure squeezed my eyes but I could still make out his hand coming up to his helmet, the face plate rising. Obsidian nothing was replaced with a visage that sliced through what remained of my sanity.

It was my own face, ravaged from years of radiation exposure, the burn of solar flares, the collision of subatomic particles. The version of me that stared back at myself had no nose, the hole where it should have been covered over by twisted, melted flesh. One eye had slid halfway down the cheek, and teeth were exposed in the thin parts of the flesh of its jowls. Still I recognized myself, and the other side of regret. She—I—had made another choice, and now she wanted what I had instead of what she'd become. The last thing I saw before the oxygen-drained blood hit my brain was a hand of melded digits reaching into the crib for my little girl. And I'd been right—the release of consciousness and life came as a relief from the agony of feeling my body freeze and crush from the inside out. I became one with the dead space beyond our world, endlessly adrift in the dark.

THE FLOCK

MARISCA PICHETTE

It started with a pimple, or a wart. She found it in the morning as she was putting her hair up in the mirror. It glared out from her elbow, cold and hard to the touch. That afternoon, she went to the dermatologist.

He glanced at it over his clipboard. "It's benign," he said, and turned her back out onto the street. So she took it home with her.

As the weeks passed, it grew. She put on long sleeves, pulling them down to her wrists. But soon the lump stuck out enough to poke through the sweaters she layered to keep it down.

She tried to freeze it off herself, but it only grew larger, splitting down the middle, two halves forcing themselves apart. She took to wearing a coat the moment September hit, but had to buy one two sizes too big just so it would fit over the projection. The elbow wore out so fast, it was a waste of money. Eventually, she resorted to binding her arm in a sling.

The halves broke at last while she was on the bus, and a horrible shrieking honk escaped her bandages. Faces turned to stare at her, judging her lack of control. She got off at the next stop and walked the rest of the way home, holding the beak closed with her free hand.

It was hard even to sleep. She could never get comfortable with it pecking at the sheets and grunting in the night. Each morning she woke to it honking as the very first finger of dawn stole between the blinds.

She pulled a piece of Scotch tape around it, but it struggled against this gag, until at last it pushed forward enough to see what she was doing, one black and beady eye peering out from her arm like an angry mole. It shrieked when she removed the tape, so she put it back in layers.

When the other lumps began appearing, she returned to the dermatologist. He tried to examine her, but the beak stirred up such a din of honking and pecking that at last he fled, leaving her alone and naked in the examining room,

bumps forming on her knees and ankles and wrists. She took some medical tape for her elbow and walked home.

Her knee was the next to give her trouble, kicking out with webbed feet whenever she tried to set her laptop down. She invested in a lapdesk that hovered just out of reach, designed specially for cases such as hers. At last she could work in peace, goosefeet bicycling lazily below.

She carried a DustBuster with her whenever she went out, to vacuum up any feathers she chanced to drop. Finding clothes that fit her now was beyond difficult. Anything adapted to her state wouldn't accommodate more than a songbird or two, and her flock was growing every day. Ponchos and long skirts were her new staple.

Everywhere she went, kicking, flapping, and jabbering accompanied her. She forsook public transportation and Ubered instead, since driving was impossible with the wings on her wrists. Sometimes she and her driver had interesting conversations dotted with intermittent honks and hoots where the tape failed. Sometimes her driver said nothing, and she apologised in the comments when she left droppings on the seat, adding a five-star rating for good measure.

She ended up quitting her job, and when her boss called asking why, her response was drowned out by honking and screeching. White wings beat the phone out of her hand. She knelt down to grab it, but one webbed foot kicked it away under the sofa. She never did manage to retrieve it.

At least then, she thought, she could rest. But she could not longer sleep. Each night she tossed and turned, shivering as the wings and feet kicked away the covers and thumped against the mattress. She woke covered in bruises and scratches, feathers in her hair.

One cold morning she slithered out of bed and padded down into the basement, careful not to wake them.

She hunted through tools, tossing aside knives and axes and rusted-out shields, her toes curling on the damp mud floor. She turned out mice from their homes in old cardboard boxes and patiently deconstructed spider webs. All the while, her flock slumbered on.

At the bottom of a cracked breastplate she found the blowtorch. It took her several more minutes to locate the sparker; the wings on her wrists didn't allow her to use flint and steel.

She sat down and placed the torch between her feet. Her legs trembled as webbed toes scrabbled suddenly to life, sensing danger. She had to hold the sparker with both hands, her fingers gone numb and cold and covered with the ticklish tendrils of webs, softer than down.

Sparks broke the shadows and the tape curled back, releasing the beaks. They set up a howling, eyes swiveling with fear to fix on the flame. She turned the torch on her elbow first, setting fire to the original head. Feathers smoked and burned.

Next were the wings. She rotated the torch to face her own wrists. They crumbled away from her skin to litter the basement floor.

Next, her knees. She roasted the feet and broke them off with her hands, feeling them crunch between her fingers.

The beaks on her ankles quaked before her fire, dying with a thin wail.

Free, she filled her hands with the dirt of the floor and rubbed it into the wounds, grinding soil and rocks into her skin, smoothing out the tears in her body. When she was done, she switched off the torch and climbed the stairs back into the house.

She paused in the kitchen, pulling a feather out of her hair.

Outside, it had begun to snow, fat flakes drifting to cover the trees. She shut her eyes, rubbing away the bumps that threatened to rise on her bare arms. It was quiet.

WHAT BONES THESE TIDES BRING

NIKKY LEE

The ocean is angry today. Its waves pound the sandbar; pummel the beach in a roar of white static. I tiptoe over the sand, basket in hand, studying what the water has brought me. Driftwood here, cuttlefish there. Into the basket they go. Driftwood for the fire, cuttlefish to trade to the carvers.

Overhead the sky rumbles, and the wind sends sheets of stinging sand against my legs. I push on. Water claws its way up the beach before the tide drags it back in silting, swirling currents that would drown even the Olwerld's strongest swimmers.

Still, I search the black sand, one eye on the angry water. One freak wave and it's over. I'll sink like the Olwerld did. Yet despite the danger crashing not fifty metres away, my gnarled fingers trail through weed and kelp, over rocks, searching for a catch.

Because when the ocean is angry, it coughs up the best trinkets.

The best bones.

At last, something smooth and rubbery brushes my hand. I double down, digging into the sand, feeling out its shape with my fingers until I recognise it. A boot.

I unearth it in a spray of sand and salt, and the roar of the ocean fades away as I run my hands over it, barely able to contain my excitement. Cracked leather, rubber sole, laces long gone. Definitely Olwerld. I burrow my hand inside the same way a bird might eat a snail, fingers scrabbling through the sand as I hunt for the morsel inside. But with every scoop I lift out, the lower my spirits sink. If there were Olwerld bones in here, I should have found them by now. I reach the heel, nothing. Arch, nothing. The toe is empty too, and I up-end the boot and beat it out on the beach. Noth—

A faint 'plick' of something hard bounces off a beach rock. I dive to my hands and knees, scouring the sand again. Where? *Where, where, wh—*

My fingers close around a tiny bone no bigger than my thumbnail. And the moment they do, I feel the weight of it hit my chest. *Yes. Someone's home.*

A gust of wind brings me back to the beach. The rain that has been threatening all morning has arrived in big, fat drops, pelting the sand like hail. I tuck the bone into the pouch around my neck and slip it under my oilskin.

"I'll wake you up soon, sweetie."

I blink open my eyes. A dim room blinks open with them. Blurred and dingy. Another blink and the room sharpens: damp plywood walls, threadbare carpet. A cast iron fireplace squats in the middle of the room flanked by an array of pots and pans. Overhead, a single lightbulb hums. It flickers. Once.

Where am I?

"Welcome back, sweetie."

I whirl on the voice, coming eye-to-eye with a weather-beaten face full of hard lines and yellowed teeth. A tangle of grey hair tumbles from the woman's head, wrapping over her shoulder in a snarled braid. In one hand, she holds a small iron-looking box, lid open, and I glimpse an array of baubles inside before she closes it.

"Do you remember your name?" she asks.

"Riley," I say, without thinking. The moment it is past my lips, the woman sucks in a breath, as if she's breathing in the scent of my name. Weakness grips my knees, and my vision goes hazy again. *How did I get here? Where is here?*

Overhead, the lightbulb's hum rises to a buzz.

"It's okay," she tells me. "Relax."

And against every instinct, I do. The building tension in my neck and shoulders slackens; the churning knot in my stomach stills.

"Good," she says. "The first awakening is always hardest."

Awakening? But before I can ask, she points over my shoulder. "Tell me what that is."

Confused, I follow her gesture to a floor-to-ceiling set of shelves on the wall behind me. Every inch is crammed with junk: old nails, curled up bits of wire, a dog's collar, several tattered and mould-covered books, a birdcage – all of it and more piled on top of each other like a hoarder's shrine. There must be close to a hundred knickknacks on those shelves, but somehow, I know exactly which item she wants me to name. Second shelf from the bottom, third item along. A small box and screen with laminate curling off its sides.

"It's an old TV," I say. "Analogue." I crouch before it and lean in for a closer look. The screen is too dusty to show my reflection. "I haven't seen one of these since I was a kid." I make to wipe the dust away, but something in me jerks my arm still.

The woman speaks again. "And that?"

My attention is pulled along the shelf. To a flat device lying beside a teddy bear with both button eyes missing and stuffing bursting through the seam of one arm. I examine the dark screen and the black mould trapped around the edge of the casing.

"Smartphone," I say, and my hands automatically pat the back pocket of my jeans for the familiar shape and weight I already know is missing. Another lost phone. I bite back a groan. Mum is going to *kill* me. Panic stabs through me. *Where is Mum?* The last thing I remember was my hand in hers, our fingers wrapped so tight, and so cold. I try to picture the scene, pull the memory out of the haze of shapes and sounds in my head. It's so close, like a forgotten word on the tip of my tongue.

Our hands clasped. Mum's fingers around mine as I pulled her along. That's right, we were running. Running from something. Something big. Terrifying. Until Mum doubled over in the street, gasping.

"Riley, slow down, I can't–"

"Post digital then." The rasp of the old woman snaps me back with a start, and the thread of memory breaks. I claw after it. Something was hiding in that moment. Something important. But the memory is gone. I blink around the room, look at the hunched woman again. Really look. Her knitted jumper has holes at the elbows. Two odd shoes grace her feet. But what catches my attention is the iron box in her hands. It's the size of a large jewellery box, vintage looking with swirling patterns on its lid, which she clicks shuts as she places something inside.

"Who are you?"

Her grin is all teeth. "You can call me Mable."

"What is this place?"

Her grey eyes fix on me, irises dark and swirling. Like storm clouds. *Like the sea.* Panic I can't explain stirs inside me. *Like the sea.* The hairs on my arms go on end. Something big looms at the edge of my memory, but like my childhood monster under the bed, I'm too afraid to look.

Outside, the shrill cry of a fantail cuts through the air.

"Go back to sleep, my sweet," Mable coos.

My eyelids droop before I even realise what she's said. *Wait, no.* I fight against the overpowering urge to sleep. But it's too late. My mind is drifting. *Wait!* I manage to crack an eye open and find my perspective's changed. It's as if I've shrunk to the size of a button, a full-on *Alice in Wonderland* moment. Mable's enormous face hovers over me, so close I can see the dimpled pores on her wind-blasted cheeks.

Wait! I try to scream, but nothing comes out. I try to rise, but my body is gone.

"You'll feel better next time I wake you, sweetie," Mable says.

And something heavy and iron slams shut above me.

Her bone is cold when I retrieve it from my bone box and spark her awake again. Unlike the first time, her body coalesces hard and fast, flaring into consciousness with a form so solid I can barely see the floor and walls through her. Seas be, she's a strong one. *And all mine.* It's all I can do to contain my glee as she glares and finally asks the right question.

"What are you?"

I sink into the old rocking chair, placing the box on my lap and curling my hands around it. "I'm a bone collector."

Her blank look confirms what I suspected. She's from *before*. The chair creaks as I rock, and I wonder how much I should reveal. How far I can push. A broken spirit is no use to anyone.

The ghost's ethereal eyes – a faint translucent silver – fix on me, clearly waiting for an explanation. So, I uncurl my hand to reveal the yellow bone in my palm.

She goes still. Perhaps she senses her connection to it. Perhaps, deep down, she already knows she's dead.

"Is that…?"

"A bone." I watch her. *Gently does it.* "Yours."

Her form shivers, edges bristling. She points to her foot. "It's *not* my–" And stops. Stares at her boot and the floor we can both see through it. She doesn't scream. Just slumps. Curls into herself on my carpet and burrows her face into her knees. She doesn't cry. *Brave girl.* Braver than others I've broken the news to.

At last, her gaze seeks me out through her knees. "How?"

I crook an eyebrow. "You don't remember?"

"I remember running. I–" Her focus drifts, expression stilling. "…there was water. It was everywhere."

My chair releases a squeak as I stop mid-rock. "Wait, you were *there*?" I say it too quick. Too harsh. Not the right tone for a ghost I'm trying to coax awake. But she lifts her head, even as her translucent limbs tense.

"Was I where?"

I mutter a curse. No putting that cat back. "The end of the world. The Olwerld. Your time."

The ghost stares at me. "It ended?"

"It did. Many died. Billions." I tap a gnarled finger on her bone in my palm and she twitches. "We woke up the ocean and he swallowed us up. Including you, it seems." *A scholar would pay a pretty penny for you indeed.* But this ghost is mine. For me.

A throaty *aarrk-aarrk-aarrk* cuts through the air, making us both jump. Gannet. Even through the door, his warning is clear. *Strangers are coming.* Without thinking, I grab the bone and plunge my power into it, grasping the spirit's essence and pulling it up and out.

Riley gasps, clutches herself. "What are you–"

I thrust her essence into the first shell I see: the Olwerld teddy bear. There's a hiss of static as I release her and the speaker inside the bear's chest crackles, releasing a slow *'I wuuuuuv yooou mooooommmmmaa'* before my power closes around her like a fist.

"Shhh," I tell the ghost inside the toy. "Don't fight. Just watch."

A haggard, bearded face greets me when I open the door. But it's not the beard nor the faded camouflage jacket that I recognise first. It's the eyes. I've not seen many living people with dead eyes, but Warden Wyman has them. There's a hard emptiness in them that chills me, and not for the first time I wonder what happened to make him that way.

"You've come I long way," I observe.

He holds up a duffle bag. "Outta juice," he says, pushing his way across the threshold. Behind him, Gannet releases an *aarrk* and darts out of his shell – a taxidermied gannet I leave on the doorstep – and slaps his way in after Wyman. His transparent feet leave no prints on the carpet.

I ignore the ghost bird – he's part of the furniture now – but Wyman's gaze follows it like feral cat sizing up a kill. Things must be bad in the settlement if he's eyeballing a measly bird spirit. I point to the driftwood table before the fireplace. "Show me."

Wyman unzips the duffle, revealing a battered radio transceiver. "Cole says the kit's fine. But the power's gone." His last words angle at me like an accusing finger.

I meet his glare, and something flickers in those dead eyes as they shift from me, to my bone box on the rocking chair, then back to me. Fear. *Not all dead then.* I smile sweetly. "Are you trying to say I sold you a dud?" My swollen knuckles creak as I uncurl my palm and wait.

Wyman hesitates, then grudgingly hands over a carved owl. The wood is polished smooth with age, the paint long faded. Still, I feel it's significance. The weight of its mana. This was important to someone once. Treasured. Like all shells are. It's no bigger than his palm, perfect for a man on the move as much as he is. It's why I sold it to him to house his ghost.

"Did you rest it as I instructed?"

He nods. "It doesn't work."

I turn the owl over in my hands, then nudge a bit of my power into it. Not a lot. Wyman won't get a free recharge unless he pays. Just enough to make the spirit inside spark.

A ten-year-old boy coalesces on the table, his cut-off jeans and singlet exactly the same as the last time I'd woken him. Unlike last time, his shape is horribly faint. A suggestion of a boy, really. More silhouette than spirit.

I purse my lips. "Rested it, did you? You all but burnt it out."

"I did rest it! Every night, just like you said." He's gaining steam, voice rising, shoulders squaring. "It worked the radio fine the first month, but now–" He hucks up a wad of spit on my floor, right at the silhouette's feet. "Useless. I paid you *six months* of supplies. You promised me the best. This ghost can't even turn on a bulb."

"Sit *down*." I snap my power at the man, brushing the inner essence that makes Wyman *Wyman*. Spirit, soul, whatever. The same part that remains *after*. It's not much of a touch, more a reminder why bone collectors are respected. Revered. Not lectured like a browbeaten sap.

Wyman immediately stops. Everything. His breath. His heart. His whole body stiffening.

"Do not lecture me, *boy*." I hold him more a moment more, then release him. The air whistles out of his lungs and his knees buckle. He catches himself on the arm of my rocking chair, nearly pitching over again. I jab his chest, forcing his attention to my accusing finger and away from the tremble in my legs. Working with ghosts is one thing, working on the living is quite another. The living take a lot of power.

"How *long* did you let it rest?" I demand. "How many *hours*?"

Wyman gawps at me. "Three hours," he manages at last. "The radio is unmanned from midnight to 3am."

Three hours? *Seas be.* It's a miracle it lasted a month. "A ghost isn't an Olwerld machine, Wyman. It needs rest. *Decent* rest," I add as Wyman opens his mouth. "No spirit can power a machine twenty-one hours day for a month without burning out. Look at it." I wave at what's left of the ghost. "It can barely keep itself corporeal." I fold my arms and harrumph. "You think you didn't get quality? Most wouldn't last a week."

The Warden seems mollified by that. At least, he's gone quiet, though his gaze fixes on Gannet again, those hard eyes watching my ghost bird in a way that puts my hackles on edge.

"We *need* the radio," he says. "Everything goes through it. Trade negotiations, supply runs, hunts, defences. It's our hub, our life-line to the other settlements."

He looks at me with that hard desperation again. His settlement is on the edge, and it is Wyman's job to see it survives. That was the problem. When men like Wyman got desperate, they got dangerous.

And stupid, I think as he glances at Gannet again. Hiding the girl had been a good idea.

"It's going to cost you," I warn. "If you want round-the-clock radio, you're going to need more ghosts." I scoop up my bone box from the rocking chair and give it a rattle. There's the unmistakable 'plink plink' of bones inside. "I have two dog shades each capable of generating three hours' power. That should be enough to let your ghost rest."

Wyman shakes his head. "Shades are unreliable. Can't have it cutting out on us. We need a steady power supply. I want another like the boy. One of your best."

Of course you do. Greedy bastard. I don't look at the teddy and the ghost girl sheltered inside it. She's the strongest I'd found in years. Fully sentient. Near solid. Like hell I'd hand her over.

"I'll need time," I say. "Bones like that are hard to find." At his growing scowl, I add, "You could offer up some of your own. Fresh dead tend to stick around."

His scowl vanishes, and the disgusted look that follows says everything. There's a reason why settlements all cremate their dead.

"Old dead," he says. "No one from the last decade."

I shrug. "It'll cost you more. Can you afford it?"

Wyman's silence goes on so long I wonder if he's reconsidering the dog shades. Eventually he shifts, pulling a slip of paper from his pocket. He hands it over. I claw it open and read, then open my bone box and tuck it inside.

"You'll see it's already signed," he says, and if I hadn't just read his offer, I might have mistaken the edge in his voice as anger. But it's not. It's fear.

I hold out my hand, and he hesitates. "A contract is a piece of paper, easily lost," I say. "This requires as handshake."

He shifts, clear uneasy. Shifts his weight, clances at the door once, as if contemplating escape – he wouldn't be the first – then sighs and holds out his hand. "It's all yours."

I grin. "I accept." And as our palms touch, my power bites down.

I feel oddly rested when Mable pulls me from the teddy. Muscles all soft and limber, like I've climbed from a hot bath. Only I don't have muscles anymore, not really. I hold my hands up and stare through them, making out a crooked kitchenette and an ancient rust-streaked fridge in the room's corner. My stomach squirrels into my spine.

Okay, Riley, be cool. I suck in a shaking breath. Or whatever it is I breathe. *Don't freak out.* The lightbulb overhead flickers, sways again in the ceiling's draft.

With Wyman and his radio gone, Mable has started…well, pottering is the best I can call it. She collects her iron box and with a flick of her wrist, sends the ghost bird into an old record player (middle shelf, fourth item along). The player starts up, and when Mable places the tonearm down on a scratched and warped vinyl record, a tinny song crackles from the speaker. Humming, she lowers herself back into her rocking chair.

"You must have questions," she says.

She's right. A dozen questions crowd my mind. It's a war between my brain and my mouth to pick one.

"What, who, the boy I mean," I gesture at the door. *Focus, Riley.* "That. What was that?"

"What you think it was?"

I want to say it looked like she and Wyman were using a ghost like a fucking battery, but that was insane. Right? Mable folds her hands over the iron box and waits. *Right?* I clear my throat, and as I do, the lightbulb starts up its hum again. *Oh sweet Jesus.*

"You use us for power."

Mable nods. "The sea destroyed the Olwerld's power. Luckily, we found a replacement." Her knobbed fingers flex towards me. "A resource we had plenty of."

Because, of course, humanity would think to exploit the dead. Anger ripples through me. Was that going to be my fate, too?

As if sensing my thought, Mable offers a thin smile that kills my anger cold. "That is the way of it now. The dead's duty is to the living, you've had your time. The living have to work with what we have."

"But—" I begin, still trying to wrap my mind around what she was saying. There were no ghosts before. At least, none that were real. I want to cry 'you can't' or 'I won't', but what comes out is a strangled, "*How?*"

Mable shrugs. "Mana, chi, chakra, spirit, however you call it, I control it. And by extension *you*." She waggles her fingers and a pressure trickles down my spine. "That's what a bone collector is. When the Olwerlder's disrupted the balance, the cities sank, ghosts rose, and this power rose with it."

Her words tumble over me. *When the cities sank...* Goosebumps prickle my neck.

Mum's hand grips mine, so cold. So wet. "Just float, Mum," I say. "I got you." My limbs are heavy, my boots dragging me down. We float in the dark, waiting for the sun to rise as the current pushes and pulls us. Wait for the sun, I think. Wait to know which way to swim.

My tongue turns thick in my throat. I don't remember seeing that sunrise.

I push the memory down and replay Wyman's visit in my head. There's so much I don't understand, but one detail sticks out above the rest. The handshake. The way Wyman slunk out of the hut after had felt *wrong*, like looking at an arm and knowing from the bend in it that it was broken.

"What did Wyman agree to?"

Mable grins yellow teeth at me. "The only thing he had left to bargain with."

Horror blossoms in my chest. *His ghost. His soul.* I stumble back, was she going to...

The bone collector snorts. "Don't look at me like that. He'll live his life just fine. All my contracts do. But when his death comes, it will belong to me."

I take in her lined face and grey braid. Wyman is easily forty years her junior. She'd be long dead herself before she could claim the goods. Unless...a sensation like crawling spiders tickles down my legs. Unless she *would* be around in another forty years. Sweet Jesus, exactly how old was she? Then a more insidious thought. *Was a bone collector even human?*

Mable raps a knuckle on the iron box in her lap. The sound of it rings through me, like she'd clapped a cymbal in my face. "Enough questions for today. Let's get you trained up."

The more skilled the ghost, the more valuable you are. This is the lesson Mable drills into me.

"Put some spirit into it," she likes to say, cackling at her own joke as I mush my essence through the machines on her shelves.

I master the record player first. Unlike the teddy bear, this machine is cold and *stiff*, like trying to turn a half-rusted screw.

Mable is utterly uncompromising. "That's because it's not a shell. It's a machine," she says. "If bird spirit can work it, you most certainly can."

Only when I realise that I've pushed too much of my essence at the machine does it finally click. I syphon off a sliver and feed it in. Bit by slivery bit. The player spins up and Mable places the arm onto the vinyl. A jazz ballad crackles out, its saxophone and baritone singer barely rising over the pop and hiss of the ancient vinyl.

"A good start," she says when she yanks me out and places me back inside the bear sometime close to midnight. "Gannet can barely manage an hour. We'll try something new tomorrow."

And despite knowing I'm only hastening my impending servitude, I can't help but feel a glimmer of triumph. It's a long night. Ghosts don't need to sleep. And Mable has somehow bound me to the plushie. So I turn and examine the tiny device nestled inside the bear's stuffing. I've scarcely brushed the machine before it releases a burst of static, then *"I'mm huuuuungry."*

"Girl," Mable warns from the sofa that also doubles as her bed. From inside the bear, I feel her power reach for me: a giant hand ready to clench me silent. "Don't make me put you back in your anchor." She taps the iron box resting on her chest. Plushies can't shudder, but my essence recoils. I don't know what she means by 'anchor', but I can guess. When I'm not busy funnelling power into a machine, the box calls to me. A part of me is in there. One of my bones. From the way it clinks when Mable carries it, there must be dozens, maybe hundreds, of others like mine in there.

By the end of the week, I've mastered the TV, the TV remote, and FM radio — even if all I get is static. The week after, it's a rusted convection oven with more holes in it than a sieve. Mable lectures me on anchors and shells.

"When I hand you on, I'll give your owner a shell to keep you in," she says. "Your anchor stays with me." She rattles the box, which I'm coming to realise she very much enjoys doing, the same way a pianist might strike a single key to listen to the note's resonance. A childhood memory washes through me at that thought. *Me sitting on Mum's lap before a scuffed old piano, hands resting on top of her fingers as they flow across the keys.*

Mable's fingers click before my face and I blink. "Leave the past alone, sweetie."

The following week, it's the smartphone. And that's when the trouble starts.

The smartphone lights up in my hand. *First try. Seas be.* I was right not to give up the girl. She's too strong for amateurs. Not even Wyman's ghost had been able to make the screen do more than flicker. I tap the cracked screen and am confronted with the lock screen. It's been years since I've seen it.

"Good, sweetie. Very good." I reach my power out to feel her essence inside the casing. It's positively vibrating with power. Part of me urges to act now, use the ghost and be done with it. But another part stays my hand. *Why not see how far she can go?* it whispers. *Think what a developed power like hers could do for you. Another fifty years, easy. Maybe more.*

I admit it's tempting. The level the girl is at now would give twenty, maybe thirty, years. Far better than the year here, month there I'd been living with for the last decade. I rub my aching knuckles. The pain was back again. Dull in its way, but growing. Reminding me of what waited if I didn't act soon.

The phone buzzes in my hand.

I yelp and drop it. It lands on the carpet with a thud but doesn't switch off.

"Sorry," my ghost says. "Thought I found a way around."

With a scowl, I pick up the phone and turn it over in my hands. It has *never* buzzed before, but the lock screen still glimmers up at me. As much as I want to know what's behind it, I've long resigned myself to the fact that there is no breaking the Olwerlders' security. I reach out my power to pull the girl from the device before she fries it – something I never thought I'd have to with *any* ghost – when I feel her dig in, like a fish fighting a hook on a line. Then she *pulls* back.

"I think I can bypass it."

My jaw drops. Too distracted by the lure of the device, she doesn't notice. Inside the phone, I sense her pushing and probing her essence through it. Until, a second later:

"Oh I *see!*"

The lock screen vanishes.

"Girl–" I begin.

She ignores me and rifles through the device. *Flash, flash,* goes the display. Things open and close faster than I can follow. When I extend my spirit to hers, I feel the hunger burning insider her. The need to *know.*

She's searching for something.

Images appear. Her ghost touch flicks through strange vistas. Sunsets over still water. Buildings tall as mountains. Stone and concrete and bright lights. Faces, so many faces. She stops on one. Two smiling adults and their children outside a house. Not a hut, a proper Olwerld house.

"It's not here," my ghost says, her voice quiet.

I use her pause to close my power around her essence, working her hold of the device loose as a parent might detach a child's grip from a toy. "What's not here?" I ask as I pull her free.

Her face is wet when she coalesces. "Answers. What happened." She sinks to the floor, hugging her knees. "It's all gone."

Overhead the lightbulb's hum returns. It flickers and I glower at it. The last thing I need right now is the ghost in my lightbulb burning out. I collect my bone box and crouch beside her.

"Smart devices take a lot of energy, sweetie," I say. "You need to rest."

Never mind that her form is still solid, and aura bright. But she nods, wipes at her eyes. Her mind's too wrapped up in mourning for the world that was to notice me open the bone box.

I send her straight to her anchor. Straight to sleep. And when I shut the lid, I slump into my rocking chair, the knowledge thumping in time with my pounding heart.

This ghost has gone far enough. I cannot afford to wait.

For the first time, I dream. Not in pictures, but feelings. Warm and muzzy, like sleeping in the sun on a summer's day. The kind of dream you know is a dream. And there is a sense of someone, *someones,* nestled close. *The bone box.* She's put me back with her other bones.

Dimly, I sense Mable move us. A rattle, and I roll into someone, catching a whiff of wine and laugher as we cross paths. A bump, and I plunge into someone else with a brisk, jolting cold and the taste of seawater in my mouth. Panic surges through me. *Not the sea.* But it's too late; the nightmare rises and swallows me hole.

"Stay with me," I tell Mum. We float on our backs. It's not survival stroke anymore. Just survival. "Just a little longer."

I hope I'm right. I'm past the point of cold. Sometimes I think I hear other voices across the water, but whenever I lift my head to look I see no one. No lights. No boats. No figures floating in the water but us. There must be others, I think. The storm had battered our suburb.

"A storm possessed," the news anchor had said. But we'd left too late. The water caught us in the street. Swept us away.

Now, the sky sprawls clear above us, stars so bright it makes the darkness between them feel bottomless. I work my numb lips. "Don't let go, Mum."

She doesn't speak.

Doesn't breathe.

She hasn't for hours.

I squeeze my fingers around hers. Her fingers are going stiff. "Don't leave me." I whisper, and I swear something squeezes back.

"I'm right here, Riley."

I start awake in the dream.

This is not how it happened. I know it's not. Because, instead of sinking, Mum shakes off her body and turns to me, transparent hands taking mine, and says: "I'm *here*."

The nightmare tumbles away, and I feel her there. Next to me.

"Mum?"

"I'm here."

I don't have room to wonder. The hows and whys of it fall away as the full realisation crashes into me. She's here. Dread clenches around my heart. She's *here*. In Mable's bone box. *No. No, no, no.* I don't say it, but with our anchors touching, she already knows.

"Oh Riley, I'm so sorry."

It takes time to prepare. I move the shells from the shelves, stacking them outside on my rickety veranda around Gannet. I caulk the window seals with pitch. Shove a rag up the chimney of the fireplace. Salt the thresholds. All of it sealed, so my sweetie has nowhere to go.

I go over my work again, just to be sure. Knives secured in the kitchenette drawers, poker outside. Nothing for her to grab onto in case she's got a touch of poltergeist.

At last, I'm ready.

I place my bone box on the driftwood table. Open it. The bones are crowded together, phalanges, carpals, metacarpals, tarsals and metatarsals, even a malleus from an ear. I trail my fingers through them all, searching for the right one. I find her hiding at the bottom, a larger patella suck to her side.

"There you are, sweetie."

Her ghost flares awake the moment I touch her. Her form is so solid it almost blocks the light from the bulb above.

"Did you know?" she demands. The tears are still on her cheeks. Damn, *damn*. I'd hoped the rest would mellow her out, but something's got her in a right fuss.

"Know what?" I ask, genuinely baffled.

Not the right answer, apparently. With her bone in my hand I feel her anger simmer under my fingers. Then grief wells up behind it, so raw it scalds my skin. It takes all my control not to drop the bone with a hiss and a curse.

"You have her!" she explodes, pointing to the patella I'd pried her from. "My mum is in your stupid box." Her fists curl at her sides. *"Let her go."*

It takes a moment to follow. Her mother? I glance at the patella, rifling through my memories. The light ghost? I'd

had her for, oh, what, sixty years? Not particularly powerful. Scarcely more than a shade. Flickers of sentience. Enough to run a bulb for an evening. But, now I think about it, I'd found them both on the same beach. *Oh hells.*

The bulb hums above us.

"Quiet down," I growl at it.

The girl advances on me. *Advances.* The cheek! Her form looms large and my temper snaps. I poor power into my hands and squeeze her anchor.

"Enough! You are dead. Your mother is dead. Your duty is to the living. Now *quiet!*"

She stumbles, legs folding under her with a cry. Mostly surprise. Maybe a bit of pain. I harrumph and reach for my bone box, picking out the patella from the pile. Best to work with her mother's shade asleep. Even if it does mean I'll have to work in the dar–

A pressure pushes against my senses, fighting off my hold. I whirl on the ghost. "Seas damn it, girl!"

She lunges at me. "I'm *not* your puppet."

I reach for my power, digging deeper, harder than I have done in many, *many* years. And there I feel it, the scrape and twinge as I hit the bottom of its well. But it's enough. I smack her away, blasting her through the driftwood table and sofa bed.

"You think you're the first to defy me?!" I step towards her, gathering the dregs from my well again. *Time to end this.*

The lightbulb explodes above us. Not a mere shattering and tinkle of glass. It blasts out, hammering a dozen shards into my back with a waft of righteous glee. A blade of it lodges in my neck. Lodges deep. My hand flies to the wound, clamping over the blood already slicking down my throat.

Fuck! Fuck, fuck, fuck!

I drop the girl's anchor and plunge my free hand into the bone box. No sense wasting such a powerful ghost on something like this. My fingers find the one I want in seconds; I know all my bones by feel. I grab it, put it in my mouth and bite down.

My vision swims. Bone crunches between my teeth. It's a flimsy carpal, easy to eat. Dust and bone fill my mouth, along with the flush of heat through my veins. Ghost essence.

In the corner, the buzz of the ancient fridge cuts out.

The ghost's essence drops into my well. A tingle washes over my limbs. *Heal me,* I command it. The wound in my throat burns, then tickles as the skin knits shut and puckers into a scar. I cough and straighten, wiping my bloodied fingers on my skirt.

My sweetie stares at me. I didn't think ghosts could go pale, but she manages it.

"You *eat* us?"

"When I must." I shrug. "When I need it."

Our gazes land on her anchor on the carpet and horror takes over. I smirk. *End of the road, sweetie.*

"No!" She flings herself forward – not for her anchor, she must know she can't hold it. She goes for *me*. Her grip closes around my wrist, and there's a surprising strength behind it. *Seas, if this girl had lived, she might have been one of us.*

I grab her anchor. Cop a glancing blow to my cheek. It's strong, but there's no weight, *no flesh*, behind it. It's like fighting a cloud. Still, she climbs *up* me, tearing at my hair, clawing at my eyes. I yell and trip over the driftwood table and thud to the floor. Pain smarts down one hip and leg. Her transparent fingers work at my clenched fist as I lift it to my mouth.

"I'm going to enjoy eating you," I snarl, and shove her anchor into my mouth.

Crunch.

Her form quivers. I feel her fight to hold herself together.

Crunch.

She vanishes. The first wave of power drips on my tongue, searing as it goes down.

"Please, stop." Her voice is small. Close by.

Not a chance. I bite down again, grit and bone dust coating my mouth.

Her essence roars into me. Where the shade before had been a flush, this is a wave. It crashes through my muscles and bones, filling my well to brimming. The contrast between is startling. I'd almost forgotten what it was like to eat a proper ghost. *Finally.* I roll onto my back. *This is what I'd needed.* More essence, more soul to fill me, *power* me.

Worth the wait, the ridiculous indulgence.

The girl's essence sloshes inside me. I laugh, my squeaking giggle the only sound in the dark room.

Another fifty years, easy.

I stand. Dust off my jumper and relish the springy suppleness in my limbs. "Ha," I say to the empty hut and reach for my bone box.

The essence *twitches* in my well. My breath snags. Just digestion. Perfectly norm—

Nausea hits like a hammer. I double over, gasping as the essence shifts inside me. She's *moving.* Working inside me, wrapping herself around my well — *around my soul* — like a constrictor.

"What is—"

She squeezes. The strength flees my legs, and I clatter to the carpet. Another squeeze. My body twitches, my control falling away. She's balled my essence up, and I feel her working, pushing, pulling, straining.

She's pushing me out. Forcing my soul out of my core.

Stop! I scream, but nothing comes out. I dive into my power, try to push back. But it's not enough. It's too tight. I'm too empty. And she's too strong.

My essence is forced up my chest, down my left arm. Into my hand. My right arm spasms. Left leg kicks. She's testing them. Syphoning power through my muscles.

Don't you dare!

My/her mouth spreads in a grin. We lurch up. Sway, stumble, sway. We stagger into the kitchen. She pulls open the drawers.

Stop!

My/her hand closes around something cold. Steel. Sharp.

She forces me down further, into my pinkie. Her essence pins me there, vice-like as she splays my/her fingers.

My butcher's knife swings into view. Lifts above my/her head. Then it drops like a guillotine.

N–

The beach is quiet today. Even the gulls are silent. Like they know something is here that shouldn't be.

I've built the bonfire high. Its heat sears Mable's skin, curling the end of her braid as I lean close and overturn the bone box into the flames. Our bones clink as they drop, then pop like burning logs. There's an odd a stomach-dropping moment of weightlessness when their connection to Mable and I melt away.

I hold Mum's patella in Mable's good hand. The other is wrapped in bloody rags, clutching the collector's ragged pinky.

Put me back! her soul rages, spitting a flow of steady curses. She doesn't stop, not even when I throw her finger onto the fire. *You will rue this day, girl. I swear it! I will end*

you! She keeps going until the fire finally cracks her anchor, cutting her off with a hiss.

The next is harder. I hold the patella to my shell's lips, feeling the warm mussiness seep through my thoughts. "You stayed with me to the end." *Both times.* "Thank you," I tell Mum, and give her bone to the flames.

I make sure every anchor is ash before I wade into the sea.

The waves whisper as they pull at my feet. One step brings the water to my waist. The next, it crowds my head, soaking Mable's braid.

Inside me, the last remnant of Mable's power begins to unravel. The knot of extortion contracts loosens, then dissolves.

Enjoy your death, Wyman. Lucky bastard is probably too caught up trying to find a working radio to notice.

I lean back and float in the sea, letting the current pull me from the shore. Gannets wheel in the blue above. One of them rides the wind on translucent wings.

I smile, feeling myself come unstuck from the bone collector's body and swirl with the water. No shell. No anchor. With a sigh, I close my eyes.

It is time to rest.

ABOUT THE PUBLISHER

Whisk(e)y Tit is committed to restoring degradation and degeneracy to the literary arts. We work with authors who are unwilling to sacrifice intellectual rigor, unrelenting playfulness, and visual beauty in our literary pursuits, often leading to texts that would otherwise be abandoned in today's largely homogenized literary landscape. In a world governed by idiocy, our commitment to these principles is an act of civil service and civil disobedience alike.

Connoisseur, Volume 1: FEAST is the first release of HEADLESS, our literary horror imprint. For questions or submissions inquiries, visit whiskeytit.com/contact/.